The Journey of
Adam Kadmon

The Journey of
Adam Kadmon

A NOVEL

by

LESLIE STEIN

Arcade Publishing • New York

Arcade Publishing books may be purchased in bulk at special discounts for sales promotion, corporate gifts, fund-raising, or educational purposes. Special editions can also be created to specifications. For details, contact the Special Sales Department, Arcade Publishing, 307 West 36th Street, 11th Floor, New York, NY 10018 or arcade@skyhorsepublishing.com.

Arcade Publishing® is a registered trademark of Skyhorse Publishing, Inc.®, a Delaware corporation.

Visit our website at www.arcadepub.com.

10 9 8 7 6 5 4 3 2 1

Library of Congress Cataloging-in-Publication Data is available on file.
ISBN: 978-1-61145-426-0

Printed in the United States of America

For Miriam

The gateway to peace is exceedingly narrow and none may enter save through affliction of the soul.

—Morienus Romanus,
De Transfiguratione Metallorum

The Journey of Adam Kadmon

1

Wandering

1 MOSES HAD LEFT DIJON FOR ZÜRICH with a light head, brimming over with optimism. The conference on the philosophy of religion in France had been merely an excuse for the real purpose of his travel — to visit Jung on the journey back to Warsaw. As the train rumbled into Switzerland, he sat back and visualized Jung in his study of wood and books, heated by a cavernous fireplace. In a spark of fantasy, he sat comfortably in a leather chair across from the great man, both laughing as yet another mystery was exposed by their insight. He imagined Jung brushing away the dinner call from Emma Jung rather than miss a moment of the brilliant conversation.

In harmony with these lofty projections, the countryside offered a glorious vista of majestic peaks and lesser hills, dusted with a patina of snow. In a positive and secure mood, Moses longed to place his feet on the ground and breath in the clean mountain air. He left the train when it pulled into Lucerne and was pleased to find a morning connection on the following day to Zürich; his appointment with Jung was not until tomorrow afternoon. Moses reached, yet again, into his coat pocket and touched the neatly folded letter that said, simply: "Dr. Jung can see you at 2:30 P.M. on August 1, 1939."

From the time he had first read the letter, he had had odd patches of disorientation. In the last month especially, he could barely concentrate on his work, as words on a page appeared to float. His stomach was in constant upheaval, moving and bubbling. Moses willingly accepted these tokens of anxiety, as he had read that the analysis begins with the letter, not the first session. Lucerne would, he hoped, give a respite to restore some balance.

A taxi made tracks through an unseasonable snowfall toward the center of town, to a small hotel in a quiet square. The ancient porter, wearing a wide-brimmed hat, half-dragged half-carried his valise down the hallway. The porter occasionally squinted at Moses, looking him up and down. He was bent with age and staggered under the weight of the bag, gradually slowing to a halt. Moses was about to offer some help but the porter moved away and faced him.

"So, you stay long?" asked the porter in a surprisingly sonorous voice.

"Just overnight."

The porter shifted the valise to his other hand and again advanced steadily until he reached the middle of the long corridor, where he paused, still holding the bag. Painfully, he straightened up and looked at Moses with rheumy eyes. The skin on his face was pebbled.

"Then you visit Mount Pilatus. Every Jew must visit."

He continued along for a few steps then stopped again.

"It is close by — a short distance from here. That is it there." He pointed east.

With black beard, white skin, heavy-lidded eyes, Moses could not be mistaken. The juxtaposition of features was a racial badge. The centuries of introspection, the self-absorption in problems made more complex by too much thought, the overattentiveness to every bodily sensation, raised the forehead and softened the eyes.

They continued to the end of the hallway and his room.

"Pontius Pilate came here to the mountain," the porter went on. "He moved for years from country to country. No rest. Then he came here, right here to the mountain, to Mount Pilatus. It was then called Frakmut. You know this?"

"No, no, I never heard this."

"Now here, coming around a bulge in the mountain, Pilate meets Ahasverus, the Wandering Jew."

He paused and grabbed Moses' elbow.

"This Jew is not our legend, you know, this Wandering Jew. He is a Christian legend. But you and me *are* this Jew. So, listen please. This is what happened. Ahasverus recognized him. He chased Pilate for hours. Finally he got him and grabbed him by the throat, screaming obscenities to the heavens at the top of his lungs and, when he could hear the last hiss of breath, he threw Pilate into the lake."

The porter glanced at his hand on Moses' elbow and removed it. He opened the door to the room and entered, still holding the bag. The room was very cold, with a smell of mildew barely masked by antiseptic cleaners. They stepped in and the porter closed the door. They stood silently in the dark.

"It's all connected. Think about it, please," he whispered. "No Pilate, no crucifixion, then Jesus wouldn't have asked the Wandering Jew for that glass of water. What our life would be, eh, if he had just given him the water and had not been doomed by Jesus to wander the earth."

He turned on a small lamp.

"There's a legend here as well. Once a year, this time of year, the first snow, Pilate appears on the mountain in the uniform of a Roman judge. If a Jew meets him, goes the legend, the Jew will be killed."

As a punctuation mark, he let the valise drop.

"I tell this to you so you can go and find him because I know . . ." he said as he moved close to Moses, "that if you plead with him, beg him, whatever you have to do, and then he lets you go, you're safe: no more wandering, no confusion, finished, the end."

"That's an interesting legend," Moses ventured.

"Legend? This is no legend. Our race wanders, we never stay in one place. If we can face the accuser and finally are forgiven, we have no need to run."

He handed Moses the key, turned, and walked out, closing the door gently behind him.

The last shafts of light failed to warm the room and the small blaze in the fireplace was no match for a bitter wind that slid through the window casings. Moses fell on the bed, wrapped in his greatcoat. A man in an adjoining room was shouting in German. It was too early for dinner and he had nowhere to go.

He felt a tickle in his throat and started probing: a swallow, some little coughs, another swallow. The possibility of being sick in a drafty hotel room made Moses tense and constricted and instantly dissolved his illusions. He rose and went to a mirror, twisting under a naked globe to look down his throat. Anxious and cold, he shuddered and hurried back to bed and slipped under the dusty covers, still in his coat. His mind floated as if on morphine: drifting on an unknown plane, aware of something other than itself. Finally Moses slept, but soon awoke in the dark, cold room.

His thoughts were crisp; images paraded one after another: work, meetings, colleagues, his daughter in her small bed. There seemed so much to attend to as he teased out each line of thought. Yet he knew that when morning came, nothing would be resolved; something might well have been stirred or pushed into the light to be examined, but the wisps of night lacked power. A mature man like Moses had done this too often to be tricked. The entangled vines of fear and inadequacy quickly smothered any insights. Even if he could hold a perspective fast, forcing it to remain, it would be lost in the whirlpool of daily life where he would be dragged down, unable to focus and attend consistently to even one thought. Among the demands of students, family, debt, and friends, only a great man could keep a subtlety from dissolving.

Perhaps, he thought, this is how a Jew wandered: by being unable to maintain his values. One day he is desperate to be a model citizen, walking down the boulevard, silently striving for success, lifting his head, hoping to be recognized. The next day he is stooped, head bowed, concentration turned inward to unravel the ancient filaments of learned thought that are the interlocking arguments of the Talmud. He is pulled outward then inward, tormented by his inability to give anything full attention.

His thoughts spun like a wheel until they stopped on the porter. What nonsense really. Could such rambling have meaning, even in his quest for convincing symbols? Why is everlasting life a curse for this Wandering Jew? Could it be to deny him the glorious Christian death, the only ticket to a blissful eternity? And why must he wander until Christ returned? He touched his throbbing temple. Maybe this is the true curse of the Wandering Jew: no respite from the powerful slide into introspection.

The man in the next room started shouting again in German. His voice was ugly and guttural, the sounds welling from his throat.

It was a glorious morning and the lake sparkled in the sunlight. After an early breakfast, Moses asked the concierge to find him a driver to travel to the mountain. He sat in the lobby to wait, and within an hour he was ushered into a rickety American car. He had been hesitant, as this was costly, but the legend was there to be grasped. How could he ignore a visit to a symbolic world on the day he was to meet Jung?

After a short, picturesque drive, the silent driver, who was tall, clean and blond, swung the car over to a gravel shoulder and skidded to a stop. There appeared little to see from this vantage point, and Moses sat quietly waiting for some explanation. There was a sheer wall on this side of the road and on the other were two large boulders with a path leading upward, out of sight. The driver got out and, with formality, opened Moses' door. He was about to ask the driver why they had stopped in such an odd place, but swallowed his words. His patchy High German would have been a foreign language to the Swiss-German of his driver.

"This is the mountain," the driver intoned slowly to make himself understood. "This . . ." he pointed toward the boulders "is the mountain of Wotan."

"Yes, yes," Moses said, pointing to the same area. "Pilate."

"No." The driver shook his head. "Wotan, Wotan."

"Ahasverus," Moses said, trying again.

"Wotan," he replied. "God of War." He said this proudly. "God of Chaos."

The bulk of the driver and his wooden stupidity were becoming menacing even though there was not a ripple of aggression on his Swiss countenance.

"Wotan," the driver said again, this time with an edge.

Perhaps, Moses thought, he had insulted some strongly held belief. Jung associated Wotan with the Nazi movement, but Moses could not recall the exact connection.

To break the verbal impasse, he crossed the road and took a few tentative steps up the path on the other side. He looked back at the driver and waved as he would to a child. The driver walked quickly over to him and stood too close.

Moses turned to reason. "This is the mountain of the Wandering Jew. Here is where he killed Pilate. Is this not true?"

The driver, upon hearing "Jew," stepped back. "No Jew here," he said, "just God of War. Wotan." He looked at Moses with clear contempt, walked back to the car, took his place in the driver's seat, and started reading a newspaper.

Moses was distracted momentarily by a sharp pain in his mouth. The pain blended immediately with a more primitive fear and confusion. Involuntarily, Moses lowered his head and whimpered. The driver glanced his way, then got out of the car and opened the door. He sensed the humiliation of Moses and an artificial servility began to appear.

"Back," he said.

He opened the door further and Moses entered, head bowed, somehow humiliated. He drove without a word and gradually Moses began to regain his composure. When they arrived at the hotel, Moses stepped from the car and reached into his pocket for the agreed amount. The driver cocked his head like a bird as if pondering.

"No money," he said. "No money."

He got back in the car and drove off.

The door opened, and there stood Carl Gustav Jung. He glided out of his room, stepping to the side, bringing his feet together with the grace of a ballroom dancer. He then stood motionless, pointing at the stairs. Moses jumped up from his chair but sat down again when he saw Jung gazing elsewhere.

A short, round woman, with a large, hairy mole on her cheek, emerged from his room and tried to squeeze past him. Her purse was clutched tightly against her chest and she was gritting her teeth. Jung did not budge, forcing her to press against him. The woman turned her head away, overcome with the horror and ignominy of the physical contact. Moses could hear her hyperventilating. With each breath her shoulders shuddered. She glanced for a moment at Moses, who peered into the distance with a vacant look.

She turned back toward Jung, who jabbed his pipe in her direction in a progressing rhythm. He suddenly erupted and shouted, "You are hopeless! The analysis is over. No progress is to be made."

His voice echoed up and down the house, vibrating in deep bass, making the words more ominous. The veins at his temples darkened into angry rivulets and he clenched his jaw in a way that made him appear ferocious.

"Get out," he yelled. "Out!"

The woman moaned, as if physically struck, and struggled to take another step. She was almost too hysterical to move. She looked again at Moses, but his eyes remained unfocused. He thought of getting up to help her, but was repulsed by the sight of the mole. She had crept barely ten feet, with one foot down the staircase, when Jung turned directly to Moses, who bolted upright from his chair.

Jung melted that bellowing mouth into a charming smile and the rivulets disappeared into the great confluence that was the man. Lightly, almost sensually, he put his hand on Moses' arm.

"Ah, Professor Aarons, please come in."

Jung saw that Moses was standing stock still, apparently unable to move.

"Professor, I am not emotional, I just *use* emotion."

He placed his other hand gently in the small of Moses' back and ushered him into his room.

Jung pointed to a sturdy chair opposite him.

"Please sit down, Professor."

He took his eyes from Moses and laughed to himself as he tamped down his pipe.

"One of my patients, you know, is a dressmaker. She called herself 'Professor.' That's right, she said she was a professor, an artist at her work."

He took a puff, then laid the pipe on an ashtray. Moses leaned forward as if to speak, but hesitated as Jung fixed him with a stare.

"I cannot see you after this one visit, Professor. I am sorry. My colleague Meier may be the one for you to see."

Jung saw the dreadful look of disappointment.

"I am far too busy, you must understand. I can't see what difference it makes. You came for a little philosophical chat, didn't you?"

"Please, Doctor Jung. I have come a long way, from Warsaw. Could I see you at least a few more times? I did come for a chat, that's true, but I have more to ask you. I need more time."

Moses cupped his hands as a supplicant.

"You are sitting here with me now, are you not? What is it that you must tell me that takes longer than the time we have?"

Jung smiled, pleased with himself, as he leaned back comfortably in his chair.

"I had a dream. In fact, I seem to have had this dream a thousand times, night after night. That's why I have come to see you, Doctor

Jung. The dream haunts me. It has spread out into every corner of my soul and has taken me over."

"Indeed," Jung said, suddenly intrigued. "Let's hear it then."

"I am naked, bounding up the spiral stairs of a tower. I am halfway up and strong winds appear, blowing above me. I am deeply exhausted and need to rest, but yet I am compelled by a desperation that pushes me into the wind. At first I cannot see, the wind is too strong, but then I break through and continue climbing the stairs in large strides. There seem to be no landings, no pause, no respite.

"At another moment, I am standing at the beginning of a long hallway, which stretches far into the distance. A man with a small horn in the middle of his forehead is next to me, sitting on a chair, reading a large, ancient parchment that is crumbling as I look. His dress is modern and elegant. I would say that his demeanor suggests a patron of culture. On the floor, by his foot, lies a decomposing skeleton, with only patches of skin, deliberately ignored and seemingly of no consequence.

"The man with the horn looks up and notices me. He points to a door now visible at the end of the long hallway. I pause, not sure what I am supposed to do. He jabs his finger in the direction of the door and begins stamping his foot impatiently. I walk down the hallway and I can see the door now clearly. It is sealed shut. It has no knob and is solid polished steel, welded and riveted into a steel door frame. I can't see any gap below or above, no opening, no keyhole, not even an edge to pry. I inspect the door meticulously, over and over, from side to side, back and forth, up and down. Each time I have this dream, I inspect the door interminably until I awake."

Jung had been listening, his eyes closed. Now he opened them and looked at Moses.

"You're at an impasse. You can go no further with your mind," said Jung. "The door is at the end of the passage — your passage, your hallway. What is unresolved is behind this door. You cannot get around it. It is as far as your mind can go."

The room grew darker as clouds covered the sun.

"This is every man's door, Professor. You, of all people, a professor of philosophy, should know this. Every man has this door."

He paused while he lit his pipe. As he leaned toward Moses, his face softened.

"The great alchemist, Goethe, points it out:

> For naught, I assembled human treasure,
> Everything that my mortal soul could digest.
> Now I come to know my worth
> And the barren desert in my chest.
> I have not lifted myself one poor degree
> Nor do I stand closer to the infinite."

He leaned back in his chair, a smile playing on his lips, as if he was pleased with himself at having quoted the master verbatim.

"There is nothing more for you to figure out, Professor. Your search is over. You can put away the books. You are . . ." He held the words in suspense for a few seconds. "You see, you are stuck!"

Jung had thrown this at Moses with force. He waited for his reaction.

Moses felt smothered, as if a thick blanket had been thrown over his head. The great arbiter of the unconscious had just slammed the door in his face. He had to stop himself from falling to his knees and begging for another chance, another meeting. Otherwise, any hope he had, any faith that he could rise above the mundane, would be destroyed. He had to seek reprieve from this spiritual death sentence.

"I have read your work, Doctor Jung," Moses said tentatively. He thought, just for a second, that Jung looked at him as someone who deserved more respect, even though his dream appeared profoundly prosaic.

"You have revealed your unconscious. From this I know you. It is your neuroses to look for answers in more words or in my psychological commentaries," Jung said, sighing. He looked suddenly tired. He started to nod his head as if asking and answering the same question over and over.

"This is the feature of your race," he said.

Jung used "race" without emotion. It was stated simply, as a matter of fact.

Moses was startled. "I can't see what race has to do with it, Doctor Jung. I am an individual. This is *my* dream."

Jung didn't seem to be listening.

"Wouldn't you say?"

Jung sat motionless.

"Well, Doctor Jung, some characteristics may be racial, but in the end I am my own man." Moses spoke timidly, as if fearful of Jung's anger.

"Psyche is not individual, Professor. You are a product of psyche. Your stairs are a symbol of ascent, no question. You are rising to something. But the collective, the collective, Professor — it goes back to an untold history of which you are a part. You have been carried along by its momentum and you are as much a part of it as I am of my race."

Jung rose from his chair and moved to the window. For a moment he looked out at the lake, then spoke, his back to Moses. "But your race is blocked, it cannot develop. The unconscious of Jews is too mature, empty of possibility. And this is the problem. The unconscious has two faces: a Janus face. It is a prehistoric world of instincts, yes, but it also holds the potential for the future. And your unconscious, the unconscious of your race is exhausted. It is lacking a future."

"Doesn't every race have this fate?" Moses ventured, lamely he thought.

Jung walked back to his chair and sat down heavily. His look at Moses was one of unmistakable pity.

"How naive," Jung said. "It is only the Jews. The material from the unconscious is stale, without a vision."

He paused, looking around the room, as if searching for the right example.

"There are many races that are different. The German movement is pregnant with possibilities, can't you see that? Deep within that movement, something is stirring."

Before Moses could answer, Jung flicked his hand, as if shooing the discussion away.

"Let us return to your dream. You see," he continued, "in this numinous dream, you have contacted Cain, the cultured man with the horn; this horn is the mark of Cain, and beside him lies his dead brother, Abel. Cain is the cultured Jew, the Wandering Jew. This is not your personal image, this is your racial heritage. The true marvel is that Cain, although doomed, is protected by God. He gives him the mark: the mark of Cain. So he survives and your race will survive even though it has no future."

Jung must have noticed the bafflement on his patient's face. He spoke slowly to Moses.

"You see, Professor, the Wandering Jew must survive. If the Wandering Jew is sentenced to wander until Christ returns, how can Jesus return for the Second Coming unless the Jew is there? The Jew is necessary."

Moses sat perfectly still in his chair. Jung leaned forward to speak, as if he intended every word to fix on him.

"You are a Jew. That is your curse yet your protection. Your race must wander, drawing on the culture of other nations. It is doomed, without a future, but ultimately will survive. This is the backdrop, if you like, the obvious, the surface of the issue. But it is to the shadow of the Jew that you must turn, the unrecognized, unwanted side. Here is where you must look to open your door, if indeed it can ever be opened. The shadow is the harm that the Jews have done, the ugliness and chaos that sprouts from a wandering, exploitative race, the ugliness that has brought centuries of hatred. It is only here, in the shadow, in the horror of the truth of it, that the door will open."

"Ah! The shadow," said Moses. "This I know about."

Jung was surprised. "Your talk is dangerous, Professor. These are just abstractions for you. Dangerous abstractions in a professor of philosophy with no psychological insight. If they remain like this, you will be destroyed because this is an aspect of your personal shadow: all the unpleasant and immoral aspects of you, which appear close to the surface, in your case. You can't talk of the shadow casually, staring at it like some cinema show. There is an old Swiss saying: 'The devil is behind a rich man but there are two devils behind a poor man.' You would have three devils, Professor." Jung found this amusing and suddenly laughed, his face red with the exertion. He stared at Moses, taking him in. He continued. "Your dream has banished you from peace. You *are* the Wandering Jew. If you cannot integrate the unconscious material that lies under you like a mountain, and cannot understand it morally, then you are as nothing."

Moses remembered little of the rest of the session. Jung's words became more and more abstract, and Moses was too exhausted and lost to comment further. Jung finally paused and dusted the tobacco ashes from his trousers. Moses stood and thanked him, aware that he might never see him again.

His breathing was syncopated with the click-clack of the train. It was almost dawn and he had dozed fitfully through the night in the uncomfortable seat. At every slit of consciousness — when he awoke for a second to readjust his position — the session was relived. In the predawn, he focused once more.

Obviously, he had taken too lightly the journey to see Jung. "How mad," he said under his breath, "I wonder what I could have been thinking?" He had believed that he was so psychologically aware that Jung would accept him as a colleague or adjourn the session for a schnapps and dinner. Instead, he had treated him with marked disdain, clearly forgetting his name as he retreated back across the threshold.

Moses opened up his diary in the dawning light and looked at the notes he had prepared for the session. He had intended to talk to Jung about the Zohar, the fundamental work of Jewish mysticism. He had initially been attracted to this thirteenth-century work by the simple fact that the putative author was his namesake: Moses de Leon. At certain times in history, it had been deemed as important as the Torah or Bible. The five volumes of the Zohar were so dense with the unfathomable utterings of ancient sages that Moses eventually attributed wisdom to what he could not understand. Yet he kept finding passages that resonated within him, intriguing yet elusive, as if a veil was about to be lifted, revealing eternal wisdom. He had rehearsed out loud what he was going to say to Jung, "You know, Doctor Jung, the richness of the Zohar's symbolism is intriguing." He quietly laughed to himself at the use of the word "intriguing." To Jung's ears, it would have implied a pathetic dilettante interest, a puffery, and discussing it with him would most likely have led to even greater ridicule.

Jung, no matter what his other qualities, was arrogant. Yet to think of him in this way gave Moses no particular pleasure. In spite of his wounded pride, he understood that it was up to him to take the confusion and disappointment and face it all clearly. For, as Jung wrote, it is one thing to have an insight, but it is a moral question whether or not it will be used.

At best, he was "stuck." Who, indeed, is not stuck? Moses' door did not have to be steel, it could just as well have been paper; he still could not break through it. The door must represent some fundamental limitation, he assumed, a basic obstacle at his very core that probably would be in his way for the rest of his life.

A tall priest stood up from the back of the train carriage and walked over to sit opposite Moses. It struck him as odd that someone would abandon one seat for another midjourney. Just as well, he thought, as obsessing over the door was taking him round in circles. He let out another little laugh; here he was, stuck again, on his understanding of Jung's interpretation.

"Oh, I am sorry to disturb you," said the priest, half standing as if to leave.

"No, no. Please sit down." Moses gestured toward the seat. "It was a joke. To myself. I'm probably the only one who laughs at my jokes."

He gave a "poor me" shrug and Book One of the Zohar slipped onto the floor. The priest leaned quickly forward and picked up the book. In the weak light, Moses noticed the man's brown skin.

"I had to move," he said, pointing behind him. "That man and woman were smoking most of the night. I hope you don't mind."

The priest rested the Zohar on his lap. His Indian accent added melodious tones to his soothing voice. His bony fingers were long and refined as they lay across the cover of the ancient book. His robes were Franciscan and he wore only sandals against the cold drafts on the train floor.

"Where are you going?" Moses asked.

He had decided a good conversation would be an elixir. He did not seek a purgative but a rewarding distraction.

"I am going back to Banaras. In the northeast of India. Where I was born."

"Ah. You have a long trip. I am going back to Warsaw where I am a professor."

The priest absentmindedly stroked the book, touching each corner, moving his fingers around the cover as if stroking the head of a child.

"There wouldn't be many Indian Franciscans, I expect," said Moses.

"There are some; seekers like me who escaped the rituals of Hinduism. Obeisance to these rituals was my punishment when I was a boy. My strict father forced them down my throat and when he died, I looked elsewhere. Others come for the same reasons, believing an answer only lies outside what they know. But, to tell the truth, I only found the same emptiness in Catholicism."

He loudly cleared his throat and quickly changed topics. "Have you been to India? You must one day visit Banaras, the oldest inhabited city in the world. It is —"

Moses interrupted him.

"What were you looking for?"

"Certainly not a cold room and inedible food." A smile spread across his face but faded rapidly. "I certainly don't know. All I do know is I won't be a Catholic priest when I return to Banaras. This is my last journey as a priest."

"Giving up the priesthood?"

Moses' companion ran his hand over his shaved pate. There was something engaging about the gesture as his fingers slid over the smooth skin. He answered the underlying question.

"There are many reasons I am giving up the priesthood. I had a dream, just as Saint Francis had at Spoleto. A voice in the dream told me to return home to where I was born. I could not stay in the monastery in France any longer."

Moses listened, trying to link this dream to his own. The air was heavy with smoke, even here.

"Were you stuck then?"

"Stuck? No, if I stayed, I might have felt constrained. But I left."

Moses noticed that his eyes glistened slightly.

"So you're not stuck? That's good, that's very good. Very good."

The train entered a tunnel and the noise made it impossible to speak. Both men looked at their reflections in the window. Suddenly, the brakes squealed as the train came to a dead stop in complete blackness.

In the silence, the priest asked, "Are you, as you say, 'stuck'?"

He leaned forward and Moses could feel his warm breath. He placed the Zohar back in Moses' hands.

"I don't know, really. I had a dream in which I came to a large steel door. I could not get past it."

"A door? Did you knock?"

"No, in fact, I didn't think of knocking. I guess I never touched the door."

"But it might have been open." The priest's voice became more animated.

"It was sealed shut," said Moses, more emphatically than he intended. He did not want his dream trifled with, although he was intrigued.

"If it was sealed shut, you could have polished the steel." He leaned back. "This is what the Sufis say: God is the mirror in which we see our true selves."

Moses knew more was coming.

"Or maybe you simply should not look behind the door. Who knows, maybe behind the door is God's hidden life. Certain things are unintelligible, you know, completely unknowable. Or maybe the dream is telling you not to pry." He leaned forward again and tapped his finger on the Zohar. "But I don't think so."

"What do you think, then?"

"I think it is God's door and He will open it when he chooses. Who knows, perhaps there is nothing behind it worth looking at. But, and this is the important issue, you are at the door. This must be the important thing, don't you see? I would say, and excuse me for being so presumptuous, that this is a point from which something can begin. The point from which you can wander?"

"Wander? A curious term to use."

"I was thinking of Saint Francis. He left Assisi to wander, to the Holy Land and other places that remain secret. When he returned, he knew what to do. He left the order and went into the mountains. If you wander, if you keep looking, then perhaps you cannot be stuck. It is for this reason I have been thinking of becoming a sadhu, an itinerant monk, when I return to Banaras. It is important not to stay in one place."

The train shuddered to life.

"This is . . ." He struggled for words. "It's funny, isn't it, how every situation reflects your state. This is my real reason for returning to India. I have prayed to God and tried to beat, if you excuse the analogy, a path to his door. Now it is time for *me* to wander." He paused and then suddenly got to his feet. "Please excuse me. This is getting too personal."

"No, no," Moses protested, "I have been personal with you."

The train continued on for a few seconds and then pulled into a busy station.

He sat down again. "I don't know. Perhaps you have been too casual with your images. Forgive me, I do not mean to be insulting. I am Father . . ." He shook his head and put his hand over his crucifix. "No. I am Seth Tripathi." He brought his hands together in the prayer position of Indian greeting and said "Namaskar."

Moses took one of his cards from his breast pocket and gave it to Seth, who examined it politely before dropping it into his shoulder bag.

"Please write and tell me about Banaras," Moses said, sincerely.

Moses then opened the notepad with his ramblings on the Zohar and, on a fresh page, he wrote the priest's name. When he looked up, Seth was already backing away. "Ah, I see the smokers have left. I will return to the assigned seat now. It was a pleasure meeting you."

He started down the aisle, then turned back. He held out his slender hand. Moses shook it, or rather, held it for a moment.

"Namaskar," he said, "is Sanskrit. It means 'I honor the divinity within you with all the powers of my mind . . .'" He brought his hands together to his forehead. "'. . . and all the charms of my heart.'" He lowered his clasped hands to his chest. He looked directly at Moses until Moses turned away. When Moses looked up, he was already seated in his original place.

2 HER NECK WAS A WIDE OCEAN of white skin. Very gradually, without glancing at him, she lifted her head to give him a grander view. Her hand rose to the top button of her dress and, sensually, she circled its edge.

Neither of them spoke, even though there was no basis for a pause. She had just asked a question and Moses had answered with another question. Slowly, theatrically, she undid the top button. She searched for his reaction while invitingly touching her neck.

Moses rose quickly and moved to the side of her chair. She cocked her head quizzically; he leaned over, moved the top of her dress aside and kissed her bare shoulder. He pulled her up from the seat and squeezed her tightly, feeling the strong muscles in her back. Somewhere in the distance, a horn sounded.

His arm crept around her waist; he was too frightened to advance further yet unable to retreat. He kissed her neck then along her collarbone. She raised her leg between his, which made him suddenly dizzy and weak. The embrace continued intensely for a moment more, then the spell snapped. Moses stepped back and held her at arm's length; she smelled of roses. As she came into full focus, it was clear, in that second, that whatever he was looking for could not be found. He let her go and shrugged, as if to say, "I don't really know."

"I'd better go," she said, quickly stepping behind the chair.

Moses could sense her increasing regret. She toyed with a ball of dust with her right foot, then took out a handkerchief to wipe his wetness from her neck.

One moment he had been talking to Martine about the outline for her essay, trying to help her make sense of Aristotle, and the next he had leaped like a madman from his chair and clung to her desperately. There was no prelude, nothing in their conversation to explain such spontaneous emotion.

"I don't know what to say," he stammered. "This is not the way — I — this has never happened to me before. Never since I have been married, Martine. This has never happened before. Never. I don't really know why it happened now."

He sat in his chair and looked out the window at the Warsaw sky. The clouds were heavy with rain and his little room was dark, with only a small light on the desk. The air was musty except for that delicate smell of roses.

"I want to see you again. Just to apologize." He paused. "Just to see you again."

It was difficult to look in her direction. He noticed she was holding her handkerchief gingerly, as if it contained the most horrible substance.

She paused at the door.

"I will be back to talk," she said quietly. She gave him a girlish, seductive smile and said, "Why wouldn't I be back?"

His eyes hurt, his neck was stiff. He locked his door and lay on the hard, cold floor, staring up at the plaster cracking from the German bombardments. He closed his eyes, taking a deep breath. The image of the massive, sealed door came into focus. It was not the first time that this image had returned so vividly: it appeared in the lull of a lecture or, bizarrely, when he heard a dog crunch on a bone. He was keenly aware that he had only the image, not a speck of the answer. Martine's visit was more a mystery than the dream visitation of Cain. The sealed door, he assumed, was still shut. In truth, he would have admitted, he had not bothered to check.

A loud shout from the street, warning of German planes, brought him back. He propped himself up and looked around at the piles of yellowing papers, wrapped in twine, and dog-eared books on philosophy. He noticed a picture of Zürich that had slipped down the wall behind his desk and was stuck in a patch of damp seeping from a cistern in the adjoining room. He pondered the worth of these books, none of which any longer held much interest, and of all the years spent making their words and his thoughts integrate into a tenuous structure. He pulled himself up and leaned on the worn sofa, and thought how today the room seemed particularly empty and miserable. He stood, straightened his jacket, donned his greatcoat and scholar's cap, and left without a glance back.

It was unusually cold for September and Moses huddled from the northern wind as he turned into Nalewki, the heart of the Jewish quarter. No sounds of planes could be heard. There was a wetness in the air that came from the ground, not from above. He raised his eyebrows to Jews he recognized but they did not reply, burdened with their own problems and the encroaching horror.

In the dark shadow of an awning he noticed a shapely young woman astride a bicycle. He smiled to himself, thinking of the words of the Zohar: "Initially the female is in the darkness."

He moved closer and saw it was Martine talking to a policeman, who was writing quickly on a piece of paper that flapped in the wind. The street was quiet; even the normally strident voices of the vegetable hawkers were muted. Now that the Germans had invaded Poland, there was a palpable terror.

Martine stepped from the shadow and appeared to be pointing in the direction of Moses. The wind picked up and blew straight through his coat. He looked down at his hands, not knowing what to do, as the fear and cold caused him to shiver. He looked up as she left the policeman and walked in his direction, wheeling her bicycle and waving to attract his attention. The policeman stood and watched, as did the few people in the street. Moses dropped his shoulders, trying to make himself look inconspicuous, but Martine came right up to him. She looked angry and bitter.

"A fine! Imagine that, a fine for not having a bicycle license! And at a time like this." She fumed.

She waited for his reaction. Moses exhaled in relief, able to assemble only a half smile.

"I'm so sorry," he managed to say.

She shrugged and walked the bicycle past him and around the corner. Moses sat heavily on the front step of a fish shop and felt the cold sweat on his back; his heart was pounding. He sank again into a familiar state of disappointment, knowing that he had no strength, no foundation on which he could stand; there was absolutely nothing there. In the past, he accommodated this deficiency of courage like a physical deformity that is ignored, but now, with the future closing in rapidly, it was an ominous sign.

Moses felt pressure on the side of his leg. He looked up to see a bicycle wheel pushed against him and Martine smiling.

"Follow me," she whispered.

He walked some distance behind her down a side street, looking deliberately at the numbers on buildings, pretending he was on some mission. She paused at a bakery whose windows were covered over with roofing iron, took out a key ring, and unlocked the door. She stepped in; Moses looked both ways on the empty street and followed.

"What are we doing here?" he asked.

"It's been abandoned by a Jew because of the boycott. My father has it now." She stepped back from the entrance. "Shut the door and come in, just for a second."

The room was black, except for a beam of light that illuminated the empty shelves behind Martine. There was a strong smell of fresh baked bread. She stepped forward, her neck in the shaft of light. She did not say a word and just stood still.

All he wanted to say was "I can't do this," but instead he asked, "What do we do now?"

Martine stepped forward, took off her coat and unbuttoned the top of her dress. "Come closer," she said in a soft voice. She moved his hand away from his mouth.

She grabbed Moses and tightened her arms around his neck, lifting her head and kissing him on the lips. Moses did not respond at first. She took one of his hands and put it on her breast, then kissed him again. Moses started to shiver in the cold room. A spasm moved up his body as if he had been seized by a fever. Martine stepped back. Her face, in the light, looked beautiful and soft.

"Are you all right?" she asked. "You're trembling like a leaf." She paused and touched his cheek. "Maybe we can try another time," she said gently.

"I am sorry really. Any man would be crazy to shiver like this. This is wrong. I shouldn't be doing this."

He continued trembling uncontrollably.

Martine continued unbuttoning her dress slowly, pausing at each button, teasing him.

"Please don't do this," he said. His eyes were fixed on the buttons.

She stepped out of the dress, folding it neatly, putting it on the front counter. Moses looked at the dress and the counter, remembering the thousands of times he had placed money on the same spot to pay for a challah.

He wanted to slide away under the door, retreat before all his values were abandoned. Her white skin haunted him, like a distant voice across water. This was a gift only a fool would abandon. He moved closer and touched the strap of her silk slip, his fingers brushing her collar bone. He closed his eyes, pushing away doubt and steadying his hand. He kept them closed as the strap slipped off her shoulder and his hand moved down her arm.

The heat rose in him like a freshly lit furnace, snaking up his limbs. He opened his eyes wide, staring at her. He quickly pulled off his coat and then his vest. He unfastened his trousers and they dropped to his thighs with a faint rustle. Then Moses slowed, his passion overruled. No thought could stop the onrush of his desire, only a superior emotion. He could not harm others.

"I am so sorry. I . . ." He fumbled to pull up his pants. "Maybe I should go out first," he said, backing toward the door, pulling on his coat.

"You go ahead. I'll wait a minute until you are away." She reached over to kiss him again, grabbing his head to hold it steady. The kiss was gentle and warm.

Instead of going home, he went back to his office, attempting to lose himself by making notes for a lecture. He glanced up occasionally at his office door, hoping she might come. But why Martine? She was half his age. Was this what Jung called an "anima" figure, his soul projected onto a female? This was not Helen of Troy, the purest form of the anima, but a common gentile peasant. Was her white skin some antidote for his weakness and fear?

Moses took a clean sheet of paper and wrote to Jung.

Dear Dr. Jung,

A young woman in my life, or at the margins of it, makes no sense, especially a non-Jewish woman. Her image, however, constantly comes in and out of my thoughts: her head slightly tilted, hair thrown back, prominent white cheek bones, pointed nose slightly askew. She has a straightforward quality and a truthfulness and innocence that I like.

Has she arrived because you told me that my search is over? It does not feel that way. Does she represent something that I crave in my spirit?

Moses reread the letter and realized it had little to do with Jung; unsure of what to do with it, he put it on his desk.

He moved the visitor's chair within touching distance in case she came. The seat cover was spotted with fallen plaster and Moses began to wipe it off with the back of his hand. In the fading light it was hard to find all of the dirt, so he carried it over to the window for a better view. He turned around to find her at the door.

"Just dusting up?" She looked around the room, as if to say that there were bigger problems to solve.

"Come in, please, sit down."

Moses returned the visitor's chair to its original respectable position.

"Have you read my paper?"

Her essay sat on his desk in the same place she had left it.

"Not in detail. But I will. Please, sit down. It appears to be an interesting approach. You are one of my best students, but you know that, I am sure."

He gestured her to the chair and felt the welling desire to kiss her neck. He converted the impulse into an awkward push of the inkwell on his desk and then sat down nonchalantly.

"How are your other studies?"

"I missed you. You are my only stimulation in this boring academy. All everybody talks about are the Germans, but you talk about ideas."

She pouted, coquettishly, her hands clasped in front of her, between her legs, swaying back and forth.

He was as lightheaded as if he was having an asthma attack and his chest pounded under his shirt. He reached over with a clammy hand and gathered in her warm fingers, gently stroking them, while her fingers circled his in a provocative caress. He enclosed more of her hand and looked up to see her reaction. She suddenly jerked away, leaving him shaking and dry mouthed. She stood and clapped her hands.

"I know what. Can you curl your tongue?"

"What do you mean, 'curl your tongue?'"

"Like this!"

She stuck out her tongue and shaped it like the end of a funnel. Moses was dumbfounded by her transition from woman to little girl.

He smiled approvingly, as if he was appreciating one of his daughter's finger paintings.

Martine stretched and smoothed down her dress, pausing too long at her breasts.

"Can't you curl your tongue?"

Before he could speak, she was on her feet and at his door, winking at him as she walked out.

Moses tore up the letter to Jung and started again. He took out a fresh piece of paper and smoothed it out on his desk, moving away books and journals to make room for a significant effort.

Moses recalled the image of Jung smoking his pipe, aloof and uninterested. He had looked at Moses when he spoke and even appeared vaguely intrigued by the dream, but he was not really engaged. Could the power of insight have made his compassion cool? Jung knew that Moses was returning to an uncertain future and a few words of support would have helped him. Instead, he treated Moses like a child, indulged for a silly song with a smile and pat on the head.

He wrote:

Dr. Jung,

You knew, didn't you, that Wotan — the God of War — was moving toward Poland. I now have read your article in *Zentralblatt*, where you wrote that Jews "as a whole" have an unconscious inferior to the "Aryan." You wrote that "the average Jew is far too conscious and differentiated to go about pregnant with the tensions of unborn futures?" This is what you said to me. So, you knew we were condemned.

Tell me, Dr. Jung, how are you able to write such words? I ask you. Please tell me. How can you speak so casually for the unconscious of whole races? I accept that you are uninterested in my work, my reputation, my loves or family. You just wanted that dream and I have often felt that if I had not given it to you, you would have grabbed it from me.

Yet we Jews need all the friends we can in Poland and it is

hard to count you among them. Tell me, are you on the crest of
the unconscious or are you just

Moses ground his teeth, feeling again the frustration and impo-
tence of his session. He sat back to read the letter, taking deep breaths
to calm himself. He was unable to finish the last line but he needed
to send this letter to Jung, if only to push the irritation away.

He took an envelope from his drawer and addressed it to Jung in
Zürich. He signed the letter, "Yours in the unconscious," but then put
a line through this stupidity and scribbled his signature. He pictured
Jung receiving the letter, rolling his eyes sarcastically and throwing
it in the garbage.

Moses walked quickly home with the envelope in his inside pocket.
Warsaw seemed no different today than yesterday; he was greeted
coldly, if at all, by acquaintances, and the sounds echoing off the
buildings were familiar and nonthreatening.

The heavy tick-tock of the grandfather clock was the only sound
at the dinner table; the entire family sat engrossed in their dinner
plates, pushing food around listlessly as he walked in. They briefly
glanced at him then returned to their inner thoughts.

"We must leave Poland, Moses. The fight is going badly. The Germans will win. They will hit our building any day now."

His father spoke in a quiet voice that spread over the table. All his
working life he had to shout over the noise of the machines that
made paper bags. Since he retired, he could barely be heard.

"This menace will visit us here." He lifted his head and looked at
each in turn. "We are fools to think otherwise."

Moses looked at the liver spots on his father's hands and the scar
on his index finger from some incident he never spoke of.

"Our assets are losing value." His father continued. "Even if we
sold everything, we might not have enough to live on for very long.

And who will buy our jewels at this time? And the boycott — this will hit us. And where might we go, tell me? All of Europe is under this dark cloud."

He stood and went to the window, staring into the street. He was motionless, his eyes focused on one point in the distance, not on movement below. He appeared to be waiting, not specifically for a mob or danger, just waiting. In the past, when Moses asked him what he was looking at, he would get annoyed. "What do you mean? I'm looking out of the window." This answer always left Moses sad and frustrated. An old man is most isolated when he stares into empty space. Perhaps the mind becomes a small residue when desires and hopes have crumbled and all that is left are immediate comforts. Was there another way to grow old, he wondered.

"So what then, Moses?"

His mother was slumped in a chair, gazing at the floor. After every few minutes of discussion, she would lift her head and ask, "So what then," or "what do we do?" She had always been sparing with words, but her laconic manner hid strength greater than that of his father. When threatened, she could strike out like a viper, and it took an observant eye to notice the intense, calculating look behind the benign face of an old woman. The venom existed because she wanted more for the family, for her son and granddaughter.

"I have some ideas," Moses ventured to say.

They all, including Moses, were speaking casually, without panic or tension. The room was calm, in spite of the subject matter, and the thick chesterfields and Persian rugs absorbed their voices. There was time yet, it seemed; a sufficient interval to devise a solution to the wave of confusion and fear that was breaking on the horizon. They watched Moses constantly; their heads turned in unison as he walked around the room, absorbing and analyzing every word he spoke. He was nominated, without election, to find an eye in the storm. His role as the man in a household comprised of two elderly people, his wife, and child, made him the only candidate. It was not important that his insecurities, piled layer upon layer, made him powerless: he was still the titular head.

To Moses, the impending arrival of the Germans in Warsaw was another door like the one in the dream; there was no way under, over, or around it. This door, too, was sealed. He could not let this image drift as an object of intellectual interest; there were only moments to find the answer. Warsaw, he knew, could not be defended for very long. He must open the door quickly, of this he was certain.

Nadia came over and swept up some coal dust. She brushed against her father, gazing at him with a weak smile. She whispered, "It will be fine. Everything will be fine, won't it, Father?"

Here was the touch that he needed: the open, loving, trusting heart of his eight-year-old daughter. Her smile spread across her face, exposing her sweetness for him to see.

"Of course it will," he said gently, stroking her hair.

Why did he bother with Martine? She had not opened his heart but only spun him around in self-loathing and confusion. The stupidity of this tawdry self-indulgence suddenly disgusted him. Martine was a pointless and pathetic attempt on his part to find softness. The more dangerous the world became, the more rapidly that softness would elude him.

His sweet Nadia climbed onto his lap and hugged him, but Martine had tainted his mood and his heart did not stir. Instead, he could only feel the heavy pressure of Nadia on his lap. Slowly, he unlinked her arms and smiled. She got off and walked away.

The conversation at the dining table suddenly became lively, with voices lilting in excitement. The name of a theater performer was mentioned and Moses overheard talk of the Landau brothers on Gesia Street. Nadia started singing and there was a sprig of laughter. For a moment, it was as if nothing had happened.

He caught his reflection in the mirror over the piano and was surprised at how ugly he looked. He walked over to examine the puffs of skin under his eyes and the heavy wrinkles on his forehead. At forty, he already looked like an old man. His large nose had red bumps and the hairs stuck out like little brushes. His distaste contrasted with the forced gaiety at the table and brought a sense of restlessness.

Moses put on his coat to go out. The room went silent and Sophie, his wife of twenty years, stood up and walked over to him.

"It is late, Moses. Maybe you should not go out. You haven't had any dinner. Come sit with us. You could get caught in a bombing raid. Every night the bombs have come. This is just a lull."

She pushed her black hair behind her left ear. She had aged quickly in the last year; at thirty-eight she had the facial wrinkles of a woman twenty years her elder. That was not why their relationship had gone cold. It was, instead, years and years of her sarcasm and brittleness that had eaten away the foundation of their relationship. She also knew him too well.

She begrudged him any activity, even a solitary walk. She tied him down, thread by thread, like Gulliver, most happy when he lay helplessly depressed, unable to move. He now sensed an argument developing about her lost opportunities and his privileged life.

"I'll be back in a few minutes. I need some fresh air." He spoke quickly as he went out the door.

He was alone. All windows were closed against the onset of night; no lights could be seen. A strong wind blasted up the street and he walked quickly around a corner to avoid its sting. He kept his eyes to the ground to avoid any rubble strewn from the bombing.

In the dull moonlight, he noticed three shadows that looked like stacked boxes against the wall. As he got closer, he could see the shadows were small boys, huddled together. They were thin and dressed in shorts and light shirts, scant protection against the early fall chill. He moved in their direction, compelled to offer assistance, until he saw that one of the boys wore a crude Nazi symbol around his neck, fashioned from two bent nails. They were talking together, shifting feet from restless energy. Moses retreated to move past them on the opposite side of the lane when he heard them laughing and saying "Jew." Suddenly, they all jumped up and ran over to him. With a quick motion, they pulled down their pants, exposing themselves.

He felt a sudden emptiness, deep and foreboding. He was unable to move as the boys danced around him, pointing and laughing, each little white penis flopping as they jumped. They moved close and began urinating on his feet. The wet, hot stream soaked his shoes as he looked on blankly, watching the streams move up his pants leg. He wanted to beg them to stop.

"Shame," he managed to say, "shame on you." But they only laughed.

They finished, buttoned themselves up, and walked away, as if they had just urinated on the wall. Their high-pitched laughter echoed in his mind.

Moses moved mindlessly away, his pace quickening with each step, until he found himself running. Weighed down by his greatcoat, he was panting, out of breath, but he could not stop. He propelled himself wildly down some lane, the wind turning the hot liquid to cold. As he ran, he moaned, his lungs wheezing. He came to a junction, moving too fast to negotiate a right turn and crashed sideways into a wall. He picked himself up, ignoring the pain in his arm, and ran back up the lane. He ran until he found his way home.

He slipped his shoes off and put them just outside the door, intending to deal with them later. Moses stopped in the vestibule to remove his coat. He sat down on the steps, gasping for air and shivering with cold and exhaustion. He did not say a word as he walked past the light conversation in the parlor into his bedroom, where he removed the soaked pants, bundling them up in the laundry bag. He took out his Shabbas suit, which he wore only to weddings, and put it on, taking time to fix the tie just right, as if he were being called up to the Torah for a blessing.

He made his way to the parlor on weak legs and sat down as if nothing had happened. His father sat in the large armchair by the shuttered window, his bathrobe partially open, revealing his white chest. Moses walked up to him and put a hand on his, largely for his own comfort. He squeezed his father's hand but there was no response. What had left his father? Was his mind softening or had he resigned himself to fate? Each day, he sat there in front of that window, staring, but never before had he looked so vacant.

"Are you all right, Father?"

"I had a disturbing dream, Moses. I was just thinking about it."

His father never spoke of his dreams.

"Can you tell me about it?"

"I was walking down the lane that runs along the back of our house. A big black dog came running up and barked. I wasn't really frightened but I saw, with relief, a little alley that ran off the lane. I had never seen this alley before; in fact, I don't think there is such a lane; we'll have to look. I went down this alley and, after a few steps, it ended. There was just a wall there, a high wall covered in vines. On the top of the wall was an animal, some form of reptile."

Moses understood the presence of the dog. Jung had dreamed of a wolfhound when his mother died, and the Germans believe that a black dog announces death. There was no alley at the back of their house. His father was venturing off the track, the well worn path he walked every day for his outing. The reptile, perhaps like the dragon in the bottle, was the alchemical symbol for transformation. The association of these images was clear to Moses: his father was going to die.

His father stood up and came close to his son.

"This is a dream of hope, I feel it. I have been moping around waiting for the Nazis to knock and now I can leave all this and go somewhere else. You tell me, you are the mystic."

"I am no mystic."

"You have that Zohar. I have seen it lying around. I know you read it."

"And you? Do you have an interest in it?"

He sat down and pulled his bathrobe tight around him.

"I have lived a shallow life, Moses. I have had shallow friends and all I have done is make money. It is too late for me now to pay attention to such things."

"But this is exactly the time for you to look."

He raised his hand.

"You, Son, this is for you. Not for me. But I feel better, it is a dream of hope. Isn't it?"

Moses hesitated and said, "I am not sure."

"It is, isn't it? It is a dream of hope and change. With all that is coming, it is a dream of hope."

Moses sensed that the rest of the family was listening, waiting for a response.

"Yes, Father," he said. "I, too, feel it is a dream of hope." But the words lay heavy on his tongue.

Moses had written four letters to Jung but mailed only two. In the first, he had thanked him for his time and sent him a paper he had written on the L'viv-Warsaw school of philosophy. The second, more recent letter, was a confused note about Jung's writings on Jews. He had never found an ending that satisfied him but had sent it anyway.

Now, Moses decided to write to Jung about his father's dream. If he replied, all the better, but it was more important to put it on paper, to clarify some themes. He was aware, however, that he really had nothing to say to Jung and there could be no expectation of a reply.

The knock at his office door echoed from the high ceiling, causing the hair on the back of his neck to bristle. It was Avrum, the head of the school, a Jew like him. They had known each other for almost twenty years but had never transcended the pleasantries. He represented a conformity that Moses strongly disliked in certain Polish Jews.

"May I sit down, Moses?"

"Please."

"I have some bad news, Moses. The Germans have arrested about two hundred of our Jewish colleagues at Jagiellonian University in Kraków. This was just last week. Today, I have been told simply, with no frills, that I must leave the academy — and so must you. They don't want Jews here."

Avrum stared at the floor for at least a full minute. Moses struggled to absorb the news, but somehow felt detached. Finally Avrum rose and shrugged his shoulders; his eyes were wet and red. Neither man spoke. Moses surveyed the room and made a mental inventory of what he would take when he left.

Martine stood at the door. Avrum bowed slightly, as was his custom.

"You have a student, excuse me."

He turned to leave, then returned to Moses and held out his hand. Moses stood and shook it.

"I'm sorry," he said, "to be the bearer of such bad tidings." And he slouched, not strode, from the room.

"Come in and sit down, Martine."

Martine was wearing a starched white shirt under a grey tunic. Her hair was pulled back, her thin lips bright red with lipstick. The heavy makeup on her white skin seemed unnecessary; for some reason she was particularly intent on looking white.

"I just came to tell you that I won't be in class next week. My mother is ill and we are going to visit her family in Lublin." She remained standing.

"I won't be here when you get back, Martine. I have been asked to resign."

"But why, Professor? Everyone likes you here."

"Because I am a Jew. That's why, Martine. There won't be many here soon, and, if the Germans take Warsaw, as they will . . ." His voice trailed off. He looked for a sign of contrition, of empathy, on her face, but there was none.

"I hope you are wrong," she said. "Maybe I can speak to my father. He knows people. . . ."

Moses pondered the unlikely possibility: Martine bringing home her professor, hiding her feelings from her father, yet convincing him to help this one Jew.

She stood there awkwardly. "I'll be back in a week. I hope you'll still be here. We have some unfinished business, don't you agree?"

Before he could answer, she was gone.

Moses gathered the papers on his desk into a neat pile. He took a clean sheet and wrote, "The end of false hope. The last drop of possibility." He dropped the paper on the floor, stood up, and left.

Dr. Weinstein came to see Moses' father out of respect for a lifetime of friendship. Other doctors, more concerned for their safety, spent their hours making hopeless plans. Moses noticed, for the first time, that the doctor's eyebrows were deliberately combed upwards to make him appear stern and officious.

"His heart is in flutter. It is out of rhythm. This made him weak and that's why he fainted. There is nothing to be done. It is mild and I don't think it will throw off a clot, but I wouldn't suggest moving him."

Dr. Weinstein immediately noticed that everyone tightened, horrified that they would be unable to leave. Stories of the "flight tax" for German Jews, destroying their wealth, and the stamping of a large red "J" on passports were more frightening as the Germans approached Warsaw. He cleared his throat and spoke again. "It is a mild flutter. It may go back into normal rhythm in a few days. Give him a hot bath once a day and keep him rested. It might be fine." He looked at the pale face of his patient. "Something else will get you. Not this."

He tried to laugh but it was out of place and he coughed instead. The doctor paused at the door, took Moses' arm and pulled him gently out of hearing range.

"This is a problem for your father. I can't come again. I hope you understand. But I think he cannot be moved. I could not see him making any long journey, not now. You might have to make plans to hide him. Or hope that things don't get worse."

He shrugged, then embraced Moses, something he had never done before.

Moses almost pushed him out the door. It was impossible to look at this face of doubt and worry when he must force the inevitable from his mind, to find a solution.

He looked at the closed door, noticed that the paint was chipped and rust was corroding the lock. Rather than confront the panic in the room, he grabbed a nail file and scratched away at the rust, managing only to cut a strip into the paint. He turned to see them all staring. Even his father had raised himself from the sofa to look at him. They came to the conclusion that Moses had made a decision. Nadia was caught up in the collective hope and ran over, putting out her arms to hug him, to carry him back into the family. She squeezed his hand. He smiled at her and joined his family.

A snowflake drifted to the cobbled street; it could have been dirt but the dull sky was too full of winter. Every Jew he passed had a vacant look and no pleasantries were exchanged. In each head, possibilities were being considered, plans were laid out. All eyes were turned to the ground in hopes of a branch or even a twig for the season to come.

Moses climbed the steps of the yeshiva on Twarda Street. He

placed his book collection inside the door on a table, where goods were piled for sale. There was not the slightest interest in his books, not just because of the gnawing poverty in the shtetl, but rather because the subject matter, the mystic Kabbalah, represented heresy to traditional Jews.

The rabbi was exasperated with Moses. "You must not turn to this material. The Kabbalah came from Jewish expulsion, when it was time to grasp at straws. It is a mistake to abandon Torah for Kabbalah now. We will be fine, this is not the time to play with magic."

He picked up some of the books of the Kabbalah and roughly pushed them toward Moses. "What is it you expect to find in this gibberish? Go to the shul and daven. Say the *Shma,* that's your mystical answer. This is what you should do. Throw these books out, they will do nothing but draw out your dark side, your golem."

Moses noticed that the rabbi would not touch the books of the Zohar. Sensing his question, the rabbi said, "This is a sin. These books, especially, mean nothing. I won't even acknowledge their existence."

Moses left the other books of Kabbalah by the door, but gathered up the Zohar and walked away. The streets were lined with porters, some carrying enormous loads but most wandering aimlessly. Many had been important civic employees, or scholars like himself who had lost their jobs, now forced to the only means available to make money, even if their backs or hearts could not bear the weight. Even then it was not easy, as a Jew had to sell everything for a cart or a carrying box. Moses and his family had, unlike others, enough saved to last six months. They also had a cache of jewels. They could not show it.

Children were rushing about in front of his home as he returned. He watched Nadia run and dance with the others. At eight, she was aware of some problem but it had no impact on her; the Jewish school shielded the children as they sat in dimly lit rooms, reading Hebrew.

"Father," Nadia said, rushing up to him. "Look what some boys gave me."

In her hand was the Nazi symbol made from bent nails. At that moment, his panic became personal; it was he and his family that were in danger, not simply "the Jews." He picked Nadia up and hurried upstairs.

He quickly gathered his family together in the dining room. He paused for a moment before he could find the words. "We have to go. The Germans will take Warsaw, the boycott is all over Poland. All of this is coming our way. We can't avoid the bombs and they will never stop. The peace we have known is over."

They were all remarkably calm, quietly absorbed in thought. Each, with the exception of Nadia, had been expecting the moment when the future was brought forward. He looked around the room.

"Sophie, decide what to take. I will go to the American embassy. Take your time, look around the house; no sense selling anything, as there are no buyers. The goyim are waiting for us to leave, then they will take what they want. Let's think of this as a long trip; we will lock up the house and hope it is here when we return. If something is precious and we can't take it, we will hide it. Bury it."

Nothing further was said. His wife went into the kitchen with his mother and started preparing food. His father went to the window and stared out. Nadia occupied herself with a wooden box on a table. Moses put the books of the Zohar underneath the wooden window seat.

"How long have you been waiting?" Moses asked the man in front of him.

"This is my third visit. Each time I wait from morning to late afternoon, unless I have to run from the bombs. See those vendors? They are making a living from us."

"What happens once you are inside?"

"You fill out papers, then come back the next day with certificates of one sort or another. Then you come back the third day. This is my third day, and, I am told, you are asked questions about diseases."

Moses was perhaps the hundredth person in a line of Jewish men, many of whom were old and bent. He recognized some, but most were hidden under hats, their collars raised against the wind. The sky was very dark and all were huddled from the cold on Focha Street, passing time with private thoughts.

"Then what?"

"Then you wait. They tell me a year, maybe more. I know one man who has been waiting three years already. In other words, you throw the dice and you wait. Maybe you will grow old in New York City, maybe you will die here like the rest of us."

"There must be a better way," Moses ventured.

He turned to see if the others in the line were listening. They were all pressed tightly together, some with hands on the shoulders of the man in front of them. No head lifted and there was little movement.

"Yes, you could have money or contacts. Contacts are important. You know any American movie stars? I don't. You tell them you are a friend of a movie star. They are all polite but they really don't seem interested. They think we are worrying unnecessarily. They don't believe that the Germans would kill us just because we are Jews. Who knows, maybe they won't."

"So why are you waiting if you have no chance?"

"We are all optimists on this line. If we weren't, we wouldn't be here in the first place. A pessimist would have already left. We are hopeful, of what I am not sure. Maybe we also think that madness will stay from our door. After all, the Jews have been sent packing before. We have survived. Maybe now we will move on, pack our bags and start again. But in the meantime I have nowhere to go and nothing to do; I cannot work and I am not religious. I wait in this line. If I am lucky, I go to America. If not . . ."

The man behind him leaned forward, pressing against Moses in a manner that ignored his personal boundaries. He whispered in Moses' ear, "We are all fools, if I may say so. If all you are doing is waiting in this line, then you might as well kill yourself now. The Germans have deported thousands, tens of thousands of German Jews to Zbaszyn. And who do you think is financing the Nazi marches in Warsaw — the Germans. In a few weeks, we will be finished. I will ask the Americans to leave now because it is worth a try, but if they say no I will leave anyway."

"But where will you go?" Moses asked. "The Germans are everywhere. Can we simply walk around them?" Moses spoke rapidly. Here, at least, was someone he could talk to about leaving. "We have nowhere to go," Moses continued. "We are . . ." he was aware for a moment of what he was about to say, "we are stuck."

"*You* may be stuck, my friend and if you are, God bless you and your family. I am not stuck. I am going."

"But where?" Moses asked.

"Do you think I will betray my family to a man I don't know? You have on a scholar's cap. Does this mean I can trust you? Can I trust a man of ideas? A man who has never done a physical day's work, who looks weak and fragile? This is a time for action, not thoughts. I tell you nothing. For all I know, you are a spy."

The man spoke loudly and others behind him shifted restlessly from foot to foot. The line was not advancing, but something moved within them that needed expression.

Moses let out a sigh, the vitality drained from him. He was no longer a distinct person but part of a mass, one of a mass of victims all aimlessly dreaming, going nowhere.

"You are right," he said. "I must do something. This is not it."

He moved from his position in line and the others quickly pressed forward to take up the space. He hesitated, but the bodies were already packed together with no room for him.

"I will do something," he said in a loud voice. He backed away a few feet.

"Fool," someone muttered.

Moses turned from them just as a few drops of rain struck his coat. Within seconds, it was pouring. He hurried away, but glanced back to see the desperate men still clinging to one another, oblivious of the storm.

3 MOSES STOPPED IN A CAFÉ overflowing with the newly rich. Some had prospered from the chaos and acted is if a further windfall was expected. Mr. Bredemeyer watched him enter, then turned his head away. When they passed in the street, Bredemeyer usually bowed respectfully; Moses was sure that he mistook him for a religious scholar.

Hopeless men, bent with hunger, sat in the dirty street outside the café. The sky was dark as rain gathered in the west, yet inside the café, the light was bright and voices were raised. Moses sat in a corner, watching the street as well as the gaiety. The patrons were all men with neat jackets and freshly laundered white shirts. None had a legitimate job, he surmised, but they certainly were in no state of despair.

Bredemeyer left his conversation, walking around the café, greeting all with a wave of his hand or a slight bow. He was a baker with unseen connections that he did not attempt to hide. He walked to the corner where Moses sat, coming directly to his table.

"Your table is bare," he said in a loud voice. "Let me buy you a coffee."

"That's not necessary, thank you. I'll just call the waiter. He has not yet moved from that other corner."

"May I sit down?" Bredemeyer took off his hat, revealing a yarmulke. "I have some business to talk about."

"Business? Not me, Mister Bredemeyer, you must have the wrong man. I am — *I was* — a professor."

Moses noticed that the two men at the adjoining table had moved, and others turned their backs to them.

"We all have business at this time. Foreign stocks, jewels, possessions, and maybe rare books. Who will buy them, eh?"

Bredemeyer sat, placing his fat fingers on the table. He did not speak for a full minute. As he sized up Moses, he rubbed his lips with his knuckles, a gesture that was both fascinating and revolting to Moses. He leaned forward and motioned Moses closer.

"You have jewels, Aarons. People are talking. Your father collected them years ago, diamonds, some say. We can get you out of here. There is a way. Have you seen Meyer, for example?"

"I don't know who Meyer is. And why do I need you to get us out? Why can't I get on the train and leave?"

"If the Germans get into Warsaw, each Jew will be marked. Looking like you do, what do you suppose you'll do? Walk to the train station and say, 'Two tickets for escaping Jews, please!'" Bredemeyer laughed. "The Germans have already bombed out the bridges and the railway will be next. You need me, Aarons. They all need me."

"But the German's aren't in Warsaw."

"Then leave!" Bredemeyer shouted. No heads turned in his direction.

"How much to get a family out?" Moses asked.

"A family? Who said a family? We can get a person out, one person at a time."

"So why don't you leave?"

Bredemeyer's hands, like two big paws, enclosed Moses' slender fingers.

"I think it will blow over. The Germans had to have Poland. It is part of the General Plan East, so they have more room. The 'lebensraum,' they call it. That's what I think, but you don't; that is why I am talking to you. I am here every day, from four to six. Here, let me get the waiter."

The room was spotless, with sofas covered in new, white cloth, though the oriental carpets were threadbare and the wood slats were unpolished and discolored. Martine's father sat in an overstuffed chair by the window, looking out onto the busy street.

Martine entered the building, pushing her bicycle into the space under the stairwell. Her father had not seen her coming and was surprised to hear the sound of her arrival. He looked out the window and saw a peddler selling bagels. He stood, lifting himself erect, as was his custom, and went to the front door. He shouted down the stairwell, "Martine, there is a Jew bagel vendor out there. Get us some bagels."

Martine went into the street and approached the Jew, who bowed slightly and lifted his wicker basket for her to choose. He handed her three bagels, holding out his hand for payment. Martine took the man's wrist with one hand and put the money in his palm with the other. She held it for a moment. The Jew lifted his eyes without raising his head and looked into the clear blue of Martine's gaze. He was frightened that anyone might see this interchange and withdrew his hand firmly but gently. He bowed again, lifted his basket, and moved on.

"Why did you hold the Jew's arm?" Martine's father was standing at the front door for her arrival.

"I didn't hold his arm, I was steadying his hand."

"No you weren't. I watched the whole thing. Do you know this man?"

"How could I know a bagel peddler? Really, father."

"Maybe last week he wasn't a bagel peddler?"

"But he's an old man, father. How would I possibly know such an old man? He was just a nice old man, that's all. I like the soft look of the Jews. They have soft faces, don't they?"

"I don't know any Jews. I have nothing against them — you know that. They huddle together and look after each other."

He noticed that Martine was avoiding his gaze, looking out the window instead. He knew this sign well; she always searched for a place to run when she did not want to talk about something.

"You know any Jews?" He said this loudly to bring Martine into the conversation.

"At the academy, I had a professor who was a Jew." Martine shrugged slightly; her furtive movements were obvious to her father. "I know that because he was told to leave the academy."

He did not trust his young daughter for any reason other than his own understanding of men.

"Come over here, Martine, and sit on the sofa. I am curious about this Jewish professor. I didn't know you even had such a professor, and now he is dismissed from the academy. These are strange times. Come sit here and talk to me about it."

Martine did not move at first, but realized that her father would pester her until she talked to him. He could go on for days like this, asking questions, prying, analyzing her every move and then using it. "Why are you fidgeting, and why are your hands so tightly clasped?"

She walked to a sofa, sat in the middle seat, looking at her father directly and strongly. This was the only way to talk to him.

He leaned forward and smiled. Even then his back remained straight, as he moved from the waist, not the shoulders. He smiled as fully as he could.

"So tell me about the Jewish professor."

"He was very helpful to me."

"Helpful to you in particular?"

"No, I am sure he was helpful to others. He must have been."

"I see, so you don't really know that. But you saw him on his own? You must have, if he was helpful to you, but you are not sure if he was helpful to others. So, how did he help you?"

"Oh, nothing special, just going over my essay, like everybody does."

"I see," said her father, leaning back in his chair. "This professor, what's his name, by the way?"

"Aarons."

"Professor Aarons. A Jewish professor, you say. So what did you two talk about?"

"Please, Father. I just discussed my essay with him, that's all! Now stop that prying. I told you he was a nice professor."

"You never said that. You never called him nice. You said he was helpful. Tell me, why do you think he was nice?"

"Because he was. Nice, pleasant. He liked me. He liked all the students. He talked about my essay as if he really cared. He was interested in my welfare and all the students'. That's what good professors do."

Martine's father looked down at his daughter, an attractive girl with clear skin and seductive eyes. She was wearing a warm dress, but the outline of her already womanly body was visible. He wondered if Professor Aarons had noticed it too?

"Sorry for keeping you, Martine. Mother's making dinner. Maybe you should see if you can help. Too bad the nice professor was dismissed. Terrible things are happening here, aren't they?"

Before she went into the kitchen, Martine wondered if taking over the Jew's bakery was one of those "terrible things."

"Mister Bredemeyer, I don't want to leave, I just want to know *how* to leave. If I needed to, how would I go? Which direction?"

Moses stood at Bredemeyer's front door.

"You shouldn't have come here. I told you to meet me at the café if you wanted to talk. This is dangerous, you coming here. So please, Aarons, leave now."

"Perhaps I can come in, I'll just be a moment."

It was late Friday night, when Jews were out walking after attending synagogue. There appeared to be a lull in the bombing. Moses had thought this would be a good time.

He abruptly found himself on the floor. His arm ached and the side of his head pounded. Bredemeyer's large shape was directly above him. Moses reached up for help and saw a walking stick above Bredemeyer's head, ready to strike. He curled up, waiting for the blow. He heard his teeth grinding and shook as if standing in a cold wind. He peered up, holding both arms out to deflect any more punishment. Bredemeyer was still poised with the stick above his head.

He was quietly hissing between his teeth at Moses, "You never come here again. You understand? This is my life you put in jeopardy, you madman. You come here again, and I will beat you to death."

Moses barely heard him. It was hard to imagine such terrible words could be said in a whisper. His nose was wet and running. He rubbed the back of his sleeve on the wetness and, even in the dark, he could see the black stain on his white shirt.

"I'll get up. Let me get up."

Bredemeyer squatted and helped Moses to his feet. He grabbed his lapels and pulled him closer. His breath was sweet with liquorice.

"Professor Aarons . . ." Again he whispered, "This is not for you. You can't survive. You couldn't be this stupid, you must be only naive. I don't want to see you again. You are finished, I am afraid, and I don't have the time to help you. You know what will happen if you come here again, I hope."

He pushed Moses out his door, slamming it. Moses tried to leave but his coat was caught in the door. He gently knocked. There were people returning from synagogue on the floor below, joking and laughing. He knocked again. The blood ran onto his shirt and he pressed his finger to his nose to stop the flow.

He attempted to rip the end of his coat but the material was too thick. He was overwhelmed by fatigue and dread, not only from the pain inflicted but from the humiliation. He leaned against the door.

Was this the door? What had the Indian monk said? Have you knocked on the door? This was not God's door, it was Bredemeyer's door. He could sit here until morning, waiting for Bredemeyer to come out, or leave without the coat and freeze. The answer was to knock on the door until it opened, not sit in a pool of his own blood.

He started pounding vehemently on the door. The people below stopped talking, peering up the stairwell to see the source of the noise.

"Bredemeyer," he shouted. "Open the door!"

The door opened instantly. Bredemeyer stood there without a shirt. He had large breasts and in his hands was a metal pipe. Moses instantly shouted, "My coat was caught, I had to knock. I am going, I'm sorry."

The whole building was silent. Moses rushed down the stairs, hearing his own breath heaving and hissing. Bredemeyer quietly closed the door. The people on the floor below turned away; he heard doors opening, then closing.

"Dear Dr. Jung," he wrote. Moses sat in a dimly lit café, his back to the broken window. He put the date in large letters, "October 1, 1939." Jung would know this was the day German troops entered Warsaw. It was also a week to the day after Heydrich issued a directive to establish ghettos in German-occupied Poland.

German soldiers were drinking coffee at the next table, although none looked in his direction. He took the paper, smoothed it out, and began writing:

> You may have received my other letters. Hopefully you will receive this. There will probably be a ghetto here but before they take us, we will try to escape. Jews were forbidden two days ago to travel without permits. This may be my last letter to you.
>
> There are moments in the day when I "remember"; not thoughts, but rather I pay attention to myself. I note my actions and follow my movements as if I stood outside and was looking in. In these moments, I feel that I have a destiny. But perhaps this

is illusion, not reality, as the destiny of the Jews is in the hands of Wotan. The Germans look at us in an awful way. What is the point, I wonder, of remembering myself when I may have no destiny?

There are times when you enter my dreams. You are sitting on a big chair, bigger than the one in your room, and you smile at me. Once, in a dream, you said, 'Get moving, professor.' "

Moses was so absorbed in his letter, prying something loose, that he did not hear the Polish policeman sit down opposite him.

"Professor Aarons," the policeman spoke quietly. "You don't know me. My son was in your seminar last year. He respected you. I am sorry to have to tell you this, but there has been a complaint lodged against you by the father of one of your students: a girl named Martine."

The German soldiers were eyeing them watchfully.

"I don't know what you are talking about. Martine was a student of mine, yes. So what is the problem?"

"You will have to come with me, I'm afraid." He leaned forward, putting his hand on Moses' forearm.

One of the Germans, clearly an officer, rose and approached them.

"What is the problem?" he said, in excellent Polish, to the policeman.

"The professor . . ." he said, "there has been a complaint lodged against the professor."

"Professor?" the German said, his eyebrows arching quizzically. "Professor of what?"

"Philosophy," Moses answered. "Modern philosophy."

"What is the nature of the complaint?" the German asked.

"A student —" the policeman began, but was cut off almost immediately.

"Ah . . . students. They can be most difficult at times, is that not true, Professor? Difficult *and* unreasonable." He turned to the police-man who was fidgeting with his nightstick.

"Let me handle this," he said politely but authoritatively.

The policeman nodded and retreated toward the door.

"Now," the German said quietly, "you will kindly come with me."

Moses could feel his head pounding wildly; all he could do was take slight comfort in the word "kindly."

He sat in a bare room on a hard, wooden chair. The walls were freshly painted and there was a strong smell of antiseptic. He had been there for perhaps an hour, during which he had for the most part stared vacantly into space, too overwhelmed to contemplate his future. Surely he was going to die. Sophie, Nadia, his parents . . .

He walked to the window that overlooked a side alley with a high gate, locked and topped with barbed wire. The activities on the road outside the gate were without meaning: children pushed an old bar-row tire, Jews braced against the wind. He sat on the chair, raising his hands to his face. He looked at the dirt on his hands, the grime having blackened the crevices and lines.

He looked up and the room was darker. Time had passed, and the window was black. He felt the press of his bladder, the ache in his stomach. He stood, moving to the far corner away from the door, pulled down his fly, looked around and urinated. The smell was pun-gent in the empty room. He felt, for an instant, there was some hope.

The door opened, admitting the young German officer. He looked around the room, then at Moses.

"What are you? An animal? Why did you piss on the floor?"

Moses jumped.

"There was nowhere else to go. I looked," he pointed in an arc around the room.

"Why didn't you knock?"

For a moment, Moses stood still.

"Knock? Oh no!" He pointed at the door. "Knock? I could have knocked, but I was . . ." He did not want to say "afraid," though that was the proper term. "I was reluctant."

Moses looked at the German and laughed — a deep, hysterical laugh of release. The German began laughing as well, in spite of himself. They kept sparking off each other; one would stop and the other would laugh again.

"I like people who choose their words carefully," the German said. Then, suddenly, he left the room, slamming the door. A few moments later, he returned with a chair, placing it directly opposite Moses before he sat down. He was thin, with small wire-rimmed glasses that magnified his pale blue eyes, and an intelligent forehead. He was balding but had a strong face, which made him look concentrated and secure. His nails were clean and manicured, and he sat back, contemplating Moses.

"You know, the Führer is a thinker but not a philosopher, like you. In fact, Professor, we have no philosophical system at all. Our philosophers, the academics, we consider eccentrics. So there is no *philosophy* of anti-Semitism. It is, you might say, a result of our need to solve our internal problems. Think about this."

Moses stirred in his seat. "But Nietzsche is your philosopher," he said.

"No, no, that association is facile, used essentially to counter the Marxists. Our Weltanschauung, our world view, is a doctrine of order that promises us stability and predictability. Order is crucial. There is an order: Germans first, then all those who are not. Jews, unfortunately for you, especially Polish Jews, are at the bottom of the ladder, lower than our own Jews. So we start with Germans, blond, blue-eyed, tall. You and I can understand this, no? It is nothing personal, Professor."

"What about Heidegger? *He's* your philosopher!"

Moses could have been sitting at his desk at the academy. Only the smell of the urine held him back from pacing back and forth, as he did in his lectures.

"No, Professor, Baeumler, Kreick, and Heidegger debate with one another, but it has nothing to do with you sitting here. Our world view is based on absolutely nothing. That, my friend, is why you are sitting here. In your own piss, literally. The search for order means that all non-Aryans are ranked, with you Jews at the bottom of the barrel. As I said, nothing personal. At the university, I was a student of philosophy and I wanted to talk to you. I'm a bit starved for conversation in this army, as you might imagine. I'm the only soldier here who speaks Polish. More will come, you know."

Moses sat unmoving, still deathly afraid, trying desperately to figure out where this was leading.

"You may be wondering why I 'arrested' you," the German said, as if reading Moses' mind.

"To save you from your countrymen," he said. "The Poles are far more anti-Semitic than we Germans," he said. "That I have already learned. And unlike us they have no philosophy, no order. With them it is visceral. Irrational and visceral."

"Save me?" Moses said tentatively.

"My professor at Berlin was Jewish," he said. "A fine man. I learned a great deal from him. Now, of course, he no longer teaches. . . ."

Moses wondered whether this man was toying with him. Cat and mouse.

"You are free to go," he said. "But if I were you I would not linger." He stood, opened the door, and gestured for Moses to pass.

Moses, in a daze, thrust out his hand to shake the officer's, but the German did not take it. He simply stared straight ahead as Moses moved past him and disappeared down the stairs.

Bredemeyer had the same violent look as before; the blood had rushed to his face, but this time he was smiling. He stepped aside, and just behind him stood Sophie, Nadia, and his parents. They all looked petrified.

Moses walked over to Sophie, hugged her politely, and then picked up Nadia. Whenever he touched her, something was added to the moment. Sophie stepped back, looking at him: "What happened to you?" she asked.

"Never mind that," said Moses. "Did you bring the jewels?"

Moses looked at Bredemeyer for guidance. Bredemeyer closed the door.

"I don't want to know what happened. I have no interest. Sophie has given me the payment. That is all. This is against my instinct; I shouldn't have let you talk me into it. I only take one person at a time. Five will be my undoing." He wrung his hands. "Time to go."

Moses cleared his throat and Bredemeyer held up his hand, saying, "I don't want to know." His face darkened and Moses backed off. He stood there with his family as Bredemeyer assessed them.

"Here is what we are going to do. In a minute I will take you down a tunnel. It is a drain under this building that goes along for three streets. When it ends, you will see two grates. Climb up the second one and you will be inside the butcher shop of a friend, who will be waiting for you. He will take you from there. Step by step, you will go on and, each time, you will be taken one step more. You have done the right thing. The Germans are watching the train station. The jewels you gave me are sufficient payment. Any questions? Good, no questions."

Bredemeyer led them downstairs into the basement of the building. There was a storage area, covered with old barrels and building material. He rolled a barrel aside, revealing a small grate. He pried open the grate with an iron pipe; below was a black hole. A short wooden ladder descended into the darkness and Moses moved to the grate and immediately climbed down. Moments later he climbed back out.

"I can see the tunnel. There is water in it, but it is not deep. We will have to crawl."

There was no sound, but the room was suddenly filled with flashlights and torches. Moses instinctively took a step back, behind a barrel. In an instant, there was a cacophony of sounds: shouts in Polish and German. The light of the torches was reflected in Nadia's soft cheeks. She had not seen him hide and turned her head, looking for him. If he did not move farther back, he would be seen. Nadia lifted her arms in his direction as a gunshot cracked loudly. He saw Bredemeyer fall. In the very corner of his view, he saw Germans advancing, surrounding his family. His mind reached out for Nadia, but he stepped farther back behind the barrel. A few seconds later the noise stopped as they were led out. The light went out.

4 NOTHING EVER CHANGED in Banaras. A stream of chaos swept Seth from the railway station to the Lahurabir district, where he planned to stay. As he walked, layer upon layer of image, smell, and sound took his mind further inward to seek a place of observation. No one looked at him or paid the slightest attention to his Franciscan robes. In Banaras, nothing is unusual.

As he walked, all his burdens seemed to lift. "Kasi," the spiritual name of the city of Lord Siva, emanated such force that his soul was nudged awake. In little alcoves, near fountains, in cracks in walls was a Siva lingam, the phallic symbol, resting on the female yoni. He basked in it all: the smoke from dung fires, the filth, the color, and the sun sparkling on fetid puddles.

He had planned to take off his robes, rest, then slowly venture out, but he could not keep himself from walking past Lahurabir. The crowds surged in currents, pulling him ever closer to the Ganges. To no one in particular he yelled, "Ganga, Ganga," and everyone around him pointed at once to the Ganges — the mother of life.

Next to him walked a sadhu, who paused to pick at a sore on his arm. His matted hair was wrapped high on his head in a Siva knot, the hairstyle of the Lord. He carried the traditional trident and was filthy, with rotting yellow teeth. The sore was festered, a deep wound, with inner tissue exposed. The sadhu turned, looking directly at Seth, his eyes like small saucers.

"Ah, you've come again," said the sadhu. "Very good."

Seth was struck silent. The sadhu stopped, squatting where he stood. The crush of people behind him pushed Seth along, but he knew, at last, that he was home. Only Banaras could supply such a greeting.

An old man, bent almost in half, stood in front of him.

"You die here, you are liberated. *Moksha* — liberation — is yours."

"This I know," he told the old man.

The man looked relieved and clasped his hands in a namaskar in front of his chest. He spoke again:

"There is a circle around Banaras, and if you die within it, you are liberated from the cycle of rebirth."

Seth recalled the Scriptures: Whatever is known as a creature, from Lord Brahma down to a blade of grass, gets liberation in Kasi.

He thanked the man and continued his way down to the Manikarnika Ghat, the place of liberation; the ghat that was there at the dawn of creation, where the sweet smell of burning bodies is ever present. He walked down the steps, the ghats, to the river, and stopped at the shore, taking off his sandals and tossing them behind him. He put one foot and then another into the warm silky water. He looked to his left. There sat a sadhu in meditation. Seth smiled at nothing in particular, and tears began to fill his eyes. A small breeze came to cool him, the sounds dimmed, the smells grew sweeter, the air felt soft, and that place became the only place on earth.

Seth slept soundly on the hard bed in the cramped room at the International Hotel. He was stiff when he awoke and saw that mosquitoes had enjoyed him well. They sat, fat and content on the ceiling, a few still buzzing lazily inside the ragged net. He got up, pressing his face against the dirty window, watching the chaos taking shape at this first light. The streets were already jammed with bicycle rickshaws, whining motorcycles, and wary pedestrians, all rushing about in a haze of dust.

He ate south Indian idlis and sambar for breakfast, looking out the restaurant window at the shimmering heat currents beginning to rise and float. Two Indian men in uncharacteristic white linen suits came into the restaurant and sat near the door, their backs to the wall. Both had waxed mustachios and dark shadows under their eyes.

The waiter moved over to Seth and whispered, "Even gangsters, these goondas, can be liberated here."

Seth looked with surprise at the waiter, more for the intrusion than the subject. The waiter continued, saying, "You wonder, sir, don't you? If all can be liberated in Kasi, do these men get moksha?"

The waiter was smiling down at him with blood-red betel leaf teeth. Seth did not know the answer but was about to venture a solution. The waiter solved the riddle, saying, "No sir, this is the answer. They will have one unbelievable pressure cooker of hell within a split second before death comes. It will be like a dream in which there is no time and the most devastating pains and miseries come. This is the punishment of evil. But even they will be liberated."

This was why he had come to Banaras. Myths and symbols were everywhere and they appeared naturally in daily conversation. This was how, he thought, he could experience the divine. Without myths and symbols, there was no recollection during the day of other possibilities, no reason to think that life is other than what it seems.

He realized it was not the voice of the dream that had brought him home. The voice was probably his, disguised to make the message more compelling. The deciding factor was the lack of mystery in the monotony of daily prayers. In Banaras, he could find the mystery.

He was about to speak when the waiter walked away. He had been here less than a day and this was the second conversation about matters of the soul. When he had come down the stairs, the manager at the desk had talked to him about meditation. He must have looked like someone in need of instruction as he had drawn the guru out of this plain man. Perhaps, he thought, it was because he was an Indian in Christian habit.

He stepped out onto the street, enjoying the blast of heat as a relief from the ceiling fans turned to the maximum. Within a few steps he was able to buy a badly stitched white kurta shirt and dhoti. Even before he could get back to the hotel to change, he felt the drops of sweat running down his back. He rushed to his room to become Indian on the outside as well as inside.

As he stepped into the maelstrom of the street in his new clothes, there appeared to be some invisible order. Though there were unsaid etiquette rules that he had long forgotten, he still had a sense of when to step out of the way for one person or not follow too closely on the heels of another. Interactions were a mixture of class distinctions, protective gestures, and supplications that he only vaguely remembered from his childhood.

Again he made his way down the lanes to the banks of the Ganges, but this time there was no particular elation or symbolism. It was deadly hot and the merciless sun beat on his head relentlessly. Around him, everyone's head was covered with a scarf. Just above the ghat, a group of monks — sadhus — huddled around an older man sitting cross-legged on a rough concrete platform. Seth put his hand on the top of his head to afford some protection and made his way up some rubble to the sadhus. One sadhu stood with an umbrella; it cast a wide shadow over the old man, under which Seth sheltered. The man just sat there, the sadhus squatting around him; nothing was said.

There were seven monks in all, who gave off a pleasant scent of jasmine. They were not ragged or filthy like others he had seen on his way to the ghat. They became aware of Seth and moved out of the way to open a path for him to the old man. They nodded at him and made gestures for him to move closer. Seth realized that he was, in a sense, caught, and smiled awkwardly. The old man looked up and motioned Seth to come closer. Seth moved within a few feet of the man and bowed, bringing his hands together in front of his chest. The man shook his head to say that this was not enough and motioned Seth yet closer. Seth now kneeled and brought himself to within a foot of this enigma, but again the old man cocked his finger and signaled for him to approach even more. Seth sat down in front of him and brought his face to within inches of the old man, who finally smiled. It was not a polite smile; it flashed across his countenance, lighting him up as if he had been waiting all his life for Seth to arrive. He raised his frail hand and stroked Seth's head, all the while pulling him to his shoulder. He held Seth like an injured child, rocking him gently to and fro.

Seth looked up into the man's eyes. He thought, "Can this be real?" The guru did not say a word; he simply nodded.

The old man let him go and Seth moved back to a comfortable distance, completely exhausted. This had all happened so quickly that he was unprepared for the emotional drain. He had come home to reunite with his Indian destiny, a process he believed would have unfolded gradually. In his time as a Franciscan he had begun to unfurl his sails and catch the winds of his own destiny. Now he was moving too fast, picked up and tossed about by forces so much larger than his small being. Within a day he had been welcomed back by a bizarre sadhu and then fallen deeply into the arms of a guru. Whatever this old man was, he was beyond Seth's comprehension. He had not said a word, no instructions to pray or meditate, no requirement to sit at his feet, but instead was a wide-open source of complete acceptance and understanding. The man was glad to see him; it was Seth who brought the blessing and gave it by his presence.

That night he sat on his bed, oblivious to the night noises and mosquitoes. Tears formed and burned his eyes. He felt a longing in his body, an overwhelming desire to prostrate himself before the guru, to lie flat with his head in the dust, arms outstretched, hands reaching for the eternal.

He lay back on the bed, shielding his eyes from the naked globe. Seeing this old man had made him understand how far he was from his own goal. He had thought that he had his finger on the secret, that some layers had been peeled back. Now, a single meeting let him know that he was further away than he could possibly imagine.

He felt his ugliness and despair. In the dull buzz of his mind, a thick, heavy doubt was in the center. He had no chance, but what else could he do?

He did not sleep all night. There was nowhere to go, so he lay there, his mind floating. Finally, he got up at first light to put water on his face, but a yellow spurt came from the tap. The pipes banged and bubbled and a dark sludge eventually plopped into the sink. He took the drinking glass from his bedside and put some of its stale water on the corner of his dhoti and tried to wake himself up by the moisture.

The lobby of the International Hotel was empty, the restaurant was closed, and he momentarily watched rats scampering across the tables before he stepped, once again, into the glaring early sun. The air was already dense and was cooking rapidly in the heat. He started to walk but quickly turned back, jumping into one of the rickshaws lined up in front of the hotel.

"From what country?" the rickshaw man asked in a singsong voice.

"Ganga, Ganga," said Seth.

The man rocked his head, in the ambiguous Indian way, to say yes, then turned up an alley going the wrong way.

"No, no! Ganga — Manikarnika."

"Breakfast, Sir. Breakfast."

The driver turned suddenly and went hurtling down another alley, bouncing wildly over the rubble strewn everywhere. He turned down yet another alley while Seth clung to the rails for balance. Then, after an endless minute, he angled around a corner and stopped. The driver jumped from the rickshaw and went into a hut constructed of rags, jammed between two buildings. A woman could be seen inside cooking chapatis. He looked back at Seth, "Breakfast, Sir. You wait!"

Seth got off the rickshaw. The alley had a strong smell of human waste. Several other rickshaws were nearby, drivers squatting on the ground, smoking bidis, Indian cigarettes. Seth walked to the nearest rickshaw, the driver asleep in a contorted position inside the conveyance.

"Ganga, Ganga." Seth pointed in the direction he believed the Ganges to be.

"Too hot, Sir. No Ganga," said the driver.

The sun beat down again on his head, worse than the previous day, even though it was still early morning. There was no shade except under the canopies of the rickshaws. He quickly returned to where his first driver had gone and climbed back in the rickshaw.

After ten minutes, his driver stepped out of the hut.

"Breakfast, Sir," he said, his teeth stained red from betel.

From the driver's throat came a hacking, which made Seth think he was choking. The driver started off and just as he turned the corner he coughed loudly and spit out a red mass, some of which landed on a vegetable vendor, who did not even flinch.

He arrived at the Ganges with the sun now turning the light white. There was little activity, except for attendants piling wood onto a funeral pyre. The sadhus were huddled together in the same place under a large umbrella, talking among themselves. They glanced up as Seth approached and one of them pointed above his head and wiped his brow. They all laughed.

Seth mounted the platform and walked over to the sadhus with his hands in the namaskar greeting. They laughed again and pointed at him.

"The man from yesterday?" he asked.

The sadhus stopped laughing and seemed to recoil from Seth. Perhaps, he thought, it was his words, referring to the guru as "the man," or his poor pronunciation in Hindustani, a language he hadn't used in years.

He felt a hand on his arm, grasping his elbow. He turned and saw the filthy sadhu with the rotting teeth who had welcomed him yesterday. "Sanskrit is the language of sadhus, not Hindi." He let out a shrill laugh and the other sadhus backed away.

"Bon marg," one shouted, pointing at the new arrival. "Avidya, avidya," they chanted. This sadhu, dressed in rags, was an avidya tantric, Seth assumed, the black magicians of spiritual practice.

The guru emerged from a building behind the platform, dressed in spotless white, his hands clasped before him. His sadhus jumped to their feet and one pointed to the Avidya. The guru walked up to the tantric and without a word put his arm around his shoulders. The tantric went soft, nestled into the arm of the guru, and appeared to melt in the embrace. The guru stroked his forehead as he had done to Seth the day before, and the Avidya tantric began to weep.

The guru pushed the tantric away from him till he was at arms' length.

"Take this man," the guru said to the tantric, pointing to Seth. "Take him and show him, then bring him back and we will make him a sadhu. Only don't make him wait for breakfast."

At this everyone laughed. Seth joined in. His whole being was laughing, and he sensed his body soften and listen.

The only light in the dark field was that of a few cow dung fires. Seth was walking, in total darkness, with the sadhu somewhere on the outskirts of Kasi. The moonlight was completely obscured by the thick cloud of dust that hung everywhere in India. Seth wrapped a shawl he had purchased around his head and mouth. In any other place this would have given him an otherworldly, or even sinister, appearance, but not here.

The field appeared to stretch far into the distance. Occasionally they would pass a family huddled by a fire, squatting, with hands extended for warmth. The light emanating from the fires was brown from the haze, and the families wore tan rags over their dark skin. The sadhu did not say a word, ignoring Seth's tentative questions. He had stopped talking to him soon after they left, walking at a rapid pace as if he were alone. They had not eaten since early morning and

Seth felt an ache in his stomach. Whenever there was a pump or trough they stopped for a handful of water, but they never sat or rested.

They walked for perhaps another hour when the sadhu suddenly stopped for no clear reason and took off his stained and ripped shawl. He folded it carefully, as if it was a sacred flag, and mounted a platform that Seth had not seen, although it lay directly in front of him. There was no wind or even a distant sound.

The sadhu sat on his folded shawl and looked inside a shoulder bag he had been carrying. He pulled out a skull whose jawbone had been removed and turned it upside down. He placed it in front of him, to the left. The head looked as if it were a bowl, not the remains of a human. He then took out three bones that looked like fingers and placed them to his right. He tapped the ground in front of him. He looked up, and Seth realized that it was a request for him to be seated.

This was the experience for which he had returned. He had left Banaras for the monastery in France at eighteen, after traveling to Italy and the important shrines. He had walked in the valley of Rieti, as Francis had with Brother Leo, and he understood why it was said that the landscape harmonized with the soul of Francis. For almost two decades, he had prayed for the love of St. Francis. At least he had hoped for the love of the brothers, but the blessing of Francis: "May the brothers love you as if you were me," never bore fruit. The coldness of his brothers and the dry words of the liturgy corroded the inspiration that was St. Francis himself.

The mystery was at last upon him, yet the sadhu disgusted him. His deep arm wound was covered with dried blood. All day it had been a gathering place for flies. The sadhu did not once brush them off, nor was the use of his arm restricted; it was as if the wound was plastered on with stage makeup. At close range, his teeth gave off a putrid smell, and when he smiled it looked as if his gums were covered with white mold. He had the annoying habit of burping loudly, the only sounds he had made all day.

The sadhu stood, removed his robes, bent over the skull and pulled out ash, which he applied to his emaciated chest and arms. He covered every part of his body, including his penis and testicles. He sat, held the ashes cupped in his hands, brought them to his forehead, and paused with his eyes closed. He raised the ashes to his mouth and chewed some, as best he could. From his bag he removed a small bottle that smelled of wine; he drank from it to wash down the ashes.

Seth was not sure what he was witnessing, but the pattern fit the practices of the Kapalikas, the bizarre sect of Siva, thought to be criminals. It is said that the Kapalikas eat from the skull bowl as punishment for an ancestor's murder of an upper caste Brahmin.

The sadhu put back the skull in the same place to his left and returned the wine to the bag. He sat still in a meditation position. Seth closed his eyes and tried to quiet his mind. He was aware of the foul odor emanating from the sadhu, naked in front of him only a foot or so away. His mind drifted and he felt sleepy, even though he was nervous and excited. Finally, the sadhu began to speak. "The goal is to overcome fear. Fear of others is the small fear. Fear of yourself is the big fear. Your meditation can go nowhere unless you can overcome the fear of yourself. Until this happens, you can have no integrity. Therefore, you must meditate in places that are dangerous to your mind. Each week you must go to a funeral pyre and gather any bones you can find. Or, better yet, find parts of a child or sadhu that has washed up on the banks of the Ganges and put that in your bag. Sit in the cremation ground, surround yourself with these bones, and meditate. Know that there are dangerous beings, living and dead, who inhabit the funeral ground. Still, you must sit unmoved in meditation."

The sadhu fell silent and returned to a meditative state. "I am about to give you a mantra," the sadhu said. "It is to be used when you meditate and when you experience fear. After I have given you the mantra, you will begin yatra, the holy pilgrimage. You will wander in the clothes of the sadhu that Guruji will give and you will visit the tirthas, the holy shrines. You will start at Banaras and then go to Gaya and next to Visala. After that, you will know where to go."

The sadhu leaned over and cleared a small place in the dirt immediately in front of them. He drew a clockwise circle.

"You must not stay in one place more than one night as you move in this direction. If you wander and have no home, you can take your mind by surprise. If you do not wander, your mind will slow and no real insight will ever come."

The sadhu looked at Seth and laughed. "Of course, you can stop at any time," he said.

He closed his eyes to meditate and Seth closed his as well.

"Your mantra is *Tat Tvam Asi* — 'all that I am.' "

Seth began reciting the mantra in his mind. He did not know how long he meditated, but when he opened his eyes the sadhu was gone. A thick fog had wound its way through the dust particles to create an impenetrable mist. The platform was too uneven to lie upon, so Seth had no alternative but to sit still in meditation. Eventually he grew tired and moved off the platform, sleeping fitfully in the dust.

At first light, Seth woke and stood, exhausted and confused. He estimated that he was southwest of Banaras. He had traveled a full day with the sadhu, but he had no idea in what direction. In a land where every inch of ground was inhabited or used, he was surprised to find neither person nor animal near the platform.

As he stepped over the area where they had been sitting, he noticed the sadhu's staff. It was a trident, used by other followers of Siva.

"*Om namah shivaya.*" The voice came from his side; the greeting of sadhus. He turned to find his teacher squatting in the dust.

"I thought you had left."

"Where is there to go?" The sadhu stood. He had a staff identical to the one Seth held. He touched the top of his staff to Seth's. "Come, time for you to set off."

"Go where? Didn't you say to go to Banaras?"

"This *is* Banaras. We are on the other side of the Ganga. It is just over that ridge."

He put his arm around Seth's shoulders and stood very still. For a moment, Seth did not notice his wound or his rotting teeth. The sadhu took his staff and pointed it to the ground, then to the sky and finally in a wide arc in front of him.

"You are *that.*"

When he said it, a crack opened inside Seth and everything around him moved very slowly and deliberately. The people no longer rushed around in wanton gestures, but all were syncopated in a movement that flowed and had a particular cadence. Seth, for the first time since he had returned to India, took a deep breath. The sadhu walked away, apparently uninterested.

Seth walked back to Banaras and meandered to the ghat. The familiar smell of burning flesh was oddly welcoming, for it made him feel he was at last moving toward the inner hope that had led him away from the monastery in France.

The seven sadhus sat in the same position and one of them stood and approached Seth.

"Go, Brahmachari." He addressed Seth as an initiate monk. "Get half a dozen plantains, a coconut, and some oranges. Come back here and meditate and then at midnight, you will be initiated as a monk and enter sanyasa in the Dasanami Order. I have been charged with your preparation."

Seth did not think twice and walked up the laneways, seeking the items he needed, which were given to him eagerly by vendors as if all knew what was to occur. Upon returning, the sadhu instructed him to lie down under a parasol and sleep. His head was throbbing with excitement and he thought it impossible that he could even close his eyes in the heat of the day in the noisy circus of the burning ghat. He was stunned when he woke up in the night with a monk standing over him with a razor to shave his newly grown hair. The monk sat him up and shaved him, leaving only a small tail of hair at the back.

All of this seemed to have a direction of its own and Seth let himself fall into the ritual. At midnight he took a bath in the Ganges and was given his robes, dyed with the gerrura color — the ocher hue. He noticed that the robes now appeared yellow from the flames of the funeral pyres illuminating the sky.

The Dasanami sadhu lit a small fire and the guru appeared behind him and handed Seth sesame seeds and asked him to repeat the chant of renunciation. "May I be free of the debt of the gods, parents, the world . . ."

The guru gestured for Seth to throw the seeds into the fire: the fire of final abnegation.

The guru now rose and cut off the tail of hair from Seth's head and threw it into the fire, where it crackled. He pulled Seth up by the hand and led him to a platform covered with a small pyre and motioned him to lie next to it. The other sadhus now drifted toward the pyre and sat around it in a reverent state. The guru first touched Seth's body with a torch and then the pyre was lit. This was his funeral pyre; Seth no longer lived.

The monks sang the mantras for the dead.

The guru approached him and said, "Victory to you, Master Sahadeva Bharati."

All the monks rose and circled him.

" 'Sahadeva' means one who is with God. May this always be true."

Well after midnight the guru talked to him about the etiquette of a mendicant monk, about sex and the other ways in which he could be corrupted. Hour after hour, he talked of problems Sahadeva would face, how he would eventually debase himself, and how he would be twisted and confused. He saw the exhausted and depressed look on Sahadeva's face and put his hand on his shoulder.

"Swami Sahadeva Bharati, listen please. I have not seen a monk who did not fall. In wandering, there is danger. All monks must fall. If you do not fall, you cannot rise."

2

Inadvertence

1 SAHADEVA BLED AGAIN. There was no pain, only a few streaks in his stools, but he could hardly ignore the dreadful potential. He had hoped that it would go away, but instead it had worsened.

He was hotter than the scorching temperature and loosened his robes, sweat tingling on the back of his neck. He moved to the patchy shade of a small tree and sat heavily on the ground. In front of him was a road of dust in the middle of an empty field.

He buried his head in his robes and cried; there were no thoughts, just an ache in his chest. His plans and hopes, woven together in a fragile pattern, dissolved, leaving him empty. The self-pity, fear, and confusion were unbearable, and he turned the pain back on himself: lack of respect for his goal, abuse of his mind, avoidance of truth. He clenched his teeth, shaking his head in self-hatred.

It could have been his dull headache, but the atmosphere appeared thick and slow. There was no sound other than the anguish ricocheting in his mind; around it went, pushing out every last hope. He wailed.

In his meditation, he had begged for whatever was needed. When he finished each sitting, he cupped his hands to his forehead, falling prostrate on the ground, offering himself up to the mystery of life, the divine.

"I surrender," he intoned. "I will go through whatever I need to reach my goal. Take whatever it is that needs to be taken. I don't care what it is, please let me advance."

Now his life was to be taken; he had offered it. It could not be retracted; the offer was too real. The surrender did not arise from bravado but from the primal yearning of his body; the desire to be complete, to do the bidding of unseen forces.

All these lofty thoughts now gave way to uncertainty and dread. The symptoms could be insignificant — minor bleeding — a cut, but he knew it was more. For too long, he had tried to negotiate with his soul. "Just another year of reading and thinking," he said, bargaining, "and I will be ready. I will attend to my soul, to the needs of the divine, in a month or in two months."

God will make a deal when the soul is at stake. If the soul is not in jeopardy, the universe loses interest, but when there is the slightest urging to rise, a tear shed for a wider view, the deal is on foot, the bet is made.

What had to be done? Were these symptoms not enough to wake him, providing the courage to break through? Was it now time to become a spiritual athlete, climbing some Everest of attainment from austerity and sacrifice? If this was the measure, he was not in the race. Or was there something else?

He sensed there was a chance to resolve it: find a direction, uncover the healing point, and traverse the path to the final goal. He had no inkling how to start or whether he possessed power to move an inch. His state was paralysis: inertia born of thought and fear. To survive, he had to find what he was missing.

Sita stirred the pot of dhal while her mother softly sang a bhajan. The devotional melody provided peace within the house and she and Sita swayed to its rhythm. They squatted together, working as a team, stacking the food for dinner preparation. There was little to discuss and Sita's thoughts rose like steam from the cooking pot. Most of the day she was in the hut, pushing the dirt from corner to corner with a sweeper of tied branches. Before lunch, she followed the road to the next village, looking for cow dung to be used as fuel. The collected droppings were placed on the walls of her home to dry.

Her father drove a bicycle rickshaw from sunrise until late. Each

morning, he pushed off toward Banaras and, at midday, he unwrapped a filled chapati from its rag, sprawled across the tattered
passenger seat, enjoying his lunch in the shade of the canopy. When
it was time for Sita to sleep, he returned with rupees, placing them
squarely in the middle of the table, showing off the reward of another day.

Like other rickshaw drivers, he was ragged, gangly, and emaciated.
Every afternoon, he stopped at a water pump, slicking down his oily
hair for his role as driver of the children of a wealthy lawyer. He
waited outside the school; they would go straight to him as he stood
beaming in front of his rickshaw. The children rarely talked to him
or spoke his name, but each week he received new rupee notes from
their mother. On this his family lived well, by village standards.

Sita's face was dark. From her temple, along her jaw line, a band
of black skin appeared as a shadow. The black also ringed her eyes,
but there was no other pigmentation on her face or her body, not a
mark or mole; her skin was flawless, although no one knew. At eighteen, she looked like her mother: short, heavy, but her face was well
proportioned, which gave her a pleasant, peaceful appearance.

From a crack between the segments of the hut, she looked upon a
barren field with the one large, ancient tree surviving on the plain.
The field was used for festival processions, but little else; even cows
refused to graze there and village dogs did not venture out in its intense heat. She gazed on the sparse view, stirring the dhal. Under the
tree she saw the sadhu.

A naga sadhu is invisible to women; his nakedness is respected as
part of his asceticism but otherwise ignored. When a naga sadhu en-
ters a village he is clothed in the minds of the villagers. Sita had seen
these sadhus before but always turned away. Today, she did not have
to avert her eyes. She looked outside the door and saw that her
mother had walked some distance away, talking to a neighbor. She
continued to stir.

The sadhu was lying on his back, his arms under his head. He was covered in ashes; his hair was matted from dirt and funeral pyre ashes. His penis was covered in ashes and lay against his thigh.

To no one in particular, Sita spoke out, "This is not what I should do. This is not what I need!" She turned her eyes to the pot.

"What is it you don't need?"

Sahadeva was in the doorway in the ocher robe. He appeared very tall and a dust swirl flared his robe. He looked menacing to Sita. She went to grab a chapati to put in his bowl, but hesitated when he spoke.

"I am sorry for startling you," he said. "I am ill. We sadhus should pay scant regard to the body, but I need to see a doctor."

He held himself tall with pride, but understood this was inappropriate. He slumped against the doorway.

"This is very unsettling," he continued with a soft voice. "Can you help?"

Sita wrapped a chapati in a cloth, handing it to the sadhu, then walked past him, out into the dust. "Come this way please," she said.

"We have no way to tell what this is. It may be nothing or it may be something. It could be in your stomach, your colon, your bowel; we have no method to be certain."

The Ayurvedic physician stood in his dirty hut. One wall was covered with bottles of sandy substances, the rest was stacked with old newspapers and bicycle wheels. There was a smell of incense and herbs, tinged with antiseptic. Into his mortar he tipped substances from different bottles, then fashioned a newspaper into a cone and poured in the concoction.

"You should take this every morning until it is gone. Then you must go to a hospital and have your bowel examined. I must tell you, it is not good."

On the last two words, Sahadeva panicked. Moisture flowed from every pore: a cold sweat. He was dizzy and the world shrank.

"Take a seat," said the doctor, pointing to the dirt floor. "Please, sit down."

Sahadeva instead staggered to the door, stepping into the glaring light. He knew that this was the end.

Sita was in front of him. It took some moments before he became aware of her presence. She put a wet cloth in his hand.

"Please come out of the sun, it is very strong today. Please, at least sit under the tree."

Sahadeva walked to the shade of a banyan tree at the center of the village and sat on a protruding root. Above him, large crows stirred and called.

"This is the end."

"You can't know this," offered Sita. "The doctor said it is not good but he said you must check. It could be nothing."

Sita took the cloth from his hand, wiping his tears. A woman was forbidden to touch a sadhu, but this was a person, stunned and raw.

"Lie here in this shade and I will bring you water."

"You must not go there, Sita. This is a sadhu and a man." Sita's mother pulled her gently into their hut.

"I'll bring him water."

"No!"

"This is a sick man, Mother, I will bring him water."

"Sita, people will talk."

Sita was immobilized. She had never disobeyed her parents, but the plight of the sadhu moved her unaccountably. She grabbed the water tin and rushed to Sahadeva. Her mother stared into the cooking pot.

The water was cool on his lips. The crows came from the trees, jumping around, looking for food. He looked tenderly at Sita.

"This is very kind. I don't want to move from here, go to a town or city and wait for days in filthy hospital halls. I don't want to be probed or poked. Some doctor will tell me how much time I have to live. What would I do then? No. I will stay here."

"Then I will feed you here," Sita said emphatically.

"No, no! I didn't come to your door for this. I will be fine here on my own. There just seems no reason to move until I understand where to go and what to do. Please don't help me."

"I will help you. That is all."

Sahadeva awoke, cold and uncomfortable. He pushed leaves under him as a cushion and gathered his robes tighter against the cold. He stared into the darkness.

It was time to reach within, to take hold of the power of his spiritual life, to invoke decades of solitude and prayer, to call upon the countless insights and the light of his concentration. This was the time to break through the barrier; if not now, then when?

He closed his eyes, repeating his mantra. As he quieted, he traveled to the place where he was still. He carefully, gently, opened the vault containing the fruits of his prayer. It was like a safe at a bank, and he envisaged it clearly in his mind. He took the handle, opening it smoothly. With the subtlety learned from all his years of Franciscan practice, he reached in to remove what he needed to cope with the overwhelming forces of illness.

"There is nothing there," he whispered, astonished.

The vault was empty, not a scrap constructed from insights, not a crumb of wisdom. There was no strength, no power, no force. There was instead an empty well that appeared bottomless.

Sahadeva was horrified. He stood up in the darkness.

"There must be some mistake," he thought, "how could all that prayer amount to nothing. Where is the power, the force to overcome fear?"

The moon was obscured by clouds, but in the blackness he saw a small, distant fire. He walked toward the only light he now had. He could discern the shape of a man sitting in meditation under a tree. The small fire produced little heat. Sahadeva sat across from the naked sadhu, with no intention of disturbing him. The sadhu opened his eyes and smiled at Sahadeva; he did not invoke the normal greeting between sadhus, he just smiled sweetly.

"I have been praying for twenty years," said Sahadeva, "and now when I know I am dying, I reach into that storehouse and find there is nothing there."

The naga sadhu smiled more sweetly. He cocked his head as if thinking for a moment, then looked at Sahadeva.

"Good insight!" he said.

Sita awoke with a shaft of light in her eyes. Her father squatted by a water can, washing his face and pouring water down his neck. Her mother was sleeping on the mat by the door. Sita watched her father's routine, trying to hurry his movements with her thoughts. The air was cool and the village was quiet. Her father took two chapatis, wrapping them in his cloth. He looked around the room, stepped out, and, in a moment, sent the rickshaw bell tinkling as he brushed off the dust of the night. Then the sound trailed off as he began another day on the streets of Banaras.

Sita rose immediately and organized her sari. The banyan tree was not visible unless she left the hut. She cautiously stepped over her mother and peeked in the direction of Sahadeva; he lay still under the tree, his back to her. She gathered two chapatis and moved toward him rapidly, noticing others emerging from their huts, staring in her direction. She hesitated for an instant, but then walked straight to Sahadeva.

He looked different, more frightened than yesterday. Something had left him. He smiled, looking at her thankfully, struggling to speak; an agonized moan came from deep within.

"Oh, god," he whispered, holding his head in his hands. He moaned again, rubbing the side of his head, as if in great pain. "My god, I am nobody, I have nothing."

Sita saw villagers staring. She felt a hand on her shoulder.

"Mother," Sita said, startled.

"Bring this man to our house," commanded her mother. "If you stay here or bring him, either way, we will be shamed forever."

Sahadeva's depression corrupted his memories and denied him belief in the future. He lay crying on a mat in Sita's hut. He lacked the presence to pray or meditate; instead he withdrew into a cocoon of despair. He twisted up, robes stained and disarrayed. His awareness was lost in his body.

Sita and her mother watched him lie there, curled up like a baby. Sita signaled her mother to go outside. She felt tenderness towards the sadhu, but her mother was fearful; it was a disgrace to have a sadhu in the house, especially one who fell apart without dignity. Sita's mother sensed news had already spread through the village and would soon leap to surrounding villages.

"This is a sadhu, Sita." She tried to explain to Sita the magnitude of the error. "This is not a man. It is better that he die somewhere else. It insults us all that he lies here like a dog. No one will want to marry you if you touch the sadhu. You will be known as the girl who touched a sick sadhu. You will carry this reputation for the rest of your life."

"This is not about me or a sick sadhu, it is about compassion." Sita sought eye contact with her mother but it was not forthcoming.

"Compassion!" her mother almost shouted. "This is about pity, and that will only lead you to ruin."

Sita lost heart for her argument. This was a greater disobedience than was acceptable. The spicy smell of her mother's breath calmed her, as it had when she was a child. She bowed slightly in submission. Her mother brushed a hair from Sita's face. She spoke very softly. "We need more fuel. Let's go together to get some."

When Sahadeva realized he was alone, he sank deeper, falling through the safety net of reason. He was focused on the aching of his labored breathing, shaking his head in pain and disgust as he gasped. He quieted himself down with supreme effort as a fresh wave of despair crashed over him, releasing a torrent of tears, causing him again to fight for breath. He was unable to slow the descent, knowing that it was not a temporary depression but an unstoppable, irreversible turn away from hope or grace.

At what appeared to be the bottom, he turned in on himself in blackness, as his soul entered a chamber. He saw the opening as if he was in broad daylight. He grasped that the chamber was not in his mind but in the recesses of his body. The place was cavernous, cold and empty but in the middle of the room was a glowing lever. It stood suspended, as if held by wires. This lever, he understood, was the choice between life and death. It was not the daily choice between courage and despair; it was the fulcrum of existence, the essential choice. The lever was not a mirage stirred by his thoughts or fears, nor did it arise from a parable or article of faith; it was there as the fundamental question and answer. Yet he realized that it was not the time to use it. It required some understanding of a riddle he had not heard. It was enough to know there was a lever; if ever he could lift it, he would live.

He calmed down. What he understood, he knew to be a universal truth: every person had this lever at the depth of despair. It was not a symbol to inspire but rather it was the life force itself. Some had seen it and yet walked away while others held it to their bosom. This representation of the life force was not what he had expected. It did not float within a beatific vision, the product of a refined awareness, precipitated by meditation or prayer. It existed in a hidden place in a chamber of the body.

"What now?" he wondered out loud.

This ailment could kill him; the continuum from bleeding to extinction appeared as certain as thunder before a storm. Yet now there was a possibility he might live; not by medicine or meditation, but by entering the chamber at the right time through the right passage.

He had no knowledge of what this really meant, but it was enough for now; he could continue.

Sahadeva stood, but was overcome by giddiness, weakness, and the light-headedness of fear. His knees grew unsteady and he lost his orientation, thinking that he was stepping off a train. He started to fall, but pressed against something soft, which yielded with his collapse. He glanced up and saw that his head was buried in Sita's breasts. She took away his pain and despair. She held his head as he exhaled in the softness, feeling totally light and free in a silent world.

2 THE HUM OF AN EXHAUST FAN blocked the sounds from outside of the room and the gunshot still reverberated in his ears. He sat down behind the barrel and closed his eyes.

It made sense they were pursuing Bredemeyer, he thought; he had obvious connections to an underground movement. But if the baker was their target, why did they take *his* family? He could only surmise that they wanted him, as well. He looked longingly toward the grate, visible from the light skimming under the door, and wondered if Bredemeyer's accomplice would wait for him at the end of the sewer.

He opened the door and slowly ascended the stairs, stepping into a well-lit hall. His father lay still on the floor, dressed in his best suit, the silk tie knotted carefully. Moses recognized a look of deep disappointment on his face; his soul had left him before he died, knowing what was about to be lost: the intellect, the refinement, and the gentle peace of family. Moses pulled him to a chair but decided against sitting him up. Instead, he took a carpet and covered him.

He sat in the chair and looked down at his father. It was better he die now, he reasoned. He knelt beside him, arranging the carpet, smoothing down his father's hair, straightening his tie. Grief welled in his chest, but he held it back, stamping his foot in defiance. Nadia, Sophie, his mother, he had to find them.

He pried open the curtains, suddenly aware that time was passing. The lights were off in the adjoining buildings and there was no movement on the street, as if everyone had disappeared with his family. He opened the front door and heard nothing except the squeak of the bookseller's sign across the street, rocking on its hinges. He stepped out into the street, looking one way, then the other. Gingerly, he started down the street toward home. Surely they would not be there: they would be at German headquarters, branded as would-be escapees. The distant drum of soldiers' boots brought him back; the sounds were moving closer. He ducked into an alleyway and via a long, circuitous route, reached home. He tiptoed to the door and bent his ear to listen: nothing. Silently, he unlocked the door and stepped inside. No one. Upstairs he checked the bedrooms, but they were cold and still. He sat down heavily on one of the beds, trying to stem the rising tide of grief, but he could not: he was bathed in tears.

As he was about to leave, he saw a letter on the kitchen table that was addressed to him at the academy. He pondered who would have taken the trouble, in these times, to drop it off at home. The paper was coarse and yellow, and an edge tore as he opened it. It was written in French.

Professor,

I hope you remember our lively discussion on the train. You invited me to write and I can think of no better way to consolidate my experience of the first day in Banaras.

I also hope this letter finds you well.

Some of us must keep seeking while others are content to live a rational life. The longing that burns in me (and I suspect in you) is not rational and can drive a man insane. He must look everywhere but has no idea what he is seeking. He merely senses its presence and, for some of us, that is enough to commit to the search.

Banaras is infused with passion for the seeking. It has set me alight and I suspect it would set you alight. The chants echo off the buildings, and there is no place in Banaras where you can escape the name of God.

Should the mystery ever bring you here, come to the Manikarnika Ghat and ask for the tall monk with the strange accent. We have a discussion to finish!

In friendship,

Seth Tripathi

How he made it back to Bredemeyer's he could not remember, but suddenly he found himself standing before the carpet covering his father. Gently, tenderly, he arranged the carpet before going back down the stairs and descending the ladder into the sewer. He heard scuttling sounds and shuddered at the thought of what was there. There was a glimmer of light far down the passage, and, without hesitation, he began to crawl on all fours. The water was warm and gradually rose, forcing him to lift his head to the top of the tunnel. He moved blindly toward the glimmer, ignoring the rats that brushed ceaselessly against him.

Moses came to the source of the light: a streetlamp shining through a grate. He continued on as Bredemeyer had instructed to the next grate, pushed it open, and pulled himself out, standing soaking wet inside the delivery entrance of the butcher shop, as Bredemeyer had promised.

"Take off your wet clothes." Mr. Idel, the butcher, was standing behind him.

"Moshe! I should have suspected. I could have walked down the street if I had knówn and knocked on your door or, better still, bought some rump."

"No, Aarons. I would have thrown you out or had Bredemeyer crush your skull. Now take off your clothes, wrap yourself in this towel and sit here so I can shave your beard. We have to make you less of a Jew while we wait for the rest of your family."

"They were caught, Idel. I tried to find them, but where was I to look? My father died. From the shock, I'm sure."

He saw Idel tense with the news. The butcher was barely able to cope with his role in helping others escape. Moses held back.

"Then all that jewelry will be just to get you out," said Idel. "It is riskier now. They are probably looking for you, so the money for all will just pay for you."

"Money?" said Moses. "Who cares about the money? The police are looking for me. I am doomed if I stay."

Idel was silent as he scraped off Moses' beard and gave him clean clothes. Moses put his passport and money on a stool. He had brought with him the first book of the Zohar, with Seth's letter tucked inside the cover.

"What is that book there?"

"I'm taking it, Idel. I will hide it in my clothes."

Idel ignored the book. "Now watch me, Aarons. This is the way you have to stand and walk." He stood upright and walked with his feet pointing in front. "No amount of changes are going to make you look like a goy, Aarons. You have become a Jew on the inside as well as the outside. Look at you — bent over, like in a synagogue. We can't pluck that out of you, but you have to try."

Moses pranced around the room until the look on the butcher's face made him feel silly. "I'm sorry," said Moses.

Idel looked at him in amazement, then shook his head and continued the business at hand. "There is a car waiting near the baby carriage store in the open air market of Karcelak. It was for your whole family, now it's just for you. I see you have your passport and some money. I will destroy the passport. Here is a new passport with a visa and an identity card in the name of a gentile. Here is some Romanian money. That's all you can take — no other belongings. You are going to Bucharest and you will need the money to buy your entry at the Romanian frontier."

"Romania?" asked Moses. "They hate the Jews even more than the Polish. You are sending me to my doom, Idel. What about Palestine?"

"Romania or nothing," said Idel.

Moses put the passport and identity card in his pants pocket. He shoved the Zohar into his shirt.

He was not alone in the car. Next to him sat a man like him, still with his beard. From almost the moment he was seated in the car, he fell into a deep sleep. He repeatedly dropped his head on his neighbor's shoulder until the man moved to the front seat, giving Moses the chance to lie across the expanse of the back seat. The car had a mattress covering on each side for protection against potential bullets. He did not dream.

The car went through Luts'k and Zalishchyky, entering Romania after stopping at the border town of Kuty. The trip had taken two days, during which Moses slept fitfully or dully watched the scenery slipping by. They had not been fired upon, although they saw similar cars with mattresses on their roofs, abandoned by the side of the road, pockmarked with bullet holes. Their driver spoke little and turned around as soon as they arrived in Bucharest. He dropped them in front of the Polish Relief Organization set up by the British Legation. Instead of going in, Moses walked down the streets of Bucharest as if he belonged there. He easily found lodging at the home of the shamus of the central synagogue.

The rabbi came that night to meet him and hear the news of Poland. He was a young man with bright clear eyes and a charming smile, and Moses immediately relaxed in his presence. The shamus brought out his best wine and the three of them sat chatting around a large wooden table. A hearth filled the room with yellow light and the burnt cedar gave off a pleasant odor.

Moses thrived on intellectual conversation, especially where he was the focus of attention. The rabbi or the shamus asked a question, then both sat forward to hear every word, looking between themselves and making appropriate sounds to convey their continued interest.

Moses explained the boycotts and the gradual narrowing of life for the Jews of Warsaw. He talked of the bombardment, the destruction of public buildings, and the recent occupation. He conveyed rumors as fact and created a horrible vision of what was to come. The wine warmed him thoroughly, and he finally said, shaking his head, "It is all confusing, why this is happening. As the Zohar says, 'the innermost core of God is unknowable.' "

The air left the room and the rabbi gritted his teeth. The shamus rose, cleaning imaginary dirt from the table, not looking at either of them. The young rabbi strained to gain composure and struggled to speak. Moses thought his mention of the Zohar had piqued the rabbi's interest. The rabbi inhaled deeply then said, quietly but firmly, "How dare you talk of the Book of Splendor in that way!"

Moses retreated, physically and emotionally, as he always did when he felt he had made a mistake.

"Forgive me. It just came out. It is not the kind of thing I normally say. In fact, I don't remember it ever coming out like this before. It must be the emotion . . . the tragedies of my brothers in Warsaw."

He noticed that the rabbi was now breathing more easily.

"The Zohar is precious to me and is always on my mind," said Moses.

The rabbi moved close to Moses. The shamus sat, relieved that the rabbi's wrath was quelled.

"You don't really know what you did wrong, do you?"

Moses realized that it was fruitless to obfuscate.

"I don't think I do. Was the mistake mentioning the Zohar?"

The rabbi stared down at him, shaking his head in exasperation. He spoke slowly. "The Zohar says, and this is on the deepest level of understanding, that man's actions change God. God's personality can be destabilized by a person like you."

The rabbi realized this was lost on Moses and gazed at him with pity. Moses raised his hand to ask a question, as if he were a boy in the yeshivah, but the rabbi ignored him and went on. "I can see you are weak, despite all your learning. I must say I don't believe half of what you told me about Warsaw and the Germans. Not half. Then to dwell on a passage in the Zohar, and quote it out of context, is heresy. It takes away from the very message of the Zohar of the all-encompassing aspects of the Almighty."

"I had a dream about this," said Moses.

"I am not interested in your dream," said the rabbi. "It's men like you who use the words but act badly. This has a negative effect on us all."

The shamus came in the morning, while he was still in bed.

"It is time for you to move on. Romania is always dangerous to Jews. Perhaps you don't realize how dangerous. We have just got out of the ghettos and now we will be thrown back in. Officially, no one has been allowed to leave Bucharest since the assassination of Călinescu but they have not clamped down hard yet."

Moses was expecting this, mainly because the rabbi was clearly annoyed.

"I would suggest you go to Constanţa, where you can probably find a ship," the shamus suggested. "I don't advise it but you are welcome to try your luck with us in Bucharest and I can help you to find some lodging here, if you like. In any case, the rabbi asked me to give you some money."

He held out a small envelope to Moses, who took it quickly, putting it in his pocket. "I am grateful," he said.

"The rabbi also left a note for you and wanted you to read it before you leave. I will be happy to point you in the direction of the port."

Moses thanked him and waited for him to shut the door before opening the letter.

Dear Professor,

The Zohar says that every man can become a mystic and the method is to: "Close your eyes and roll your pupils." This refers to the practice of meditation common in the east. But there are different levels and Tiferet, the center of G-d's personality, is only available to the gifted. I tell you this so that you know your limitations. This is not for you.

The Zohar says that G-d has emotional reactions to the

intentions of man. At least try not to harm others; you are capable of this. I do not think you are a bad man. Simply weak.

Moses folded the letter, putting it next to Seth's letter in the back of the Zohar. He went out of his bedroom where the shamus stood, as if waiting for him.

"I must go east. I certainly can't go north or west," Moses said.

The shamus explained the route. "Find your passage on a freighter through the Bosporus. You will need an entry permit if you want to stay in Turkey or go to Palestine. We can't give that to you. You might buy one at the port but I doubt it. Or you can go to the Middle East or through the Suez to Ceylon. The canal is still open."

Moses pondered. "Palestine is in chaos. There it would be hard." He touched the Zohar and felt the protruding edge of Seth's letter. "I will go to Ceylon," he said. "And then to India."

He noticed that the shamus was looking at him intently. Moses softened his voice. "Yes, India . . . that is where I shall go." He paused. "It was kind of you to take me in," he said. "The rabbi said the answer is to be found in the east. I can meditate for every mile of the one-hundred-and-seven-mile Suez! Thank the rabbi for his good advice."

The dugout seemed as if it would break. It tilted dangerously upward with each wave, whacking flat on the fall. Moses watched the ocean debris swirl under the boat filled with Indians squatting on the wooden rails. Dizzy from the heat, he wrapped his shirt around his head to protect himself from the pounding sun. Two hours after departing from Jaffna and the Indian coast was still not visible.

Moses tried to shift his weight, but there was no room to move. He had been pushed into the overcrowded bow with Tamil families returning from Ceylon. All were too preoccupied to notice his European shoes and coarse, woven pants. His beard had started to grow, his hair was long and unkempt, and with the shirt on his head, he could be mistaken for an Arab.

The ease with which he had made his way from Bucharest, the smooth progression from place to place, led to magical thinking. A tattoo on a Turk's back was a sign that he was on the right journey. For the first time in decades his mind floated unrestrained and he was carefree, living on his wits, making friends with one and all by his refined intellect and philosophical discourse.

He lifted his head to the wind, smelling the salt spray of Palk Strait. The dugout rose and crashed, but Moses was not afraid. He sat still. Time flattened.

He noticed an old man, cramped in a corner, grimacing with each fall of the boat. He was Indian but looked like a Jew: his white beard was long and luxuriant, his eyes insightful but cautious. He reminded Moses of the carriage vendor at the Karcelak market in Warsaw. Or his own father.

He pictured his wife sitting next to him, complaining, "Moses, the boat is rising too high. Moses, I'm hungry." The connection between them had soured. He had stayed in the marriage for Nadia, and to avert the immense fatigue that flattened him whenever he thought of the disapproval of his entire society.

He visualized Nadia asleep in her bed, the covers perfectly arranged in loving care. The peace of innocence and her delicate smell made her room a haven for Moses who would sometimes sit there for hours rather than argue with Sophie. It was too painful to think of Nadia now. He had to suppress the memories and remorse or he would not survive.

He waded ashore at the tip of India, Rameswaram. The sand of the beach quickly gave way to the swirling dust of the street and the stench of burning dung. The transition from the beautiful richness of Jaffna to the starkness of Rameswaram was startling. Flies buzzed around his wet pants and he stood at the edge of the beach, unsure of where to go. He turned to others leaving the dugout and said "Hello," but no one turned to respond. He walked from the beach and all he saw were waves of heat shimmering on an open road filled with wobbly oxcarts covered with shades to protect the drivers from the brutal rays of the sun.

Suddenly thirsty, Moses looked around for water but saw only half-built buildings with metal rods sticking out in disorderly patterns. He had no choice but to continue walking and looking.

"May I help you, sir?"

Moses spun around to see an Indian with a handlebar mustache.

"You speak English?" asked Moses excitedly.

"That's what I am speaking, sir. The English of the king."

"Thank God someone can help me. I am looking for a Buddhist monastery where I can rest."

The Indian's head rocked from side to side.

"Please sir, this is an Indian country. This is Hindu; no Buddhists here."

Moses had taken the shirt off his head but now put it back as the sun hit hard on his scalp.

"Well, then a Hindu monastery."

"There is no monastery for travelers, sir, unless you are a pilgrim. There is a Siva temple, an important shrine, but no place for food and lodging."

"Well then, where do I go for food and lodging?" asked Moses.

"If you have money, sir, there is no problem. You can stay at the Lakshmi Lodge. Very nice."

The man raised his hand in a gesture of grandeur.

"But I have almost no money," Moses explained.

"Then, sir, there is no place you can stay."

Moses waited for a further response. The Indian was moving away.

"But what then am I supposed to do?" implored Moses.

The Indian shrugged, looking squarely at Moses. "I am sorry, sir. I am not your mother." He turned, having lost all interest, and walked away.

At the entrance to the Siva temple, two sadhus lay half asleep in the sun, sprawled out like drunkards. As Moses tentatively entered the temple, he saw a small fountain of water and squatted to drink his fill. He then cupped his hands, pouring water over his head, wetting his shirt. Lingams, the phallic symbols of Siva, as well as androgynous busts of Siva, were along the walls. Moses wandered to the back of the temple until his arm was grabbed.

"Only Hindus," he heard.

He turned to find a sadhu standing close to him.

"Food?" asked Moses.

"You have food? Thank you, sir," the monk cupped his hands.

"No. Where can I *get* food?"

The sadhu silently pulled him back to the entrance, turned into a fiery arch by the blazing sun. He walked out and the sadhu let go, moving back to his place by the front of the temple, where he lay down. Moses noticed a small shrine on the ground to Siva Nataraja: Siva in the dance of creation, decorated with flowers and with bananas at its feet. Moses looked around, then paused to listen. There was no sound except for the sadhu rearranging himself at the door. He looked into the temple and there appeared to be bodies lying in the dark near the walls. He waited, moving his hand closer to the food. There was no movement from within the temple and the sadhu was already sleeping. He put his hand on two bananas, placing them in his pocket.

The sadhu immediately rose to his full height. He gave Moses the greeting of India, the namaskar, and smiled. Moses smiled in return and walked away. The sadhu called out, "Siva will destroy your illusions. You now have no choice."

*   *   *

The train from Rameswaram to Tiruchchirappalli, or Trichy for short, was overcrowded, forcing Moses under a bench. His long legs were tucked up to his chest but he was glad to have this space, even if so confined.

After an hour on the train, which continually sped up then jerked to a stop, he desperately had to urinate. He observed that as the train slowed, interrupted for a few minutes by people or cows, passengers would jump off, squat and relieve themselves. He slid out from under the bench, moving to the train door, observing this phenomenon, as he became sweaty, quelling the body's urge. The train came to a sudden stop and he jumped to the side of the tracks, along with two old men, squatted down, Indian style, and fiddled with the buttons on his fly. At last, he was able to unhook and smiled as relief came. He looked up when he heard the train creaking as it took up the journey. Moses stopped midstream and grabbed the rail by the door, pulling himself back onto the car. This was too much. He looked around for a place to finish but the car was full of families, lying about and squirming. He had no choice and moved to the door of the moving train and unburdened himself freely off the train, spraying food vendors and people walking beside the train. No one seemed to notice, or care.

He made his way back to his space, lying down contentedly. Soon his eyes closed and, for the first time since his escape he forged a plan. His thoughts sped up, as did the train, blowing away a mist. He would find his way to a university and seek an academic position; he was, after all, an academic who had published extensively. In the meantime, he would stop in Trichy and try to find work. How was he stuck, he wondered, if his mind could so invent a new path?

The train rattled into Trichy and he stepped down onto the platform. As he walked out into the dusk, the air was cooler and cleaner than in Rameswaram: the streets were flat and ordered. Here, he thought, was a proud city with a purpose. As he meandered, the light faded and the streets darkened rapidly. He looked for a protected area to spend the night and soon found a bed of weeds between two buildings. Without difficulty, he found water to drink, ate some rice, lay back, and drifted into the deep sleep of a weary traveler on a luxurious bed.

The dark clouds failed to hold back the light of a full moon. Several ragged children noticed Moses asleep and crept quietly in the shadows, examining him with curiosity. Europeans were usually well dressed, upright, and clean shaven, yet here was one with matted hair and dirty clothes, sleeping on the street like a beggar. They sniffed at him and touched his clothes. He sneezed, and they jumped back and laughed. Moses stirred and mumbled. They panicked at the sight of this waking giant and ran off, leaving one girl squatting near him, transfixed.

The girl moved closer to Moses, observing him tossing and turning. She inched toward his outstretched feet and slowly, at the same pace that all things move in India, untied his shoes and took one off. Moses suddenly jerked upright; not from the touch, but from a nightmare in which he was being chased. He saw the girl and roused himself, unsure if she was part of his reverie.

The girl jumped to her feet and ran away, unaware she was carrying one shoe. Moses yelled for her to stop as he set off in pursuit, waving his arms. She ran faster, toward the Rock Fort Temple, bounding up the steps while Moses followed, wheezing loudly from the effort. He was running from desperation, sensing that he would unravel if he lost his shoe. He heard her pounding up the stone stairs as she ran ever faster. He struggled to the top, emerging into the night air. In front of him was a stretch of grass and, in the moonlight, he saw the door of a small building on top of the fort. The girl was nowhere to be seen. Without hesitation, Moses crossed the grass and lurched into the opening. In front of him stood the girl with an old Brahmin priest who held the shoe in his hands.

"The temple is closed, sir." The priest spoke in halting English. "Tomorrow. Come back tomorrow."

The priest handed Moses the shoe.

"This girl stole my shoe," Moses protested. "I am not visiting the temple, I just wanted my shoe back."

Moses pointed at his presumed oppressor, a girl of perhaps fifteen, dressed in rags. The priest placed his arm around her shoulders.

"No, sir," he said warmly. "She was taking them off for you. To be comfortable. She is a good girl. She would not steal the shoes of a stranger. Go with her. She will find you a place to stay. Not here."

The priest saw that Moses was still angry and tense.

"Go with Satya. She will find you a place to stay."

Moses walked with them down the procession of temple stairs. The priest descended half way, then turned back without a word or gesture, while Moses and Satya continued down until they walked out into the night. Moses propped himself against the temple wall and put on his shoe as she walked on, glancing back periodically as if telling him to follow. They walked until they reached a teeming mass of huts on wooden stilts, perched precariously over a swamp of stench. She gestured again to Moses, and he negotiated the planks, which twisted in a spiral, moving inward toward the middle. Moses accompanied her into a hut and she gestured for him to sit.

Moses saw that her face was the shape and color of an almond. Her eyes were moist and expressive, and her lips were full and seductive. She had flowers in her hair. Despite her beauty, she was more a child than a woman; she was not much taller than Nadia. He was about to thank her when an old man with a bare chest entered the hut and unfurled a frayed cloth that floated on the slats. He motioned for Moses to lie down. Moses shook his head in feigned politeness, but the old man insisted. He looked out past the man to the other huts and realized that it was hopeless for him to make his way anywhere. He said thank you several times, did a few namaskars, and put his money, passport, and identity card in his shoe, which he used as a pillow. He kept the Zohar next to him. The old man lay outside the door and the girl a few feet from Moses.

No inhabitants in this sea of shanties seemed interested in his existence. They were focused solely on survival, with no time to speculate on who he was or why he had suddenly appeared among them. Satya, however, took his comfort as an important mission. Quietly, on the first day, she took his shirt, leaving one of her grandfather's instead. She beat Moses' shirt on the banks of the Kāveri River, later returning it, neat but still dirty. She presented it, folded, as if from the best laundry. He held the shirt up, nodding his approval, even as he noticed a button missing.

Throughout the morning, the old man came and went. When the sun was at its zenith, he laid a banana leaf before Moses upon which he ladled cooked rice. On the second day, he added vegetables to the rice. Satya sat across from him and stared, as if waiting to find some task to perform. If Moses looked back, she turned away and made an attempt at cleaning with a broom of twigs. Occasionally, she came close, pushing a hair from his face as he patted her bare arm.

On the third day, Moses walked from the shanties down the road called the Chinna Bazaar into the center of Trichy. After several unrewarding efforts to find a job, he went to the General Post Office, where he was immediately offered work, for a few rupees, writing shipping labels in English for the parcels that went by mail train to Madras before a three month journey to Europe.

There was only one document in English on the notice board: a promulgation of the Defence of India Ordinance that required every European male to be registered. He was sure the postmaster read English but nothing was said to Moses about registration. There was, in fact, no interest in Europe at all and he was unable to exchange his meager European currency.

Moses sat at a wooden desk, stacked with blank labels and paper. The postmaster stood behind, translating the Tamil handwriting into English, intoning a name and address, "Missus A. Dharmananda, two Edward Street, Leamington Spa, England."

The sight of clean paper and a pen in his hand agitated Moses. Thoughts constantly floated to the surface of his consciousness. Too many words burst forth at once, streams of sentences to Jung, fragments to Nadia. He rubbed the bridge of his nose, trying to concentrate.

"Mister Krishna Shivastra, his lovely wife and children, eleven Haikin Street, Belgravia, London, England."

The image of Satya came through the fog. He smiled as he wrote. Satya was uncorrupted, a white cloud in a stormy sky. He had followed her that morning as she walked with friends to the cantonment, watching tourists from the Guru Hotel come and go. He heard her giggle, her hand to her mouth, as a fat German lady struggled to get off a rickshaw. The lady looked helplessly in her direction and Satya turned away, her eyes to the ground in shared humiliation.

Satya's grandfather treated her tenderly, despite their wretched lives as untouchables. Each day she cleaned and cooked, waiting for her grandfather to return from his coterie of old friends, a group that crouched in the dust, smoking bidis.

Moses was like one of the guests at the Guru Hotel, except he was in her hut. The exotic life of oddly shaped white people, smelling of soap, was alluring like the trappings of royalty to a commoner. A small kindness to her was enough; Moses was now the object of her hidden desire to rise above her destiny. Within three days, he became the bearer of great potential.

He finished the last label to Mrs. Anda in Fontainebleau, formerly Mrs. Satyananda of Trichy. He noticed a letter on his pile in English to Professor Anand, Banaras Hindu University, Banaras, Uttar Pradesh. He showed it to the postmaster, who whisked it away, although the words remained embedded in his memory. As he returned to the hut to rest and eat, the words "university" and "Banaras" enlivened hope as he thought of a future and finding Seth, the tall monk with the strange accent at the Manikarnika Ghat.

He took several rupees from his wages and placed them before the grandfather. The old man looked at the notes for some time, then held each to the light, examining them for imperfections before putting them into the folds of his dhoti. Nothing in his manner suggested that Moses was more a benefit than a burden. Yet each night, he rolled out the sleeping mat for Moses, watching him fall asleep with Satya by his side.

When it was cold, the girl curled up beside him. Her hair reeked of cooking smoke and her shoulders were dirty. The fourth night, she shouted in her sleep and he stroked her hair. He was pleased with this rare chance to give solace to a young girl; he felt pity for her and all the others who inhabited the subhuman neighborhood of stench and human waste.

As he stroked her hair, she became Nadia. This time he let some of the feelings and pent-up tears come.

On a particularly hot day, Satya ran to Moses as he returned from work, jumping gleefully. She tugged on his shirt, giggling and pushing him into the hut.

"Diwali," she shouted at him repeatedly.

Moses had wondered why firecrackers were being set off. This was a joyful festival and Moses felt his spirits rise. Satya lifted a bag from a corner of the hut, pulling out an old but clean sari. She lifted it in wonder, then held it against her to check the fit. She turned to face Moses with a questioning look. He smiled and nodded approval.

Satya turned her back and took off her dirty clothes. Even though she was naked, she acted as if she was alone in the room. Moses initially shared her mood of modesty, turning away, but then he sat on the floor and stared.

That night, he reached out as he had before, touching her arm; patting it gently, then stroking it softly. He moved up her arm, cupping her shoulder. He positioned himself closer, then moved his hand down her back. She stretched her arms and his hand moved up her side, feeling the curve of her breast. He was not aroused but lost in the feel of her skin. She drew closer and he felt her warm breath. In the dim light, he saw her looking at him. She turned on her back, but he withdrew his hand. She joined her hands under her head and stretched, moving closer. She found his hand, placing it on her stomach, pressing it firmly. He felt its emptiness. His mind dulled and he turned his back to her. This was wrong and dangerous, his mind told him, and as she moved closer he edged away.

He had been desperate to touch her, to slide his fingers along her skin, but now that it was offered, he rejected it. He was not being sensible, merely vulnerable; too fragile to be lashed by the feelings swirling chaotically just below the surface. Sadness blanketed him. He was alone in the middle of India without a family or future, and almost destitute. All his learning, all those years of conceptual thought, reading, and postulating lead nowhere. He was no different than those who defecated into the swamp.

As he cradled himself in unhappiness, Satya hugged him gently, stricken with guilt. She thought her seduction made this great man sad and she cried, hugging him more tightly. Moses felt humiliated to be comforted by a child; delicately, not to offend her, not to cause her harm in any way, he pushed her away.

He rose and walked out onto the platform. He looked back and saw Satya feigning sleep, curled up, her knees raised. He saw the skin of her fragile neck gleam in the moonlight. The air was still, but silence could not settle with the incessant barking of dogs. He went back inside, lay down on his mat, and again stroked Satya's arm and shoulder. She pretended to sleep, ignoring his touch.

His fingertips tingled as he touched the labels. Desire passed through him like a current and he looking longingly at every woman that walked into the post office. He was enthralled by the soft facial down of a young girl and the prominent cheekbones of her dark Tamil mother. The desire was sensual, not sexual, and blossomed from an overwhelming need for human contact.

He was still in this same state as he returned to the hut. He was sure that he was being watched, and caught a ragged woman peeking out from her hut. He had not seen another white man in this area. When he first arrived, the children had stared at him with wide eyes; some cried as if in panic. Wiry, emaciated dogs barked at him until he stared back, causing them too to panic, whimper, and turn tail. Now, after a full week, he was surprised to still be an object of curiosity. He had thought he was part of the scenery, ignored by all, including the dogs. Except for Satya.

That night, when Satya lay next to him, he surprised himself by pushing her away. She moved closer, putting her arm around him. He pushed her farther away and said "No!" She rose, checking on her sleeping grandfather, then moved to the middle of the hut, facing Moses. Slowly, she took off her clothes and stood in front of him. She moved toward him but he put his hand up and shook his head. She got dressed and lay down next to him. This time she turned her back to him and Moses quickly entered a deep sleep.

In the morning, he went to the railway station rather than to the post office, to check the routes and timetables to Banaras. He realized he had to leave. The train left in an hour and he hurried along the paths and planks leading to the hut, to collect the first book of the Zohar.

The old man sat in the doorway, blocking Moses, who tried to make himself understood with walking fingers and train noises. The old man shook his head, pointing to the hut. Moses did not understand but felt a sense of urgency. He entered the hut and grabbed the Zohar, breaking its binding as he crumpled it to fit into his pocket. He smiled, and waved to the grandfather as he left. The man ran down the walkway, grabbing Moses' arm, pulling him back. Moses easily broke free, but the old man began yelling to the other faces peering out from nearby huts. As Moses walked briskly away, he noticed men coming out, also yelling at him, making threatening gestures.

He went quickly to the station, looking over his shoulder. No one seemed to have followed. Should he have left more money? He had eaten the old man's food and used his hut for shelter, without so much as a thank you. The hustle of the station drew him from his thoughts. He grappled with the complexity of finding the right train, quickly leaving the issue of Satya and her grandfather behind.

Moses found a seat on the overcrowded train, and squeezed himself tightly against a window. A family opposite him dismantled a stack of food pots, rearranging their bodies to claim a space for the meal. There were loud footsteps above, from passengers on the roof, and the train's whistle split the air.

Moses stared into the bright dusty station, watching the flow of colors, waiting for the journey to commence. The tea vendors, or chai wallahs, patrolled the platform, crying "Chai" as if it was a lamentation. More passengers climbed on board and the family eating its lunch defended the shrinking space by pressing hard against others.

He saw a commotion on the platform, the sounds muted by the general din. A parade of ragged police were followed by several soldiers, carrying rifles that looked as if they had never been fired. Bringing up the rear was a gaggle of little boys, laughing and jumping in excitement, mimicking the strutting soldiers. The police and soldiers paused outside the carriage next to Moses, shouting; there was a chorus of "neys." The procession disbanded, soldiers spreading out on the platform with guns at the ready. The police entered his carriage; he saw the tops of their caps over the passengers but not the animation on their faces. As they came closer, he thought they looked more frightened than determined.

The passengers scrambled aside as best they could in the restricted space until there was a path directly to Moses. A policeman, little and wiry, but carrying a long wooden baton, or lathi, stood facing him. He was very agitated, his eyes opened wide and his teeth clenched. Without warning, he struck Moses on the shoulder. Pain radiated throughout Moses' body, and he rose to his full height, trying to intimidate the little policeman. Other police jumped on Moses, pushing him against the window, knocking the air out of him. The soldiers streamed into the carriage, waving their rifles as the police piled on top of each other, securing his arms.

Moses was dragged along the platform by two policemen; the small, skinny men pulled him so quickly that his feet dragged. They threw him into a small building, replete with barred windows, just at the entrance to the station. One policeman entered and, without further warning, beat Moses with his lathi. Moses covered his head but the blood dripped down his face and onto the dirt floor. The stench of urine permeated the room, rising on the cloud of dust stirred by the beating. Moses sensed he was about to faint as he detached his mind from the beating; looking through the grime-covered window, he watched the little boys bobbing up for a view.

He was left alone. The back of his pants was ripped and his money and papers were either taken or lost. He felt for the Zohar, then raised himself, searching the room for this last link from the past. His thoughts gathered impotently, trying to assess the significance of the loss. The immediacy of the beating, the putrid smell and choking dust momentarily dispelled his concerns about the Zohar. He drifted into the agony of his wounds, touching tenderly each area of pain to see if any bones were broken. He tried, from a corner of his awareness, to steady and catch his breath. The wave of panic was held at bay and his breath slowed as a policeman entered.

"How hot it is in here," said the policeman in English, looking around at the bare walls and dirt floor. "They could have put you somewhere nicer, eh?"

The policeman banged on the door, which instantly opened. He shouted and a stool was brought in. He was cleaner than the others with a twinkle of intelligence in his eyes.

"So hot! Especially for an Englishman."

"I am Polish," said Moses, "but I speak English. Why am I here?"

"You are right! We should have taken you to a cooler place. I don't know why they put you here."

"Why am I being held at all?"

Moses rose to face the policeman as blood continued to stream down his face.

"Perhaps you don't know, sir." He paused. "Where should I begin?"

He took off his cap, and mopped his brow with a clean cloth.

"Very simply, sir. You violated a little girl, who today took her life."

The entrance of the jail was intimidating with watchtowers and a massive chain-link gate. Inside, the dirt courtyard was encircled by cells; each had a dirt floor, a wooden sleeping platform with no mattress, and a bucket. The door was a gate of iron bars, and the swirls of dust blew through the cell without hindrance. The walls of the jail were unpainted.

Moses sat on the bed, dressed in disintegrating prison garb. His hair and beard were disheveled, caked with his own blood. The warning to expect the indignity of dysentery caused him to push away the brown dhal; the bowl was already covered with insects.

The sun angled into his cell, causing the temperature to rise. Moses climbed under the bed for shade, curling up in physical agony and shame. Had he really hurt such a beautiful child? A child no different than Nadia. He could not find the answer, but plunged instead into a self-hatred that was like his cell: dirty and restraining. He was not Polish or a Jew, not a husband or a father, nothing but a discarded husk, crushed and beaten.

He drifted in and out of sleep that night. In the morning, with the help of daylight, he pulled his mind out that night of the mire, examined his wounds, and located himself in his surroundings. He climbed back onto the wooden bed and, with gusto, ate a hot meal of rice and vegetables. He was grateful for a section of orange.

As the morning drifted on, he dozed. He was not sure, in the recollection, if he was asleep, but Nadia appeared, smiling at him. At this moment, guilt overwhelmed him again, this time a veritable flood, as if it had been massing behind a dyke. Satya's death and the loss of his daughter merged into one, and he acknowledged the terrible consequences of his actions. Or inaction.

In his mind, he walked to the door of his dream, seeing himself projected in its reflection, as the Franciscan had, once long ago, suggested. He saw his frailty, weakness, his pathetic mental tricks, and the cold spaces that filled his being. He inspected himself from head to foot, seeing the mental sores, the self-pity. Gazing into his own eyes, he saw that a light still flickered. He accepted this blessed insight as if it had been whispered clearly in his ear: he must find integrity.

The courtroom was a small, hot chamber, made oppressive by a low ceiling. After four days in jail, he had had fifteen minutes to speak to his lawyer, an elderly man in an ancient suit, draped over his emaciated frame. He did not inspire confidence. Moses sat in the dock while his lawyer and the prosecutor stood near the judge's bench, talking quietly. He turned and saw wretched beggars on the back rows, probably there for the shade. A prison guard stood by the doorway, picking his nose. The air did not move.

A large man with a turban entered, took a dirty cloth from his back pocket and smacked the judge's chair. Dust rose in little bursts and settled. The lawyers were laughing. His lawyer walked to him, leaning on the wooden rail of the dock.

"You are free to go, sir."

"That's it?" said Moses. "Days in jail and it is over in one minute?"

"There is no crime. The prosecutor now admits that there is no provable connection between the girl's death and your alleged action." The lawyer shrugged. "You can return to the jail for your belongings or you can just go."

"I have nothing there, but when I was arrested I had a book and some documents. Can I have them back?"

The lawyer called the prison guard, who slowly ambled across the room. They spoke briefly in animated voices and the guard turned and left.

"Wait here. He will bring you the book and documents and then accompany you to the railway station. I advise you to leave."

"Thank you," said Moses. "I . . ."

"You need say nothing. This is my duty. Just sit here now and wait. That is all."

The lawyers walked out of the court together without looking at Moses. The beggars left, unsure of their status in the empty room. Moses sat still in the airless room, his shoulders drooping, taking short, deep breaths. He shook his head in disbelief. The retainer switched on a fan above the judge's bench and a slight breeze reached Moses. The moldy air, mixed with dust, was almost refreshing.

The jailer returned with his money wrapped in a rag. Pages were missing from the Zohar and his passport and identity card were damp. Moses began to count the rupees, but the jailer took his arm roughly, pulling him from his seat and out of the court. He handed him Indian pajamas, waiting for him to step in the shadows and change out of the prison uniform. As they walked, no one looked in their direction. Moses was dressed like an Indian and the now full-grown beard and unkempt hair gave the appearance of a light-skinned Indian rather than a European. The guard accompanied him to the crowded station where a mass of humanity huddled around the ticket window. The guard yelled and barged his way through, moving aside women with children, pushing Moses to the window. The jailer spoke to the attendant then grabbed Moses' money rag, taking out some rupees. He turned to Moses, pointed at a train making loud hissing noises as if it was ready to depart, and said, "Banaras."

3 A COOL BREEZE BLEW THROUGH the hut and Sahadeva kept his eyes closed to savor the tingle on his skin.
He had been covered in the night with a fine cotton cloth,
smelling of fragrances. He opened his eyes a fraction and saw that
the hut was empty and the sun had risen.

As he looked out of the hut, Sita entered and the light behind her
sari outlined her legs. She smiled when she saw he was awake. In
her hand was a metal cup that she offered to him; it was cool water
with a hint of rose.

"And how are you today?" she asked, in a delicate voice.

"I am better, thanks to you. I don't know what disease I have, but
it has shown me something very important."

He stood.

"It has shown me that I am of no significance."

"Of course your life has meaning," offered Sita, "all our lives are
in the hands of Siva."

"Yes, but what I have seen is more than that. It is that I can make
no mark — however slight — on history. All I can do is live the
small time remaining and then disappear. There is no one with my
name to live on. Even if there were, they would forget me. Forgive
me if this sounds maudlin. It is not. In fact, it is a relief. It makes me
feel older, but not as desperate."

He looked at Sita, now squatting and sweeping a layer of dust off
the dirt floor. He tried to speak but coughed. He cleared his throat
loudly.

"I am a sadhu. To this I am dedicated, but never have I been so
looked after, so cared for, and so absorbed by another person."

Sahadeva wanted to tell Sita that she was his Brother Jacqueline, the spiritual mate of St. Francis. He stuttered, "There is no more than I can say except . . ."

Sita stood and did a namaskar. Her voice was barely audible. "Please say no more. I have had the touch of another. I never expected as much. But we both know that you must go."

"I will go back to Banaras. I need to be with my order and see my guru, to rest, not wander."

Sahadeva returned the namaskar, bringing his hands close to Sita's, touching the tips of her fingers.

"I will go now."

Sita was surprised. "I did not mean for you to go now. You are welcome to stay until you are better."

"That may be a long time. I am able to go now."

He left the hut, turning back on the road to Banaras.

The tears welled in her eyes as she watched Sahadeva move down the road. She looked to see if her mother was watching, and when she realized she was alone, she flung herself on Sahadeva's sleeping mat and fell into a well of tears. Her chest ached as she gasped for air, but she did not try to restrain her grief. In a moment, she pulled herself from the spiral of sorrow, and raised herself to glance again down the road. Sahadeva was walking slowly, but every few feet he turned and stared back. She lowered her head so he would not see her.

The ordered path of her life was now disturbed. Instead of an arranged marriage and a lifetime in the village, a new road appeared for her. As she thought about Sahadeva, she shook her head, acknowledging the impossibility of the situation. He was a sadhu; no contact with women was possible. Sahadeva was dead in the eyes of the world and his presence in her hut, the touching that had occurred, was completely forbidden by scripture.

Her feeling for Sahadeva was mostly pity, she told herself. For a moment, she wondered if love could exist at the same time. She stood, remembering his smile, and saw him in the distance, the sun still flickering on his ocher robe. Her deepest longing was for integrity: a deep commitment to strength of mind and understanding. She was already imbued with these characteristics. Without theories or beliefs, she acted with force of character, causing others to mark her actions.

She looked along the road to see if he was still visible, but he was gone. She noticed movement by the tree where the naked sadhu had lain. It was Sahadeva, staring in her direction. She ducked, without being detected, then rose to face her dilemma. Sahadeva wiped his brow, then quickly dropped to the ground. She was not sure if he had lowered himself or fainted. Very quickly, she walked toward him.

Sita's mother was behind the hut, looking for sticks to supplement the cow dung. She instantly saw why Sita was walking along the road.

"Sita, come back!"

Sita walked with determination, glancing back at her mother with an anguished look, hoping that her chains would be released this one time.

"Sita, you cannot go there. You must come back." Sita's mother paused. She knew her daughter's destiny was in the balance. Relationship with a sadhu was scandalous. Too much had already occurred; more than one eyebrow in the village had been raised. She lifted her sari and ran toward Sita.

Sita broke into a run, rushing to Sahadeva. Her mother, unaccustomed to running, and in an attempt to keep her dignity before those villagers who might be watching the spectacle, slowed to a walk. She turned and was dismayed to see dozens of women outside their huts, waiting to see the outcome of this unimaginable situation.

Sita reached Sahadeva just as he stood up. He knew why she was coming. In a weak voice, without commitment, Sahadeva cried out, "Sita, you must not be here. Go back!"

She removed the sari from her head and stood before him, panting. Her face was covered in dust, streaked with tears. She was almost ready to accept the impossibility of their relationship and the harshness of his words, when she saw a smile light up his face. She squeezed her hands together, laughing loudly; she knew what he had decided. Sahadeva was soon caught up in her laughter, and when Sita's mother came up behind them, clenching her teeth in anger, she thought they had both gone insane. She was about to speak when Sahadeva stepped back, addressing them both.

"Forgive me. Please let me talk to you both." But when he spoke he was clearly addressing the mother.

"I know I cannot be a sadhu. Never as a priest or a monk have I experienced the peace that I have had with Sita beside me. I will disrobe in Banaras and return. When I have done so, I will come to your house and ask your husband for Sita to be my bride. If he says no, I will find some work in the village so I will be near."

The mother looked at Sahadeva for the first time, seeing past the robes and the tradition. "No, this is not possible," she said. "We already have a boy in mind who is studying to be a lawyer in Lucknow. We have spoken to his parents. You cannot come back. We don't want you here; you have brought shame to our family and this will never be forgotten."

"I am coming back," Sahadeva insisted. "I will come to your door."

Sahadeva gave his namaskar, turned dramatically, and headed off down the road. He did not look back.

4 ZELAZNA STREET IN WARSAW was the "Jewish Street," while Chlodna was known as "Aryan" Chlodna Street. It was the place where the iron gate defined the boundary of the ghetto. It was the end of the old life and the beginning of another, dangerous and alien. Although a world away, leaving the station at Banaras had a similar significance for Moses.

He paused on a bench under the shade of station rafters where bicycle rickshaw drivers vied for customers. An Englishman, inappropriately dressed for the weather in a tweed jacket, riding pants, and high boots, was set upon by boys and drivers, all pulling at his luggage while speaking soothingly to direct his movement. The man yanked his bag from one, only to have it snatched by another. Moses half thought to make contact with him, using his offer of help as an introduction, but he had no real interest in another's affairs. Instead, he wanted to gather his strength and set off in search of the university and the priest he met on the train.

Moses bent to drink from a rusty tap on the side of the road. He wet his rag, wiped his face, and looked around. Banaras shimmered in the heat. The streets were chaotic, as people appeared desperate to be somewhere else. The air was filled with dust sparkling in the bright light, and the tinkle of rickshaw bells was pervasive.

Moses stopped to buy some oranges, noting that the bag was constructed from sections of the Uttar Pradesh Municipal Statute. He moved to the side of the road to escape the juggernaut of traffic and strolled along slowly and deliberately, craning his neck, as would any tourist. Only three days ago he had sat in misery on a wooden platform in a small cell, in a state of anxiety and fear. Strolling and eating an orange were to him sublime luxuries.

At every turn there was a deformed beggar, with gross body twists and protuberances unseen in Europe. Moses could not help but stare with curiosity and bewilderment until he felt nauseated. He looked for respite and walked down the stairs of a small restaurant where he ordered a cup of Indian tea. He asked the owner in English for a scrap of paper and a pencil. He was given a triangle of paper from a bag and a stub of lead pencil.

Moses composed a new letter to Dr. Jung.

Dear Dr. Jung:

If you no longer remember me from my visit to you or the letters that I sent from Poland, you certainly will remember the man who wrote to you on a scrap of Indian paper. I have come a long way from your door and I am writing from Banaras in India.

Moses asked for another scrap of paper and this time was given pieces of packaging with one side free of text.

I came to you with a dream. I was stuck at a door. Now I see that I could not move because of guilt. No wonder I have such a door! If I was free of this guilt, I could open that door, of that I am sure.

There is nowhere you can write to me, even if you were so inclined. I will find a way to move on. The answer is probably here in front of me.

Moses read and reread his letter, as he sipped his sweet milky chai. He shook his head, understanding that when he saw Jung he was at a primitive level and this dawning guilt was the breakthrough he needed. He sat back in the rickety chair, satisfied. The blend of noise, smells, and dust formed a one-dimensional surface, as he became more relaxed. He had enough money for a week and by then he would have contacted the university and found, he expected, some type of position. He could set out eventually and find the priest and talk more about the door and his fresh insights.

He sat there for a few more minutes, until the noise of Banaras intruded. He was alone with the owner in the restaurant and they looked at each other.

"Who are you writing to?" asked the owner.

"I guess you could say a guru in Switzerland. At least some people think he is a guru."

"There are many false gurus. We Indians know this. You see those sadhus across the street there. The short one there, you see him? He is an impostor and is a sadhu only to get food. A sadhu should be one who has renounced the world in search of spiritual understanding, not one who uses the spiritual to provide the goods of the world. Don't you agree?"

"How do you know the real sadhus from the fake?" asked Moses.

"There is no real way of telling, but you can sense it. Have you been to the Ganges? There you can see many sadhus who have eyes fixed on the divine."

"I have come to find one monk at the . . ." Moses reached for the Zohar and opened the letter from Seth, "at the Manikarnika Ghat."

The owner gave him uncomplicated directions to the ghat. Moses slowly stood, stretched, and thanked the owner before entering the moving mass of people headed in every direction. He headed away from the station and toward the Ganges.

Moses walked until he saw the lanes that the restaurant owner explained were passages to the great river. He stepped briskly through the throngs.

Among the cows and sadhus, people squatting and standing, he noticed a man having wax removed from his ears with a frightening instrument and a barber shaving a small boy's head. Next to the barber was a man in a wooden chair, reading an English newspaper. Moses walked up to him, in need of conversation and assurance. The man was wearing a bright orange turban but Western pants and shirt. He had on refined, wire-rimmed spectacles and appeared gentle and civilized.

"Do you speak English?" asked Moses.

The man looked at Moses, examining him from head to foot. "Yes, I do. Are you English?"

"No, I am Polish. Perhaps you can tell me how to get to the university. I want to apply there for a job."

"The Sanskrit University?"

Moses moved closer and squatted. He could not find a comfortable position and put a knee to the ground for balance. He shook his head.

"No, Banaras Hindu University."

The man looked at him carefully, trying to understand why such a ragged European would want to visit one of India's great universities and apply for a position.

"It is far from here. You could walk, but it would take long. Asi Road then Lanka Road. Better that you take a rickshaw."

The man saw that Moses looked desperate, and pointedly returned to reading his newspaper. His dismissive loss of interest told Moses the conversation was over. Moses thanked the man and stood up, standing there awkwardly.

He took several steps, then turned back to look at the man. The man raised his head from the newspaper, got up, and walked over to Moses.

"This is a dangerous area," he said. "You should go now to the university if you are going."

The man turned, and entered a small building with no windows above the ground floor. Moses wanted to call out to him, but he understood there was no connection to be had; the man was uninterested in the convoluted problems of a Western man in India. Still the fact that he had given Moses a warning, when little else was offered, seemed important.

Moses tried to size the place up for danger. The Indians were underfed and small; when he bumped into them accidentally, they bounced off him like children. There were no menacing characters, and the only quick movements were boys chasing one another under the legs of cows. He had not seen any police since arriving, and there were no signs of aggression. The chaos was contained within an intricate web of conventions, and it appeared unlikely that the pattern would fray.

The afternoon dragged on, the light lingering. He noticed small cooking fires being lit in the shops along the lane. He approached a street vendor, purchased a chapati and dhal and leaned against a building, eating and scanning the street for visible threats. Occasionally, a fierce-looking sadhu walked past, but his eyes were focused elsewhere.

Moses continued down the lane, feeling cool air, as if he were emerging from a tunnel. He stepped into an open area, high above the Ganges. The stars were clear in the twilight and the river sparkled below. In front of him lay the steps to the Ganges, the ghats. He had found his way, as had Sahadeva months before, to Manikarnika Ghat.

A flock of widows dressed in white saris passed in front of him singing "Hare Krishna." Otherwise the area was serene, with little movement. He sat on a wall above the ghats, watching the diminishing rays of the sun turn golden brown on the sacred river. The activities of night began slowly. A fire was lit by a sadhu sitting under an umbrella, and the smell of burnt dung immediately filled the air. A few old men walked into the river to bathe, holding their hands together in prayer, then immersing themselves in the holiest of waters. He was ignored and began to relax.

A pile of blankets lay next to the wall on which he sat. He wondered why such a valuable commodity went untouched in a place where a twig was a treasure, and he glanced around for signs of an owner. He left the wall, walking in a wide circle to see if anyone came to claim them. He stopped at a dripping tap across from the wall, noticing that a sadhu walked past the blankets, giving them a wide berth. Moses moved closer to the blankets, continuing to check around him. A cooler breeze came across the water, carrying more pungent smells, including the unmistakable odor of burnt flesh. He noticed that the other side of the wall on which he had sat was used as a urinal, and he nodded approvingly that this spot had all the amenities he needed.

Even though it was early evening, his head was heavy from the exhaustion of the day. He had spent a sleepless night on the train from Trichy. He sat on the ground with his back to the wall, his head soon nodding. As he lay down, he reached over to the bundle and pulled the blankets around him, using some to cover his feet, others as a pillow.

He was in a basement. He knew he was dreaming but he was interested in a message that drifted toward him through the jumble of images. His wife came into the room and sat on the floor, in the darkest corner, as a witness but not a participant. He took a step toward her, noticing another figure whose face was blurred until he came closer. It was the visage of his father. His eyes were sad but he spoke without emotion. "Moses, there is no passion on this side. There is no interest in the living but I came. I am not sure why. Perhaps to tell you that you will be dead in six months."

The jolts to his body did not blend with his dream, and he emerged from sleep to find two men in the dim light hitting him with sticks. He raised his hands to deflect the blows and strained to see their faces. The dark men in the weak light moved too fast, and all he could do was shrink the target. One of the men shouted at him in an Indian language, but he heard clearly what the other yelled in English. "From dead people — these are from dead people!"

His attackers paused to catch their breath and Moses quickly rose. His back and legs were numb but he could tell he was not badly hurt, only bruised. He puffed out his chest, flailing his arms, screaming in English for help. The two men moved back and stopped hitting him, looking at each other in confusion.

"What have I done to you?" Moses implored.

A man stepped forward from behind them, moving them aside,

taking their sticks, which they surrendered willingly. They bowed to the man who patted them on the shoulder and the man moved closer to Moses.

"These are the blankets in which dead children are wrapped. Only an animal would lie on these. Only an animal, not a man."

In the light of the embers of the sadhus' fires, Moses recognized the orange turban and the man who warned him away.

"I didn't know. How was I supposed to know?" Moses pleaded. He backed away, feeling his bruises.

"Your ignorance is the only reason they didn't kill you. The *only* reason. Now go."

With the dawn sun the air warmed quickly and the coolness of the night was rapidly pushed away. He walked away from the ghat, gently feeling his bruises, pressing his fingers against his ribs. He was depressed more from the dream than the beating. The dream was too specific and organized to be a metaphor or a sign; it had the objective quality of a definite message from the other side. Yet he could not take the words literally.

As he walked, he searched for alternative meanings. It could mean he must change or die. Yes, he thought, that was it.

He moved along the road with renewed vigor. Here was a message of hope: a chance, a gift to help him make his way.

As he felt his bruises, he noticed that his money, passport and identity card were gone. It could have been when he was beaten or when he jumped about to look menacing. In a fold of his pajamas he had a few rupee notes and decided that it was very much the time to make his way to the university. This would be his new home and he no longer needed a passport or papers. At least he had the Zohar.

The rickshaw driver looked at the few rupees with contempt, lying back in the seat of his carriage, pointing to the sun to indicate that it was too hot to travel, at least at that price. When Moses implored him, he waved his hand as if pushing away a fly. The other rickshaw drivers were either sleeping or bedded down in their carriages.

"How much?" asked Moses.

The driver did not answer but then he saw that Moses was wearing a watch. It was a Swiss watch with a brown band that he was given by his father for his first academic position. The driver pointed to the watch. Moses laughed and went to walk off. The sun moving quickly to its zenith and the throbbing heat of India sapped his strength. Moses returned to the driver, removing the watch.

"OK, the watch."

The driver inspected it, holding it up to his ear to hear the ticking. With his head he motioned for Moses to get into the carriage while he carefully put the watch on his wrist. Moses climbed in, noticing that the watch was upside down. The driver stared at the watch, holding it again to his ear for confirmation that it was real. He put his foot to the pedals, laboriously pumping his legs.

The campus of the university was indeed a long way. After a half hour, Moses was feeling dehydrated and exhausted, even though the rickshaw canopy was raised. The driver slowed at the entrance to Banaras Hindu University and Moses stepped off as the driver immediately turned back to Banaras.

Moses entered the spacious grounds, which were green with hearty foliage. The buildings were attractive and spaced out pleasantly and he walked through a world of students and professors, all engaged in their pursuits. Asking around, he found his way to a building housing the philosophy department. He knocked at a door labeled "Dean," entering without waiting for an answer. The room was piled high with stacks of papers bound with twine, and a man with thick, black-rimmed glasses sat behind the desk.

"Excuse me, I apologize for walking in like this. I am a professor from Poland. A professor of philosophy. I have had a difficult passage here, which is why I look so disheveled. It's a long story, my money was taken among other things."

The man rose, pointing Moses to a seat.

"Please take a seat. Are you here to see Professor Anand?"

"Professor Anand? Yes, indeed, I am here to see Professor Anand." Moses recalled the name from the letter in Trichy. "Is he in?" He spoke with more confidence as he sat in the soft armchair.

"One moment, please."

The man rose from his desk and walked around it to a door. He entered, and Moses heard him speaking in a loud voice, in what he assumed was Hindi. In a moment, the man came out and opened the door wide.

"Professor Anand will see you now."

At first Moses did not realize that Professor Anand was the man with the orange turban. He shook his hand and they both put hands together in the namaskar greeting.

"Please sit down, Professor. Can I get you some water?"

"Water would be wonderful." Moses no longer was aware that he was penniless and ragged.

Professor Anand yelled through the open door. Moses expected a response, but the retainer did not reply.

"So, Professor, how can I help you?"

Moses recognized Professor Anand and was unable to speak. He was about to apologize, but thought that perhaps the professor did not recognize him. He looked carefully at Anand and there was nothing in his eyes that flickered with recognition or anger.

"Well, I am a professor of philosophy and I am interested in living in India. You see —"

"Forgive me for interrupting, Professor. I am very interested in talking to you, except that I have an urgent meeting that I must attend. There is no position for you here, unfortunately. Not a part-time position nor any chance of lectures. This is with the greatest respect to your scholarship and understanding, which I am sure is vast. We only employ Indians at the moment, and, in any event, all our positions are filled for the next two years."

He said this in a soft, modulated voice, with a smile on his face.

"Yes, but, I have no other place —"

"Forgive me for interrupting again. I am terribly sorry. I must get to the meeting. I do hope you enjoy India and please feel free to look around the campus before you leave. Perhaps you can send me some of your work."

Anand worked his way around the desk to the door.

Moses stood in panic.

"Professor, I have nowhere to go."

Anand was at the door.

"Oh, that is no problem. Perhaps you should start at the great Siva temple on your tour. That is the place to start."

He opened the door and left. Moses moved to follow but the retainer approached him.

"I am sorry, this is a private meeting."

He pointed toward the door and Moses left.

Students spoke to Moses enthusiastically and freely, yet if he raised even a hint of his predicament they slowly stepped away, excusing themselves politely. That they spoke to him at all gave some hope that someone eventually would come to his aid.

He saw two older students on a bench in the shade and approached them smiling. One of them moved to make room for Moses and patted the bench for him to sit down.

"A lovely campus," said Moses, "very interesting."

"You know, the border of Kasi is only a hundred feet away. If you're going to die," said one man laughing, "you better hurry back across the border. That way, at least, you will be liberated. The way you look, you shouldn't be sitting here."

Both men laughed louder, rose from the bench, and walked away, their laughter echoing among the buildings.

As Moses stepped away, he noticed two guards with spindly legs popping out of their militaristic short pants moving in his direction. Each wore a green peaked cap and a belt across his chest, much like a Polish policeman. He saw that they were looking at him suspiciously, so he picked up some scattered pages from the ground, putting them under his arm as if he were a student or scholar. He knew that his stay on the campus was over. His hair was long, his beard dirty, and his clothes were stained and ripped, while the students and professors were clean and well fed. He probably had published more than most who now walked past him, but as he wandered toward the exit he pondered the fate that had reduced him to this, the lowest state of his life.

He saw a professor strolling across the campus and ran in his direction. The man saw Moses coming and walked faster. When Moses increased his speed, the man reached into his pocket, dropping a rupee note and a half-eaten chapati. Moses formed words but stopped instead for the money and food. He went to the cool of the Siva Temple and ate the chapati, which still had the taste of dhal on the edges.

Perhaps it was eating another's food droppings, or, more particularly, the humiliation of being a beggar among scholars that made Moses realize that he had to leave. He had to discover a base to reestablish himself and to assess options. He glanced around the temple, thinking of how decades of scholarship had brought him to this position. He addressed the Siva idol at the end of the temple. "Yes, I know. Faust was right," he said, quoting, "Base fool with all this sweated learning / I stand no wiser than I was before."

Moses left the temple, following the semicircular road to the exit. He departed the campus and again entered the sacred rim of the city of Kasi.

3

Destruction

1 MOSES HAD ONLY ONE PLACE to turn. In the heat of the day, with barely controlled desperation, he walked back to the Manikarnika Ghat.

The sadhus at Manikarnika did not look at Moses when he spoke. He even tapped one on the shoulder but the monk ignored him. Moses was dizzy with exhaustion but he had to persevere. He sat heavily under the umbrella where Sahadeva had sought shelter weeks before. He was not, however, welcomed and had no more status than a scurrying rodent.

He was sitting on the book of the Zohar and now pulled it out of his pocket; it was tattered and the cover was missing. He picked at the frayed edges of the book, reinserting pages in the right places, removing loose threads in the binding. He gently dusted off the top and sides, blowing away the lint from his pocket. He removed the letters from Seth and the rabbi in Bucharest.

"What holy book is that?" a sadhu asked Moses in clear English.

Moses initially stuttered. Then he replied with the calculation of a desperate man, "This is a secret book. You should not have even seen it." Moses put the Zohar back in his pocket.

The sadhu looked at him suspiciously. "There is no secret book printed like that. Why do you try to trick me?"

Moses noticed that the sadhu appeared to be a man of intelligence with wisdom in his eyes. He tried another approach, "It is the Zohar, the book of Jewish mysticism."

The man seemed to lose interest, so Moses came to the point. "I am trying to find a man who was a Franciscan priest. His name was Seth Tripathi. He was very tall and I think he wanted to become an Indian priest."

"If he did become an Indian priest, as you say, he would no longer be your friend. He would be dead to the world. Your search is hopeless."

He saw Moses' expression of despair. He regretted talking to him and now wanted him to leave. Still, there was someone he had seen who fit the description.

"There was a tall Indian, with an accent, who is now a sadhu," he ventured. "He took off on Yatra down Madanpura Road, toward the university. You can look that way. You can ask in every village." He turned his back on Moses.

The road from Banaras was dense with traffic. At each juncture the movement slowed as a new mass was being absorbed into the whole. A procession, holding high a plaster of Paris Ganesh, attempted to merge with the main current at the same time as a funeral march arrived from the opposite side of the road. The elephant god and the dead man were the only objects above the thick fog of dust stirred by thousands of restless feet and worn bicycle tires.

All movement eventually halted from the glut of rickshaws, trucks, and human bodies. The crowd tried to move, but each step was so small that progress was indiscernible. The chant of the pallbearers — "Ram Nam Satya Hey" — had to be maintained, but was suitably dampened to account for the diluted situation. Moses tried to make his way through the occasional spaces, finding the Indian bodies soft and pliable as he jostled for any opening. The Ganesh devotees were lost in a wide-eyed trance and continued their frenzied drumming and chanting, pounding the dirt further as they stood in place. Their purpose contrasted sharply with his lack of meaning and direction; he was only moving away from Banaras, looking for the proverbial needle in a haystack, because there was no other option.

Wind caught the disturbed dust, swirled it in eddies at the side of the road, then threw it hard in the faces of the crowd, causing them to splutter and cough. For a moment, the singing stopped as hands and clothes covered mouths and noses for protection. The smells of urine and feces, usually an undercurrent, were whipped up with the dirt, bringing tears to people's eyes. Moses tried to stand still, but was carried along suddenly as a new momentum moved up the hill, away from the city of Siva. Another blast of hot air stirred the floating dust; Moses heard his teeth crunching on the particles of dirt.

The huge crowd seemed to lose direction, drifting first one way then another, toppling several on the outer edges. The anguished screams of those who fell made everyone strive to stop swaying, but the force already generated could not be curtailed. In desperation, Moses reached out to steady himself on the man swaying in front of him. The man did not resist the contact, allowing Moses to come closer and grab his waist. They shuffled forward over uneven ground as the wind gradually died down, revealing that the wisdom of the crowd had taken them squarely up the road.

The man glanced over his shoulder and was visibly surprised to find an emaciated European there. He turned slightly toward Moses, who let go of his waist.

"India has many hazards," observed the man. He was tall for an Indian, just a few inches shorter than Moses. He was dressed in the ocher robe of the itinerant monk and Moses relaxed at the sound of English.

By gradual side steps, the two disengaged themselves from the crowd, moving to the side of the road, away from the slow-moving current.

The monk stared at Moses, who looked away under the strong gaze.

"The closed door. I remember," said the monk.

Moses looked at him carefully and a smile of recognition crept onto his face.

"Seth! Seth! I have been looking for you!"

Moses grabbed the monk's arms, pulling him closer in delight.

"Seth! They said I couldn't find you!"

Moses laughed, repeating the name.

"My name is now Sahadeva Bharati. I am a sadhu. You found me because I was returning only weeks after I left. A failed sadhu."

"Sahadeva," said Moses, pulling him even closer, giving him a soft embrace. After a long moment, they stepped back to contemplate each other.

Their gaze dropped momentarily as each considered the purpose of this extraordinary meeting. In a place as vast as India, it was only the gods in the form of destiny that could throw two people at each other this way. Yet destiny did not always deliver a propitious result, as they both knew.

"Professor. You are a professor, right? From Warsaw. I wrote to you when I first arrived back here. A well-dressed professor, the last time I saw you, if memory serves. Now dressed in rags, walking from Banaras? How did this happen? How did you get here, on the other side of the world as they say? I hope my letter had nothing to do with it."

"A long story," Moses sighed. "And your letter did have something to do with it. I escaped from Warsaw and came here with the same inspiration that took me to Jung in Zürich." He realized that Seth had never heard of Jung. "I was hoping to find a job at the university."

He saw that Sahadeva looked skeptical.

"I didn't come here for a job. I came here because of you and this book." He pulled out the Zohar. "At my heart, I long to understand the mystery. I thought it was here." He paused to note Sahadeva's mood, then blurted out, "Actually, I have no money. Nothing! I am lost here, bereft."

Moses shrugged, waiting to see what the next crucial second would bring forth from this man, whom fate had brought his way.

Sahadeva pulled him farther from the road, into the welcome shade of a tree. This admission from Moses, a show of weakness, softened Sahadeva's independent resolve. Here was someone, Sahadeva realized, who, out of necessity or maybe interest, might listen to his own drama. And, in the telling, he might be released from the anguish emanating from his recent brush with mortality, and his pricked passion.

"I, too, have nothing," said Sahadeva. He grabbed a twig, tracing circles in the dirt. "I came here with a deep yearning that I felt only India could answer. In a very short time I have been defeated. The yearning has been twisted into misery."

Moses grasped that an emotional connection with Sahadeva was the bridge to his future. He nodded sympathetically, making small sounds of concern where he thought appropriate. He glanced up furtively to see if his response was reassuring or whether his underlying desperation, which could not be masked, was repulsive to the sadhu. He was relieved to see Sahadeva was smiling.

"And the door?"

Moses sighed deeply. "The door? Ah, yes, the door. You do have a good memory. For a time, I thought it could never open, but now I think I may have a key."

Moses felt that if he spoke further of the door it might lose its significance, drift away as had so many fragmented, unexplained images in the past. But he could not contain himself.

"I think the key may be found in guilt, feeling guilty."

For other sadhus, psychological explanations were foolish; the truth is written and applied. For Sahadeva, the sweet luxuries of analysis and introspection were valued at the monastery, and now he found it a relief to let the mind wander, build castles in the sky. He sank into the conversation as one does into a warm bath.

Moses continued, "Guilt provides a key. I haven't really had a chance to analyze it fully."

"What is there about guilt that opens the door?" Sahadeva squatted on a tree root and took out some cooked rice, handing a portion to Moses, who filled his mouth immediately. He savored the chewing, then attempted to squat next to Sahadeva.

"Guilt makes me reflect. It always returns, and no matter how much I squirm, there is no way out."

Moses took his own conversation seriously, understanding that the squandered image of the door may indeed be the speck of dirt that would turn into a pearl. Again, he tried to stop talking, but the words flew out along with a few grains of rice.

"But the fact is, the door is still closed."

Sahadeva hesitated. Although he craved a good, even controversial, conversation, it was apparent that Moses lacked any real insight. The man was disheveled and filthy, and it was clear, even to the ragged boys that stared at Moses in amazement, that to give him the slightest encouragement would make him immediately dependent. He noticed that Moses gazed at him expectantly, waiting for some sign of acceptance.

Sahadeva rose and Moses immediately stood.

"Well, I hope you find your door."

Moses sensed he was about to be dismissed. He had seen the same look in Jung's eyes; the beam of consciousness had been turned off. He spoke rapidly. "Tell me, then. Why have you been defeated? You came here to be a sadhu and you are. What else has happened?"

It was obvious to Sahadeva that this was a desperate attempt on Moses' part to rebuild what had crumbled, but, piqued by the question, Sahadeva could not help responding.

"I'm not particularly well," he said softly. "In fact, I may be very unwell."

He felt an odd joy in his telling. He was about to expand on his fears, when a strong gust of wind made them pause and duck their heads.

Moses spoke as the wind quieted. "Tell me more about your illness. I have, for the first time in my life, absolutely nothing. So, here is a good set of ears for you."

The traffic had thinned. Sahadeva stepped back on the road to Banaras and Moses followed.

"You may come with me if you like. Shortly I shall no longer be a monk. In fact, I'm on my way to disrobe. I can share my food with you and perhaps find you a place to sleep. If that is enough, come along."

"Agreed," said Moses. "Where are we off to?"

Sahadeva did not bother to reply. He noticed that Moses' step was lighter now, his head back, sniffing the heady mixture of spices and excrement that was India. Moses looked at Sahadeva, patting him on the back.

"Our meeting," he said enthusiastically, "has to be destiny."

Before they had walked a mile, Sahadeva contemplated leaving Moses in the dust. The excitement of sharing his concerns was flattened when he realized that they could not be relieved by elucidation. What was he to say? That he may die? That his years of meditation and prayer were no different from a lifetime spent accumulating useless objects? Strange, he thought, that he had even harbored a momentary hope that the burden could be lightened by companionship or a sympathetic ear.

Sita. His heart ached for Sita. She was uninterested in his fears, uncritical, accepting him, holding him steady. He had mistakenly believed it was merely her attention that was a salve but now, as he glanced at Moses, he understood that it was Sita, and everything that was Sita, that placed him on higher ground.

The lifelong call to expand, and his new aspiration to find the lever of life that briefly sparkled as he thought of her, was quickly snuffed by his own anguish. Meditation could not save him from his illness, nor could a philosophical or religious framework of words. His only guide was the reality of the situation: the stark, very real potential for his annihilation. Nothing else. In the past he had meditated on death to focus concentration, sitting in French graveyards to sharpen his mind. Now that the reality of death was palpable, he withered in the face of it, unable to find any resources or direction. The lever was as distant as Moses' door.

He heard Moses breathing heavily over the din and snuck a glance at his wretched fellow traveler. The man's face was unattractive, oversized ears on a face twisted at the mouth, as if he had just swallowed a lemon. He loped along like a predator searching for carrion, his eyes bulging in anticipation of any form of satiation. Sahadeva shook his head and wondered, not for the first time in their short meeting, why he might die and such a soulless character live. Then, almost immediately, he felt guilty for his thought.

He was about to stop and explain to Moses that he was best left alone, but hesitated. At least Moses provided some diversion and, perhaps, could be of some benefit, although he dared not think of how a neurotic European, without money or hope, could advance any cause, least of all his.

As they advanced toward the Ganges, sadhus greeted Sahadeva; Moses waved back as if they were saluting him. Sahadeva realized that there was a limit to this association and, if Moses should humiliate him, he would brush him off like a speck of dirt.

He found Moses a place to sit in an alcove at the rear of the busy ashram behind Manikarnika Ghat. Sahadeva was able to obtain food for Moses, brought to the ashram by devoted families. The monks did not look at Moses, stepping over him as if he was a corpse.

Sahadeva went immediately to have the darshan of the guru, the blessing of his presence, to obtain his permission to disrobe; the desire to be free of religious countenance was pressing. He blamed himself: he had abandoned Catholicism for Hindu teachings that promised blissful realization of the omnipresent Brahma, with the right practice. All that he had obtained from becoming a sadhu was entry into a living hell in which he would surely die. He hoped that if he escaped it, he might pull himself from the raging vortex that was sucking him down.

He was told the guru was in an inner room outside which disciples were perpetually crammed, waiting for a glimpse of their master. Sahadeva stepped over other monks and moved toward the door. Occasionally the door opened, and the monks outside peered in for the slightest glimpse of the guru. He inquired of the senior monk when he would be allowed into that sanctum, but the monk simply shrugged, pointing to the floor for Sahadeva to wait. The air was hot and stale, making it difficult to breathe. Some monks slept while others sat upright in meditation, oblivious to anything but their own inner absorption. A fly flew back and forth, and Sahadeva noticed he was not the only one following its movements in a vain attempt to keep the mind active in the thick sludge of the atmosphere. He tried to speak to a little monk sitting next to him who was busy peeling his toenail. Sahadeva uttered only a preliminary sound when the monk lifted his finger to his mouth to enforce silence, then returned to his bodily preoccupation.

He rose to leave, but noticed that even more monks had crammed into the space in front of the room, making any exit impossible. He closed his eyes, attempting to steady himself, but the heat made him sleepy. He kindled his mind by silently intoning the name of Sita. Soon her image came and he pictured her running toward him, a smile on her face. In his mind, she lifted the sari from her head, and wiped the dust from her sensuous lips. The heat anesthetized him and he slid into the space before sleep and behind awareness. In the daydream, Sita came closer and unwrapped her sari. He realized she was not getting undressed but was holding something underneath its folds that was meant to be hidden. She produced a shiny lever, the lever he needed.

A sudden commotion pulled him awake. The door opened and everyone sprang up standing on tiptoes, waiting for the guru to appear. Sahadeva was unable to move past the bodies of tightly packed monks, who were oblivious to anyone but their master.

Many shoes and sandals were stacked by the door, indicating that the guru had visitors other than sadhus. He saw that this mound was the only place with some elevation. He crawled between the legs of the expectant monks who did not look down, suffering any discomfort to maintain their position. The smell at this level was totally oppressive. He made his way to the mound, climbing precariously on the pile to see the guru.

The guru stepped out unexpectedly and Sahadeva instinctively gave him a namaskar. The old man looked around, then his gaze fixed strongly and particularly on Sahadeva, balancing on the pile. The guru did not speak but Sahadeva heard in his head, "This is not for you. You can go."

He looked down, realizing that he had totally and irretrievably demeaned himself by standing on the shoes, receptacles for the lowest and most disgusting part of the body. Such an action was like piling the shit of dogs in front of the guru and standing there for a blessing.

He turned to the guru, but he had already moved away, leaving Sahadeva alone with his disgrace. None of the other monks looked his way as they all strained for the attention of the guru; one deep glance or special word could immediately elevate a practice or, it had been said, bring instant enlightenment.

The guru's words or his own words came again, "This is not for you."

He knew this already, from the moment he had met Sita. Perhaps he was too western, he thought, but then a small spark of awareness told him that he simply lacked the capacity for progress. Sahadeva jolted, as if touched by a live wire. He reached for an explanation as for a branch over a cliff, but found nothing. The thought stood steady and bright like a direct illumination, with a message that was incapable of being doubted. If this was the case, then he was hopelessly lost. If there was no progress to be made, then there was no future and no possibility of any resolution.

Stunned, he walked into the main hall of the ashram and announced to a senior monk that he wanted to disrobe. Without comment, he was given a small bundle of food and some rupee notes. He saw Moses perched by a window, looking at the movement on the ghats. The steps were lined with bathers taking the afternoon ablutions. Sahadeva sat next to Moses, clearing his throat again and again in an effort to speak.

"We will have to leave here. I am no longer a sadhu. This life, I have been told, is not for me."

"That's probably because you're more western than Indian," suggested Moses.

"Do you think so?" Sahadeva struggled to keep sarcasm from his voice.

"Absolutely! Jung said the practices of the East are not for the West. You have to be part of the culture to be part of the religion. You have been a Franciscan monk, so you are not really an Indian. With all your years in the West, you're almost as much a visitor here as I am."

Moses was about to continue when Sahadeva raised his hand. Moses continued anyway, "Maybe your unconscious is not pregnant with possibility. That's what Jung said to me."

"I really can't talk about it now," Sahadeva stood up and rearranged his robes. "I have lost hold of myself."

He did not wait for another comment from Moses and immediately left the ashram, uttering the words of the sadhu, "Let's go. Let's set off."

There was no breeze to push away the dead air of the afternoon, yet they moved as quickly as traffic would allow, inhaling in shallow breaths. Neither knew where they were walking as they meandered toward the open road. After a few minutes, Sahadeva stopped.

"I must quickly go back and leave a message. Someone may come to look for me. Please wait here. I will be right back."

Moses looked at the monk.

"Who are you expecting?"

"Someone who may come looking for me. I told her I would look for her, so it is unlikely she will come, but if she does I must tell them to have her wait. I will check back from time to time."

"You, a monk, have a woman?" asked Moses, incredulous.

Sahadeva was surprised at Moses' stare, the twisted, suggestive smile on his face.

"I *don't* have a woman," he said emphatically.

Sahadeva held up his hand, to stop any further conversation, and walked back toward the ashram.

Moses squatted in the shade, perplexed. How could a monk find a woman while he was ignored by women? Often he smiled at Indian women, who looked at him as if he was a circus clown in full make-up.

Wind gusts and traffic exhausts swirled debris where he sat. The leaves and soot rose and fell endlessly. He stood, to rise above the dirt cloud, and watched the continuous stream of rickshaws. He realized the sun had moved and substantial time had passed. He stepped into the street, as much as traffic would allow, looking in both directions for Sahadeva. It occurred to him that maybe Sahadeva might never come back. Maybe this was the polite Indian way of rejection: say you will be right back and keep walking. If so, he would have to start out on his own once again. He moved from the shade and then, as if blocked, turned back, unable to go on. He had no sense of where to go.

Another strong gust of wind blew up the street, bringing more dust and debris but, this time, carrying the pleasant odor of cardamom. Moses rubbed his eyes, which watered from irritation.

"Crying like a lost child?" asked Sahadeva.

Moses turned to see Sahadeva out of his robes, looking like a merchant in a clean white dhoti and kurta.

"No," Moses said. "Just some dust in my eyes." He put his hand on Sahadeva's shoulder. "Just some dust."

"Let's go then," said Sahadeva. "I have someone to visit; that is, unless you have other plans."

Moses walked by Sahadeva's side and gradually Moses told his story. Sahadeva questioned him on how he had escaped, but Moses spoke in generalities, saying nothing of Bredemeyer or his family.

"The Germans were in Warsaw, but I managed to make my escape through a sewer under the streets."

He also left out Trichy.

It was apparent to Sahadeva that Moses had a stronger sense of self-preservation than he had thought. He was not the weak man he had supposed but a survivor where others would have been destroyed. It was interesting to Sahadeva that Moses had been propelled not by philosophy or theory, but by a great will to live, a motivation the former sadhu now questioned in himself.

Sahadeva watched the emancipated European striding along with a certain strength, waving his arms as he spoke. He struggled to understand the nature of that strength and, as he listened to the story, thought that it must be bravery. Moses was brave; his appearing in Banaras showed he had courage. He had let life carry him here and had not resisted its movement. He could have stayed in Bucharest or reentered Poland, but instead he had come to a completely unknown land.

When Moses spoke of his feelings, his voice suddenly rose. He became agitated, gesticulating broadly, even shouting, before reining himself in and lowering his tone. When he spoke of his escape or, most important, when he mentioned his daughter, his voice was measured and soft.

The paradox was that while Moses appeared passive, letting himself be carried along on whatever current, his story indicated a man who took risks and was able to endure deprivation and fear. It occurred to Sahadeva that he might have misunderstood or underestimated Moses. It was he who had the locked door, not Moses, and if the man could only quiet his mind Sahadeva was sure that some basic character would shine through, a pivot around which he himself might turn.

2 SITA WAS WATCHED SUSPICIOUSLY by her mother, Rohini. When she went to gather cow dung, Sita felt eyes on her back, peering from the window. If she went beyond the imaginary line that formed the village boundary, Rohini would run to drag her back. The thud of Rohini's heavy steps on the packed earth echoed through the village, rising above other sounds, causing all to turn and stare.

Rohini could not dispel the embarrassment that was now the subject of jokes and exaggerated stories, so she maintained a bowed head, avoiding the casual contact that was her usual world. The day Sahadeva left, little boys that darted like sparrows in an open sky crept up behind her and threw mud on her sari. She had cradled each of them as infants and, when she faced them, their laughter turned to remorse and, awkwardly, they tried to brush the stain. She was not angry with them but confused that the force of ridicule was now a typhoon, blowing away years of accumulated good will and sentiment.

Sita's father had little interest in the views of others but was fully aware his family was being scrutinized, both from curiosity and scorn. When he paused with other drivers from the village in the heat of the day, he would be delicately excluded from the conversation. The others listened, but no thread from his comments took hold; his words appeared to pause in the air, then plummet to the ground.

Each night, after dusting his rickshaw until moonlight reflected in the fenders, he crawled into bed and prayed. As a child, his only feeling, beyond fear and hunger, was the uplifting love of Siva. When he was subject to ridicule as a child, he sang devotional songs, bhajans. As he now silently recited chants to Siva, his spirits rose comfortably on the pleasant waves of worship. His mind shifted from Siva and focused on Sita in a bridal sari at the side of a well dressed man with an oiled mustache. He stopped chanting, opened his eyes, and reached over to shake Rohini.

"Are you awake?" He heard her breathing lighten. "We will have Sita married. Tomorrow I will contact the family of Prad."

"We live under a cloud," Rohini whispered. "They won't want us."

"I will start borrowing for the dowry. Lord Siva has given me this idea."

The invocation of Siva to prove a point was unusual: as they were so deeply religious, it was assumed He was the source of all inspiration. They knew, without expression, the only reason they had not been subjected to greater humiliation, or even stoning, was their abiding love of the divine. Whenever great saints and gurus came to the village they called Sita's family close, and it was Sita's father that was given the blessing of serving them a cool glass of water. For his great devotion, he had been given the nickname "Bhakti," one who is devoted to God.

The idea of marrying Sita was a constant topic of discussion between husband and wife but was always postponed because of the impossibility of an essential social requisite: raising money for the dowry. They feared borrowing money because of the horrible complications it implied, and the pestering nastiness of the money lenders. It now appeared that borrowing money would bring less suffering than the shame they experienced when Sita sat on the root of the tree, lifting her head constantly toward the road in hopes of the return of the sadhu.

Sita now sat on that root, feeling the approaching presence of Sahadeva, although she had trouble visualizing him. Since the monk had left, Sita had been unable to attend to her chores. She pondered hidden meanings behind mundane actions and her senses were heightened, causing her to stop and marvel at the taste of a pomegranate or the sunset filtered through the soot.

Sita had not been restless or unfulfilled before Sahadeva had entered the village. Her destiny had excavated a track so deep, wide, and well marked, that there was no reason to doubt the next step or eventual goal. She was contained within a society, village, and caste that survived because each knows his place and what to expect. Yet, the moments with Sahadeva had made her aware that there was another possibility: a wellspring brimming with sweet feeling.

As days passed, Sita watched the road. Tales of Sita spread beyond the village quickly, retold when she was seen on the road, unmoving, looking into the distance. The balance of sentiment shifted from Sita as a foolish girl in love to plain foolish. Her marriage prospects dried up as she stood frozen, like Lot's wife, making it impossible to proclaim her virtues to a potential husband as a woman of commitment, honor, and duty.

Sita had no regard for the terrible impression she was making but felt dreadful about the torment of her parents. She could not, in spite of this, cease staring down the road. Even when she forced herself to turn away, the words of Sahadeva drifted through her head like a melody and she was carried away by the reverie.

3 SAHADEVA AND MOSES SPOKE INFREQUENTLY, even though they had expected the outpouring of words would be curative. Each was absorbed in his own thoughts and the only conversations were utilitarian: to find food or shelter. Occasionally, one or the other formed words, but decided against interrupting the quiet camaraderie that was forming. After a week of small talk, they spontaneously started a more significant conversation.

"I think . . ." Moses began, but was surprised to see Sahadeva shrugging. "You were about to say?" pushed Moses.

"I am almost out of the money from the ashram."

The word "money" aroused Moses from his self-absorption. He paused, looking around, as if to get his bearings. They had wandered from one end of Banaras to the other: from Cantonment, to look longingly at the beautiful hotels, to Banaras Hindu University, to the south of the city.

"Are we out of money, Sahadeva?"

"Sahadeva, you call me? I should be called Seth again. No, we are not out of money. Not yet —"

He paused a moment, then continued, "Not yet, but we will be soon. I can't beg any more. I could, but I am not a sadhu and I am too well dressed."

Moses was aware that in India, there was almost nothing that could evoke sympathy in one man for another; deformities, disease, blindness, or just plain wretchedness, were commonplace. He knew begging was hopeless, as the only duty of a householder was to provide for the itinerant monk because each man one day could become a sadhu.

Sahadeva glanced at Moses and laughed.

"I'll keep the name for inspiration. Sahadeva means 'one who is with God.' Now who am I with?"

As he was about to speak, the klaxon horns of several trucks gave a deafening blast. Both men covered their ears.

"The trumpets of heaven," offered Moses.

"I doubt if they are declaring any victory for me. They are probably calling me instead. After all, my goal is in ruins and I am no longer with God."

Moses was surprised to hear such laments from one he assumed was his spiritual superior, a man who had sought enlightenment and faith in two religions. The visage of the wise Indian monk evaporated, and Moses saw in its stead the man, Sahadeva, with a lined and weary face.

The reality of Sahadeva's illness constantly crept up on him, no matter what thoughts he used to keep it at bay. In the middle of a conversation, or while eating, he would grimace as a cold sliver of doubt pierced his resolve. The thought pattern was repetitive: he would die with dignity.

"Integrity is the key, you know." Sahadeva turned to Moses.

"The key to what?" asked Moses.

They were a few kilometers from Sarnath; Sahadeva gestured in the direction of Sita's village. The sun was sinking and the dust held the remaining light.

"I will go into the village up ahead," said Sahadeva. "I have business to attend to. Why don't you wait there under that large tree. I will come back for you in a day or two."

"In a day or two? What am I supposed to do for a day or two? And what if you don't come back? How am I supposed to know where to go?"

Sahadeva put his hand on Moses' arm. "You have come this far without me. Why don't you meditate? I will find you some food."

"No!" Moses insisted. "I am coming with you." His face flushed and he sounded desperate.

"Come, then." Sahadeva released his arm and headed toward the village.

"What is in the village?"

"A woman I love."

The morning light created the first shadow in the hut and Sita rose instinctively to look out the window. The sight of Sahadeva walking toward her made her gasp for air, as she leaped to the door. Bhakti also observed the sadhu and a white man and, from Sita's reaction, assumed this was the source of their disgrace. Sita's father rose to his full height — not exactly an imposing sight — puffed out his chest, and tensed his muscles as he stepped outside to confront the sadhu and westerner. He often saw Europeans in Banaras but never one so tall, dressed as an Indian. Neither man appeared strong, but both were clearly determined.

"I am sorry to cause you alarm," said Sahadeva, addressing Bhakti. "I don't intend to cause any trouble. I just want to talk to Sita."

The rickshaw driver stood still. He was unused to variations in his life, his daily regime. The two men, he sensed, had the potential to overwhelm him, alter everything. He did not speak.

"Can I speak with her?" Sahadeva asked, his voice conciliatory, almost a whisper.

Sita stood in her father's shadow, waiting for him to answer, but as he was unwilling or unable to speak, she stepped forward. Her father suddenly awoke and grabbed Sita's arm, pushing her back, causing her to fall. The explosive movement caused a change in positions: Bhakti jumped in front of her and Rohini ran from the hut, stepping between Moses and Sita. Sahadeva realized that his intrusion was too abrupt.

"I am very sorry," he said, as he stepped back. "Forgive me."

Sahadeva walked away and Moses followed, fixing Sahadeva with a frown.

"What's the matter with you? Why did you run away?"

"I wasn't welcome. It was too startling for the family."

"But what about you. You want to see the girl. What are you supposed to do now? Leave and never see her?"

Sahadeva failed to understand the question.

"I'm not sure what you mean. This family was shocked to see me. They need more time. Perhaps another day we will go and see her again."

Sahadeva walked rapidly down the road, away from the village. Moses lagged behind, realizing Sahadeva was annoyed. He tried to placate him, saying, "I scared them off, not you."

"No. They are petrified of all outsiders. Not just you, but me as well. I came into their life as a sadhu, which is like their beacon, a religious beacon, and then I fell in love with their daughter."

Sahadeva glanced over his shoulder, as if expecting — or hoping — Sita might be following. Moses recognized that he had gone too far and changed the topic.

"Can we sit for a moment, before we go back to Banaras?" asked Moses.

Sahadeva pointed to a concrete pillar by the side of the road and they sat down. Sahadeva looked at Moses blankly, as if sadness had created a wall between them.

"You don't understand. I can't cause a problem for them," Sahadeva closed his eyes, holding back tears. "They were devastated and confused by my presence. It is not possible for me to go further. Can't you see? Should I burst into the house and force myself on her?"

"Do you really love this girl?" asked Moses.

Sahadeva was bewildered by the question; his feelings for Sita were unclear. She provided, when he was drawn to her breast, the singular opportunity to let go, the peace of assimilation. He could not dissect the elements: what belonged to Sita and what was his own dread.

"Well, do you?" asked Moses, wondering why the answer seemed so difficult. "Either you do or you don't."

Sahadeva stood and looked down at Moses. He spoke with anger, "I don't know what I feel. I can't break the traditions of these people, just step over centuries of culture and impose myself."

Sahadeva awoke from a dream in the dark of night in which Sita was sinking into the ocean. He was not sure, on waking, if it was she. The woman had long hair flowing to her waist. She was dressed in a white gown and was standing on a wooden platform gradually sinking into a calm, aqua sea. He rose, putting the dream to one side for later consideration, aware that Sita was now contained within his essence, so that her absence could not be assuaged by moving on or busying himself in activity.

He had no perspective on the phenomenon that was Sita. His primary goal had always been to accumulate merit by the strength of his effort. When there were discrepancies or pain he redoubled his discipline, banishing speculation. The process of becoming a monk, eastern or western, required an unequivocal single-mindedness that, by its nature, left no room for personal desires or imagination. His illness had shattered this belief, forced him to see that nothing accumulates. It was a short step to conclude, as he did, that he had dedicated his life to absolutely no purpose. There was no solid foundation, no fundamental plank of truth, that supported him; he was suspended in thin air. He wondered why he should struggle over what was right and wrong? If anything, he realized, it was time to stop trying hard, forcing his mind along a narrow path. Had he learned nothing from this? Was he doomed to continue banging his head against the wall or could he let himself, for the first time, merely drift, floating on the waves of circumstance, learning from the currents?

Sahadeva had always lied to himself that his emotions were controllable. He now let them range free and they came out of their hiding places, coursing through his veins, entering each organ, waking them. These feelings were good, he understood; without them, the experience of life belonged to others. Maybe he could take the chance, go back to the village, and risk everything to see Sita. He observed that the lever was *in* life, not in denying it existed or shutting it out by cajoling the mind into submission.

The monsoon clouds seemed to accumulate over Moses, who was still asleep. Sahadeva had no comprehension of how this man, lost in all respects, slept soundly on uncomfortable, uneven ground, in a contorted posture. He watched Moses for a moment, surprised at his stillness.

Without speaking, Moses awoke, rose and shook Sahadeva's hand, as if at a business meeting. Although surprised, Sahadeva opened to the warmth that flowed from Moses and smiled in return.

At dawn, Moses and Sahadeva walked into Banaras. The rain clouds were gathering high above the city, waiting to open, to drench the unprotected. They gazed intermittently at the pending storm, noting potential shelter. The sun still blasted through the clouds and many rickshaw drivers had already pulled their conveyances to the shade. Sahadeva pointed to a rickshaw driver, asleep with his feet hanging out, and Moses immediately recognized Sita's father. Sahadeva motioned to Moses, who stepped a few feet away.

"What should we do?" asked Sahadeva. He somehow believed Moses to have greater subtlety in matters of the heart.

"I thought you were no longer interested," Moses said.

"I never said that," Sahadeva said. "I said I could not trample centuries of custom."

"Forget custom," Moses said. "What do you, Sahadeva, want to do?"

Moses was surprised to see the little man who had so intimidated Sahadeva. In sleep he looked even more vulnerable. A man in a yellow shirt carrying a large cockatoo walked between them and the rickshaw. Sahadeva whispered to Moses, "This is auspicious. A cockatoo overheard the conversation between Siva and Parvati."

The bird squawked loudly at the foreigner, jumping on the hand of its keeper and flapping its clipped wings. Sita's father awoke and jumped out of his rickshaw. The father shouted loudly over the piercing scream of the bird, and within seconds, other rickshaw drivers formed a menacing circle around them.

The man with the bird walked on, leaving Sahadeva and Moses to face the drivers. They held back as Moses towered over them, looking dangerous with his ill-fitting clothes and wild hair. Sita's father yelled to the others in a dialect Sahadeva did not understand. One of them grabbed a bicycle pump from inside a rickshaw as they stepped closer. Sahadeva looked for an escape but noticed that Moses was standing still.

"How incredible," thought Sahadeva. "In the middle of this danger, he finds a way to compose himself and stand his ground."

The smallest driver pushed Moses in the chest. Moses looked at Sahadeva in amazement. The attack was without power, like a shove from a small child. Moses pushed back and the man slid backward, falling in the dirt. The other drivers stepped back in shock at the quick dispatch. They failed to see that all the fight had now left Moses. He stood rigid, but in absolute panic, his arms immovable, dropping limply. Sahadeva again marveled how solid Moses stood in the face of danger.

The drivers looked at one another. It appeared that Moses was mocking them, ignoring their threats, standing tranquil in spite of their effort to look menacing and fierce amid the rising chorus of their threats.

"We better go immediately," said Sahadeva, breathing heavily. "A crowd is forming; it will be more dangerous than these drivers."

Moses firmly stood his ground.

"Please, come," Sahadeva implored, tugging him away.

Sita's father was yelling an explanation to the gathering throng. The other drivers fell silent, moving away from the confrontation, back toward their vehicles. The driver with the pump raised it threateningly, but it was an empty gesture.

As they fled, Sahadeva felt like a buoy cut loose at sea; all this had now made Sita unreachable. Words could not mend the humiliation that Moses had inflicted on Bhakti. He would be consumed by anger that would rationalize his defeat; it would fester, causing irreversible damage to the relationship.

Sahadeva glanced back, reassured they were not being followed. He wondered how Moses could display such strength and power. Could it be, he thought, that we are variegated, like plants; some have innate courage while others, like himself, are weak?

They did not speak as they wandered through the Muslim quarter near Lahurabir. Moses nodded to men stacking boxes of colored dyes. One of them stepped close to Sahadeva, unnerving him and he involuntarily raised his hands, as if expecting a blow.

"We could use help unloading and stacking these boxes. Do you need some money?"

The man spoke to Sahadeva, ignoring Moses.

"Yes, of course," said Sahadeva. "I could use the work."

Moses had already sat under the shade of an awning, not expecting to do anything but watch.

Within seconds of exertion, sweat poured from Sahadeva. As the boxes leaked their contents, streaks of red and yellow formed on his clothes. After an hour, his knees weakened and he sat on the ground, as the dye and sweat turned brown on his face. He breathed with difficulty in the heavy air. Rain had yet to crack the claustrophobic atmosphere; the clouds were so still, the sky was a painting. Occasionally, a drop fell and all would look to the heavens.

Moses stepped behind Sahadeva, drawing a circle on his dye-stained shirt. The two men laughed for the first time in weeks as a flash of lightning ripped through the clouds. Sahadeva walked to the fountain at the crossroads, took off his shirt, and poured yellow tap water over his head and back. The few rupees were given willingly; the men were fed up with his limited stamina.

They crossed the road to the "Quality Restaurant," spending the rupees on a small meal of chapatis, dhal, and sweet milky chai. Their mood lifted, Sahadeva talking about the weather and work they might get tomorrow. They had no plans but an unspoken association had formed; it was now mutually assumed that the future would be undertaken in common.

In a very quiet voice, barely audible, Sahadeva spoke of himself.

"I have been very ill, Moses. In fact, I still might die. I don't dwell on it, really. Well, maybe I do. It is too massive to look at directly. How can you look at death? But I do know that I have terrible bleeding."

Moses listened carefully, wondering what a man of God could want from him, a person of no strength or integrity.

"As each day passes, the fear in my mind recedes. It used to stand on my shoulder. Now I think of it less. But anytime there is a pain, or something goes wrong in my body, I immediately associate this as part of the bigger problem. Perhaps the most important thing for you to know is that I no longer have an anchor. When I realized I might die, I was cast adrift. I cannot bring myself to meditate because it has disappointed me."

Moses looked at him with understanding, putting his hand on Sahadeva's brown arm. This was the first genuine communication for Moses since escaping; he had not permitted himself the hope of such intimacy. Since leaving jail, he was painfully aware that his naïveté might cause more suffering. Now, he settled into the convivial role, of listener and confidant. He adored philosophical conversations and was at ease with Sahadeva's abstractions.

"Moses," Sahadeva paused, until Moses looked at him. "Sita is important to me. It is as if she is part of me. Nothing had meaning when I realized I could die, but now it is just this possibility that makes me want her. God has unveiled her to me at my most vulnerable time. She is the life force to me, and if I do not see her, nothing else can ever have meaning."

Sahadeva looked about at the human chaos, walking a few paces into the crowd, as if looking for an answer. He returned to Moses and spoke loudly, so he could be heard over the deafening hum of the traffic.

"If I don't find the life force in me, I will surely die. She is what I need to find it."

With this, he walked away. Moses expected him to return, but he turned a corner. This was Sahadeva's full answer, there was nothing more for him to say.

4 THE CLOUDS JOINED, forming a dark, ominous mass; the village was black in the starless night. Dogs yapped at the sky, covering the small sounds he made. He heard a low growl and could make out the shape of a small dog in his path.

They had walked to Sarnath within half a mile of the village; not by design, but randomly, from the desire to keep moving. Once they had picked a place in Sarnath for the night, across from the Deer Park where Buddha gave his first sermon after enlightenment, he left Sahadeva sleeping peacefully. Moses did not want to venture out in the night, but he had no choice. This friendship was his lifeline and it was inconceivable that he could survive on his own in the vicious reality of India. Moses recalled how pity had derailed him in the past, but the wave of emotion rose too high and fast for him to resist. If Sahadeva must have this woman, then Moses would see that wish fulfilled. He thought of Nadia and felt the suffering of love that was lost.

A faint glow of moonlight illuminated the village and Moses saw a half-moon peeking from the clouds. He walked down the road that led to the huts. There were small cooking fires still glowing in huts and the smell of burning dung was mixed with spices from dinner. The air had a cardamom smell, reminding him of chai, lifting his spirits.

He stopped at the entrance to the village. His feelings for Sahadeva had deepened; he needed a companion to talk and listen to. With Sahadeva, India was tolerable. Sita had destabilized Sahadeva: he was moody and irritable, snapping at Moses for no reason. His mind was so adrift that Moses felt the growing bond between them was under threat. Occasionally Sahadeva walked off, returning dazed, unsure of where he had been. Just this morning, he spoke for the first time of returning to France and rejoining the monastery.

Moses walked to the back of Sita's hut, to peek through the window. The father was cleaning a bicycle wheel, the mother and Sita sloshing water in metal bowls. There was a cooking fire near the door and Moses felt the heat radiating from the hut. Sita had her back to the door and Moses examined her closely: a short, large-boned girl with a dark peaceful face. He was not sure of what to do or even what he wanted to do. She was the soul of Sahadeva, as strange as it looked, and he perceived, his own salvation.

He leaned closer for a better view. The father sensed his presence and turned to see Moses' face framed in the window. Seconds passed and neither changed position. Moses realized it was too late to move and froze. For a moment he hoped — foolishly — that Bhakti would forget him; pretend he wasn't there, to avoid trouble.

A second later, Moses felt something hit him. Rohini had thrown the broom of sticks at him, striking him on the head. He smelled dog feces on the sticks. Sita and her mother were at the window, staring at him.

He heard shouting in the distance and understood he was in grave peril. He wiped the sweat from his face, spitting involuntarily; he could feel the feces on the back of his hand. He went to the front of the hut and looked inside; the family was there, backed against the wall, the father sheltering Rohini and Sita, who was closest to the door. He could hear a crowd forming, yelling loudly at one another, as if undecided what to do. Without thinking, Moses leaped into the hut, grabbed Sita by the arm, and pulled her toward the door. Strangely, she yielded, but her foot dragged across the cooking fire, strewing embers. He pulled her from the hut and down the road toward Banaras; she put up no resistance.

Moses saw that the crowd was surging down the road without direction. He glanced at the hut and saw it was now ablaze; the fire rapidly consuming the branches and twigs. As it burned, he saw two small figures in the flames. He pulled Sita more quickly to make sure she did not look back. Soon he ran and she loped next to him. Then she balked, gazing toward the village and the still-burning hut.

"They escaped. Don't worry," Moses panted. "They did escape."

Even though she did not understand him, he felt she sensed his reassurance. She did not utter a sound as they progressed toward Sarnath.

"They are fine. Sahadeva, you have to be with Sahadeva." He intoned his name slowly and deliberately. "That's the way it was meant to be."

Moses paused, listening in the dark. The only sound was thunder.

"What have you done?" Sahadeva was walking in a circle, repeating the same plaint. "Have you no sense? You can't just kidnap a woman in India. We will all be killed now."

"I meant no harm. I was just trying to help." Moses spoke, glancing in the direction of the village. "Let's go, then. Let's escape!" Their breathing was shallow, all senses escalating, like the closing bars of a raga.

"We will have to go!" shouted Sahadeva. "You give us no choice! No choice! We can't return her like a borrowed pot. The whole village will come after us and every man will hunt us down." Sahadeva spoke directly to Sita, repeating the same message in Hindi.

Sita had cried quietly when she arrived, but, as Sahadeva shouted at Moses, she sobbed ever louder. Sahadeva moved to comfort her, but she kicked him away with her foot. Sita's yelling drew a few beggars, squatting, as if watching a cricket match.

"Stop it!" yelled Moses.

Sita quieted down for a moment, then wept.

Sahadeva watched Sita struggle for breath and stepped between them.

"Let us have a minute together, please," said Sahadeva. "I want to talk to her alone."

Moses walked down a lane, moving furtively. He arrived at a square with an old fountain, sat on the edge, and looked up at the haze of a million dung fires. He wanted to give Sahadeva time to calm her.

Four bent figures walked into the square, dressed identically in the white sari of the widows of Banaras. All were decrepit, of indeterminate age. They stopped before Moses, startled to see a European. After staring at him for a few moments, they crossed the square to a building. The smallest one, almost bent in half, raised her walking stick menacingly at the door. She moved away and approached Moses, speaking in very slow Hindi. Moses was able to discern the sense of her message from the gestures, that they needed help getting through the locked door.

He shrugged and the women laughed. Moses saw that they were ridiculing him, imitating his gesture.

"Go away," he yelled, half rising to menace them.

The one with the stick pointed at him, then pointed at the locked door. She did this several times, moving slowly from one to the other so the meaning was apparent.

Moses shivered as her insight brought him back to the door of his dream. He understood instantly that the harm he had caused had now fortified the door against any tampering. He turned his anger on himself as the same woman came closer, appearing to stare through him. Moses pushed her away, unwilling to be exposed any further. She fell heavily to the ground.

The other women panicked and struggled to move away. The small woman rose up and stood there, with the sari off her bald head. She was holding her arm, as if it was injured, and limped slightly as she came toward Moses. The smell of betel nut and decay was on her breath. She took her stick, tracing a face in the dirt: two eyes, a nose, and mouth. She looked at Moses, spit on the face then rubbed out the eyes.

A cold chill filled him and the curse settled into his cells. The doubt that expanded inside him ripped apart his hopes and he knew that tomorrow, or the next day, destruction would somehow take hold and crush him.

"I was only joking," said Moses softly.

The woman looked at him with contempt.

"You can't do anything to me, anyway," Moses offered, aware there was something else he should have said.

He moved to the fountain, sat on the rim, closing his eyes. He heard noises and opened one eye to see children running along with a stick and a hoop. There was no sign of the old widows. He stood up and walked away.

As Moses walked up the road to Sita and Sahadeva, he visualized every moment of the catastrophe at the village. The curse was over-shadowed by the tragedy; Sita's mother and father had been caught in the blaze, dying a horrible death.

"What am I?" thought Moses. "What kind of man could I be to do this? Everything I touch creates horror."

He was unable to feel remorse and was bewildered by his lack of feeling. His mind rushed to offer a range of justifications, but he brushed them aside, struggling for some contact with his feelings. He was guilty of death.

His eyes hurt and he was about to rub them, when he remembered the curse. He let the dirt sting and resisted raising his sleeve. The discomfort passed quickly, replaced by fatigue. He walked to an open drinking pipe, took off his shirt and washed away the dog feces, rubbing the shirt sleeves together to remove the stains. He put the wet shirt on, refreshed by the coolness.

Sahadeva and Sita sat talking together, huddled close. Sahadeva was touching her as he talked, holding her arm, grabbing her hand. Moses searched the road for a sign of retribution but no villagers could be seen. The turmoil of movement and sound appeared normal. He did not want to interrupt their conversation and sat across from them on the ground. The sounds of Sarnath dulled him and he was quickly lost in observation. Above him, the enormous black clouds massed and swirled in the night sky, preparing for a major assault. An endless stream of rickshaws still passed in the dark, carrying oversize machinery and men with red Siva markings on their foreheads.

"What a strange place," he thought. "What would have happened if I stayed in Warsaw? Would I have caused the death of a young girl and now two Indians? Or would I have done worse?"

He walked over to Sahadeva and Sita.

"Can I talk to you about the door?" Moses addressed Sahadeva, as if Sita was not there.

"Now? You mean the ｛ ｜r in your dream? You want to talk about the door now?" Sahadeva ｜ ｝ook his head, incredulous. He looked at Sita, then Moses, and laug ｜d. "Are you mad?" Let's go now. Sita will come with us. She has r.o choice."

Sahadeva was sure he had lost more weight and that some part of him was wasting away. As they walked in the black night, he tightened the drawstring, and felt that his hands were caked with dirt. He clapped them together loudly. As if in response, a crash of thunder caused them all to jump. Moses and Sahadeva laughed, looking at each other wide-eyed. They kept laughing and the infectious laughter caught Sita briefly; she glanced at them in amazement, giggling involuntarily. The sky boomed again and this set them off afresh.

Famine turned to a feast. Moses hugged Sahadeva then pulled away, dancing with his arms outstretched, stopping only for a second to encourage them to join in. He moved toward Sita and extended his hand. At that gesture, the atmosphere changed and the whole affair ended abruptly. Sita moved away with a solemn look.

"You are my friend. I would give you anything," Moses yelled at Sahadeva, from the remnants of the mood.

A bleak sadness descended upon them. Sahadeva smiled at Moses.

"You don't need to give me anything, Moses," he said warmly. "I have everything I need."

Large, fat drops of rain began to fall, increasing rapidly in intensity. Countless dogs barked plaintively. The sky opened wide and, in moments, the dirt road was a river of mud flowing toward the Ganges.

The rain forced Sahadeva to postpone his confusion. He was with Sita at last, but in a way that was incapable of resolution. If he returned her to the village, he would be hanged, and Sita further dishonored or rejected, but if he ran, the village would chase him to doom. For Moses to demand emotional loyalty at this time was so bizarre that he found no words to argue and certainly none to comfort him. He had to force Moses to see the horror of his actions, but as the words rose in his throat they dissipated like fumes. He stepped under the rough shelter of a vegetable vendor and the pounding of the rain on the roof momentarily soothed him, reminding him of his warm room in the monastery. "Forgive me, Moses. I am tired."

Moses visibly softened. Sahadeva spoke again. "We are all tense. We must get moving. The villagers will come after us, as surely as a dog looks for a buried bone. We must go somewhere. If we stay here, we are lost."

The village turned in on itself and reflected. Tragedy was the common fiber and usually the pain of others was most often ignored. This gruesome death went beyond their experience of suffering, however, causing the image of Sita's parents to rise in every mind. The sight of Sita's father meditating or performing Arti had given the village hope in the face of crushing doubt and a paucity of inspiration. The meditative rickshaw driver, the devotee of the Lord, and the gracious mother who respected her husband, serving him with strength and duty, were idealized more now than in life.

All spoke of nothing else, and, in the last moment before sleep that night, each reflected that an act or gesture must be made to affirm the pride of the village. When that awareness turned to confusion, they were left with the momentum for action. The missing Sita became a fulcrum for their determination. To ignore the deaths, or to forget Sita, was a denial of the bedrock of their lives.

All that night, it rained with raw intensity. The clouds crossed rapidly, bringing fresh supplies from the Bay of Bengal. The rain washed away the soot; the ground would soon be cleared.

The three weary fugitives spent the rest of the night shivering miserably in a corner of the railway station. Sita slept apart, her back to a wall, while Moses and Sahadeva lay close to each other. Moses slept fitfully, possessed by fear. He visualized ugly deaths: being pulled apart by rickshaws or hacked to pieces. The new fear mixed with residual panic, imprinted over time and only recently subdued. Fear seeped into his chest, constricting his breathing. He coughed repeatedly, spitting and hacking, gasping for breath.

Throughout the night, Moses awoke and paced the platform, watching families eating as if it were noon, sadhus meditating, and old people bent over, meandering but going nowhere. The sadhus were motionless in meditation, breathing invisibly. Moses discounted meditation: his attempts at it only produced whirlpools of his own mire. He pondered how people of limited intelligence, lacking subtlety of mind, could develop insight.

When he lay still, staring at the rafters, listening to the rain, his thoughts teased out each strand of the problem, holding it up for scrutiny. He could abandon them, leaving them to their fate. This would be to their advantage, as his presence made them far more conspicuous. But on his own, he would be a blatant target, visible against any backdrop, unable to rely upon Sita to plead for them or Sahadeva to talk smoothly in religious idioms, to appease potential attackers.

He glanced at Sahadeva, tossing in his sleep, and felt a twinge of guilt. Sahadeva was lost in limbo between shattered aspirations and the hidden joy of having Sita. His response to their predicament was to look longingly at Sita, then look over his shoulder. The dilemma facing Moses was too familiar; it was identical to Warsaw: the impossible task of taking responsibility for others. This time he had created the problem, bringing down the wrath of villagers on all three of them. He was led to ponder if he also had drawn the Nazi horror on himself, his race: had the act of being weak, fearful, and confused invoked Wotan from its bestial sleep?

A large crowd on the opposite platform waited for the train to Calcutta, now hissing and clanging as it approached the station. That noise was dulled by the rain crashing on the roof and the shouting of the crowd. He saw that the travelers had luggage: large brown bags of unimaginable belongings, held together by twine. It dawned on him that the station was the most obvious place for the villagers to look. It had to be. If they tried to leave Banaras by any other method, every rickshaw driver would pass a message. The train was the only means of rapid exit and, accordingly, was hopelessly transparent.

"Of course," thought Moses aloud. "How crazy to think we could sleep here and use this as an escape route."

He was about to wake Sahadeva and Sita, when he saw a European man, well dressed and clean shaven. Two Indian porters were by his side, holding leather bags weathered by use. The man saw Moses and waved. He spoke to the porters, then walked over the bridge separating the platforms, making his way to Moses. He stood there, smelling of snuff. He looked Moses up and down, the gesture one of curiosity rather than derision.

"I could tell, even in that garb, you were European," he said in French, but Moses detected a Polish accent. "What sort of man are you?"

Moses was overcome, as if found out; he stuttered, trying to find a response.

"Why, I am a Pole, like you," Moses replied, taking his interlocutor by surprise.

The man stepped back, dusting off his jacket, as if removing fragments of Moses' desperation. His distance indicated he already regretted the encounter.

"Polish?" he asked Moses. "Are you a Jew?"

"Yes, I am a Jew, but I am Polish."

"You are a rare sight, my friend. A Polish Jew. I doubt if many are left." The man took out a French cigarette, tamping it on the back of his hand. He saw that Moses was in a trance, stunned by his statement. "You have obviously been away a long time."

The train whistle, meant for cows on the track, deafened everyone in the station. The man held his hands to his ears, noticing that Moses had not moved. He turned to leave, but Moses grabbed his arm.

"I must have news," Moses blurted.

The man pulled his arm free.

"I come from Vilanov, outside Warsaw. I saw Jews placed in so-called refugee centers, then sent in deportation convoys to Treblinka. To what end, I don't know. There is a ghetto in Warsaw; Leszno Street runs down the middle and it appears that typhus and hunger rather than the Nazis rule the streets." He paused. "So, I assume that is what brought you here. To avoid the ghetto." The man looked again at Moses, and Moses imagined his thought: "Did you do yourself a service by fleeing?"

But the man saw Moses was no longer listening and walked quickly away, crossing the bridge to board his train. An inaudible announcement blared on the loudspeakers, inciting new commotion. Moses stepped back, leaning against a pillar. He felt as if his soul was trying to slip its boundaries. He was about to shout, just to re-lease some anguish, when a train on their side of the platform came barreling into the station, steam rising to the roof. Indian soldiers stepped off, disheveled from the night journey, scratching them-selves and rubbing sleep from their eyes. The sight of authority and guns galvanized Moses. He shook Sita, then Sahadeva, who rose softly, as if gliding up through satiny water. They looked at Moses, who squatted on one knee to address them, "I think we made a mis-take by coming to the train station," he said.

"Yes, you are right," Sahadeva agreed. "I have a brother in Patna who works at the railway station. I haven't seen him for decades, but still, he would receive us. Here we are too obvious."

Deliberately Sita walked to a water tap in the center of the station, cupping her hands to drink. She lifted her head, glanced around ca-sually, and walked back to Moses and Sahadeva as if she had be-come part of the conspiracy. Wordlessly they left the platform, sheltering in the entrance to the station.

"I know where to go," said Sahadeva, shouting over the rain.

Sita and Moses stared at him in surprise.

"To my ashram or another ashram. I don't know. But this is where we should hide. Let's get there before Banaras awakes."

They moved to the Raj Ghat, close to Kasi Station. Sahadeva glanced up at the temple of Adi Keshava, sitting high on the Raj Ghat Plateau, looking out at the confluence of the Varuna and Ganges Rivers. Behind the temple was a dilapidated building used as an ashram for widows. The women sat listlessly all day, singing devotional songs, emptied of life and possessions except for a few coins necessary to pay for funeral wood. This ashram was dedicated to Mother Chaumsathi, the goddess of many widows, sent by Lord Siva to Kasi.

They entered the ashram, walking up the wide steps and into the darkened chamber. The widows, looking like bones in their white saris, ignored the intruders. Sahadeva tried to speak to a widow near the entrance, bending to whisper to her, but she stood and walked away.

"She doesn't hear me," said Sahadeva. "Perhaps she is blind or deaf. Maybe she is looking only at ghosts, but she doesn't see me."

Sahadeva addressed more widows with the same result.

"For some reason, they are not paying us any attention."

"That is good, isn't it?" offered Moses.

Sita cleared her throat. She had barely spoken since her abduction, silently following Sahadeva's directions without complaint.

"This place frightens me. Do we have to stay here?"

She spoke loudly and her voice echoed into the recesses of the large room. Moses could not understand her words but saw a fresh fear on her face.

"This may be the perfect place," said Moses. "One of us can go for food and we can hide here until we are ready to leave. Then we can travel to your brother."

At the end of the entrance hall, a steep circular staircase descended into darkness. Without hesitation, Moses walked down, using the walls for direction. He motioned Sahadeva and Sita to follow and they joined him on the first landing. The stairs were hewn from the rock and as the dim light from above faded, they plunged into the blackness. The air was damp and cold and, for the first time since coming to India, Moses shivered.

They continued, the walls dripping and clammy, until the stairs ended and the bottom landing opened to a corridor with a faint glow at the end. Water wept from the roof and Sahadeva assumed they had descended under the Ganges. At the end of the corridor, they found two sets of stairs: one that ascended and was lit by torches and another that dropped lower into darkness. Moses was about to climb toward the light, when he was stopped by Sahadeva.

"Wait, Moses. We can't walk aimlessly. We must have a plan."

Moses looked at him in surprise.

"How could there be a plan? How about this? I go up and you go down. Take a torch from the wall. We will meet back here in half an hour, as best we can calculate."

It was clear that Sita was on the verge of tears. She took a deep breath of the cold air, but before she could exhale Moses said, "Sita will come with me," and he made a gesture for her to follow. Before Sahadeva could protest, Moses bounded up the steps with Sita in his wake. They found another corridor that was also lit by torches. Moses walked to the door at the end of the passage and pulled it. It opened quietly on its hinges and a stream of foul smelling water gushed out. Moses stepped inside, then slipped, falling backward. He scrambled to his feet, soaking wet, his teeth chattering. There was a dry platform across the room, with another door.

"We must try that door," said Moses. "We have no choice."

Moses did not wait for Sita's approval and he plowed through the water, using the wall for balance, until he mounted the platform. The wooden door was shut. Moses yelled to Sita, "Come. We will try this door."

Sita had lagged behind, but now moved up to him, her sari soaked. With Sita's help, Moses pushed the heavy door open and warmth radiated from a burning hearth. Two widows squatted, attending to a cooking pot; the room was a kitchen at the center of a semicircle of rooms and passages.

A widow, with gentle hands that had seen a lifetime of caring, removed Sita's wet sari and her undergarments, placing them on a cooking tripod by the fire. She did not protest, standing there naked in front of the fire, as Moses politely turned away. His clothes were taken as well, and placed on another rack by the fire.

Moses looked at Sita, who was staring into the fire. Moses started at her feet, then inspected her legs. She glanced away, unaware of or ignoring his gaze. Her back was smooth and flawless, not a mark defaced perfect brown skin. Her shoulders were rounded, but muscular, her arms firmer than he remembered. He noticed her long delicate hands and the shape of her breasts: full on the bottom with a sweeping arch up to her nipples. As she turned slightly, he could see that the areolae were perfectly symmetrical. There was a line of muscle on her stomach that gave greater authority to her breasts. He looked at her strong legs and the wide arch of her buttocks.

Moses realized he had stopped breathing during the inspection. He gently exhaled, then examined her again, laying his gaze upon her as if it was his fingertips. He felt his chest bursting. The beauty he craved in his higher self was awakened in the magnificent form of Sita. This was not the pounding of his sexuality, as it had been with Martine. Instead, he was cracked like an eggshell with an outpouring of sensitivity and refinement. For the first time since leaving Warsaw and Nadia, he relaxed the knots around his heart, and felt the pain and longing soften. This strong woman held a quality that gave him renewed meaning and hope.

He did not move when Sahadeva entered from a door at the other end of the room, picking up a white sari from a stack in the corner, unfurling it, as it billowed in the warm air from the hearth. Sita stepped back and the sari floated over her shoulders.

In the flickering light of the fire Moses watched, as if it was all in slow motion. The beautiful brown body of Sita was covered by the contrast of the white sari, lifted into position by Sahadeva's long bony fingers. The Indian's gaze was loving, like a father's, as he worked with Sita to make the right adjustments. In this slowing of time, he saw Sahadeva smile at her with moist, soft eyes and she returned the feeling with such intensity that the room seemed to grow brighter.

Sahadeva noticed Moses crouching naked by the fire. Deliberately, Moses stood, revealing himself to Sahadeva and to Sita. Sahadeva was not sure what to do and his face contorted as he looked for clothes. Moses raised himself particularly straight, looking directly at Sita. It appeared to him that she was smiling, glancing at his body. Her gaze felt like feathers and he became aroused. He lingered as his penis grew, pulling back his shoulders to display himself proudly. Sita and Sahadeva turned away, but the widows, still crouched by the cooking pot, stared at him intently.

"It's warm in here, isn't it?" he said loudly.

He directed this toward Sita with some force, hoping she would turn to him. Sensing his intended purpose she turned away, her back to him, stepping toward the widows, who continued to stare, unfazed, while stirring the large pot.

"Yes, yes," said Sahadeva, ignoring the message of Moses' body. "I think we had better dry your clothes. In the meantime, take one of these saris and wrap it around you."

Sahadeva took another sari. He walked to Moses, wrapping it around him like a Polynesian sarong.

"This should be enough for now. Sit down and have something to eat. We need our strength."

A widow brought a steaming bowl of dhal to each of them. Moses sat back, in the warmth of the blaze and the contentment of being close to Sita, savoring each mouthful. He ate noisily, leaning against the wall, with his legs spread. His gaze never left Sita, following her as she sat next to Sahadeva.

"We can't stay here forever," said Sahadeva. "It is false to hold on to this moment. We need to move forward."

"What for? Where else can we go? Anyway, we are all together here, you, me, and Sita."

"Are we a group now?" asked Sahadeva. "The three of us? Before you were happy with two of us." Sahadeva appeared angry, a reaction Moses was expecting.

"No. It is really you and Sita now. I'll find my own way."

"I doubt it." Sahadeva stood, kicking his bowl accidentally. He now was visibly angry. "You dragged me into a maelstrom for your own benefit, so I would be pleased with you or probably . . .," he shook his head in understanding, "to get us into a situation with no way out. So I would be stuck with you. And now there is no way out. She can't return, and you and I will die together."

Moses also stood, raising his voice, "I was just making up for your cowardice," he cried, "You wanted her, so I brought her to you."

Sahadeva was about to shout at Moses but hesitated, thinking that Sita might still be unaware of the death of her parents. Instead, he changed the topic. "I am going out to see what I can."

He walked up the stairs at the back of the kitchen, which led directly into the hall of the ashram. He stepped into the glaring light of morning and saw that the Ganges was thronged with bathers.

"This must be a Monday morning," he thought idly.

As he left the ashram, a temple official, a pujari coming from the Ganges, seemed about to give him the greeting of sadhus, but Sahadeva bowed his head, ignoring him. He wondered if his shaved head evoked the greeting or if he was now notorious.

Sahadeva walked to the adjoining Prahlad Ghat and then up to Daranagar Road, a busy artery of Banaras. He had a bounce in his step both from the food and the fact that he and Sita were together, even under such impossible circumstances. He crossed the road, weaving through people, rickshaws, and bicycles. The sounds of the street and the dusty smells reminded him of why he had returned to India. He passed a stall of dyes and, as he had when he was a boy, stopped to absorb the rainbow of colored powders. The shopkeeper smiled at Sahadeva and he turned away, his step even lighter.

His telltale bleeding continued, although in the last week of wild excitement he had not given it further thought. Now, as he meandered along, he was struck by the chaos that lived behind his thoughts. The panic pulsed like music, and the cadence was slow and steady; sweat rolled down his back. He looked up and saw the sky building to another monsoon explosion. There was a lever; he had seen it, and it was available to cure him and extend his life. The lever lay in his body, not his mind, in uncharted places: perhaps in cells, stubborn and obstinate, or an organ uninterested in his insights or aspirations. The lever was the life force, the spark of the Divine that made it impossible for any man ultimately to be an atheist. Yet his body would not listen, apparently uninterested in maintaining its own integrity. If he escaped, there could be a future where he could sink into the body, releasing fear and pain. He knew that whatever there was to be understood, it could never be grasped by words or his mind.

He turned off the main road, walking toward the Tatheri Bazaar, hoping to find cheap clothes. His plan, hatched as he walked, was to dress Sita in men's clothes, cut her hair, and leave with her on the train to Patna. His plan did not include Moses.

He did not see the rickshaw driver emerging from a side lane until, at the last moment, he saw the front wheel about to collide with his leg. Sahadeva jumped aside, pushing over a small child who was quickly swooped up by a frantic mother, and lost his balance, falling headfirst into a stall of oranges. He was not hurt and stood up immediately. The rickshaw driver moved ahead as if nothing had happened but then looked at Sahadeva. The recognition was instant for both of them. Sahadeva thought to run, but the world became smaller.

The driver stepped from his rickshaw, leaving it in the middle of a swirling throng. There was much yelling and cursing from the crowd and a tall Muslim man with a neatly curled moustache made threatening gestures with his fist. The driver walked to Sahadeva and held him with both hands.

"I know you," the driver said. "You came to our village with the murderer. Yes, I know you."

Sahadeva could do nothing other than shrug. He looked for a place to run, but was held in the driver's iron grip. The bedlam of those delayed by the incident gathered momentum and a man on a bicycle bent, picking up a rock to throw if the driver did not move. The driver knew the road rules and the awful consequences of impeding the desperate push of traffic. He let Sahadeva go, returning immediately to his rickshaw. He pushed off, moving rapidly away.

Moses put his hand on Sita's neck.

"There was a bug on your neck. I think I got it."

Sita attempted to make sense of his words, then returned to cleaning the bowls, while Moses stared at her neck, comparing touch with sight. In Poland, he had jumped at Martine with a primitive lust. Sita engaged him in an outward expansion toward beauty.

The widows left the room, climbing the stairs to the main hall. Moses casually meandered into the adjacent rooms, verifying that he was alone with Sita. In the shrine room, he came upon a large chair, in which one would seat a guru or sage. Moses dragged the large chair to Sita. She looked at him in surprise, knowing that he had gone too far by disturbing their hosts' furniture.

"Sit here, Sita," he said, patting the chair. "You sit here in this guru chair. Let's pretend you are the Devi."

Sita was horrified at the words "guru" and "devi" coming from this horrible man. Moses, with his wild hair and beard, looked insane, and she waited for him to strike like a rabid dog. She hoped Sahadeva would return shortly. She spoke to him in Hindi, hoping he would understand.

"Please, Moses. I am embarrassed to sit in the chair. This would cause me very much pain. Please." She shook her head.

He motioned her closer.

"Well, just stand next to the chair," he said. "Come closer, I am not going to bite."

"*Kripya* — Please," she pleaded, visibly shrinking.

Moses interrupted, speaking with a commanding voice, indicating by inflection what he meant. "Oh come, Sita, I am just trying to play. Sit down, would you."

Sita walked to the chair and tried to drag it back to the shrine room. She strained with both arms, but was not strong enough. Moses stood and watched. She paused for a moment and looked over at Moses. He was about to speak when she turned and pushed the chair a few inches with her back.

"You don't have to sit in it," Moses said.

Sita glared at him defiantly, straightened her sari and pushed again. The chair creaked, moving another inch.

Sahadeva rushed back to the ashram. Panic increased his speed. People jumped out of his way to avoid collision. His running was frantic; he lost control as he strained for safety.

A little boy ran next to Sahadeva, as if they were in a race. They rounded a corner just as the sky opened with a torrential downpour. The boy laughed gaily at the rain, raising his arms in excitement while running effortlessly. Sahadeva jumped over newly formed puddles, increasing his stride. A sudden muscle cramp made him conscious of the madness of his running and he slowed, the boy running around him in circles. Sahadeva shook his finger at the boy and said, "*Chelo, chelo!* Go away."

The boy was small but looked, as some Indian children do, as if he were a miniature adult. The boy was unable to stop laughing, his eyes wide with wonder at the sight of the man running. Sahadeva arrived at the ashram and stopped, propping himself against a wall, gasping for breath, his legs rubbery. He balanced for a few minutes and then collapsed on the ground, his back to the wall, head between his legs, struggling for air. At last, he forced himself to stand.

The boy walked away, evidently losing interest, and Sahadeva entered the ashram, walked through the hall, and descended the stairs. His bowels hurt and triggered despair as he contemplated ten possible explanations; he chose the worst as a confirmed diagnosis.

He did not see the boy enter behind him, following in the shadows.

Sahadeva opened the door and saw Moses and Sita sitting peacefully, engaged in their own tasks. They could well have been in different rooms and appeared unconnected and uninterested in each other. Sahadeva walked over to Moses and squatted next to him.

"We must talk, Moses. There is a problem." Sahadeva spoke so calmly that Moses did not look up.

"What is it, Sahadeva?"

"I said we must talk. There is trouble."

Moses looked at his friend, noticing his bloodshot eyes and red face. Instinctively, Moses recoiled, moving back against the wall. He had no interest in hearing Sahadeva; his world now had some order, fueled by beauty, warmth, and a full stomach. All he wanted was to look at Sita and not move from this hole in the ground occupied peacefully by the widows. He knew the monsoon was probably raging outside, and if asked, he would have said he could live here indefinitely. Sahadeva brought a sense of disruption, and to hear bad news would destroy his first real peace since escaping from Warsaw.

"Talk to me later, would you? I feel relaxed. At last. This is a place where I could do some writing. You know, Sahadeva, it has been several months since I opened a book. Maybe you could teach me Sanskrit."

Sita shrank into a corner, as if trying to make herself smaller. Sahadeva turned and walked over to comfort her. Moses was oblivious of their concerns and fears and moved toward the door. To their surprise it opened, and the little boy darted in and stood looking at them. He was perhaps eight, with a small barrel chest and short legs, but his face was very dark and his nose protruded, giving him the look of a fully grown midget. His appearance made no sense except as the tip of an onslaught. But this man-child, in the center of the room, was so bizarre and incongruous that they only stared.

The boy spotted the precarious pile of bowls, stacked by Sita. He kicked them over, jumping and laughing. Sahadeva tried to grab him, but he leaped away, with his back to the hearth. He saw this as a game and beckoned Sahadeva to chase him. Moses opened the door and Sahadeva seized the boy, throwing him out effortlessly, as one would heave a light object.

A few minutes later, the boy popped his head from behind some boxes of flour. They had not heard him enter. Moses yelled "What?" as he watched the boy emerge, covered in flour. The boy realized he had gone too far and crouched down, cowering. Sita walked over and took him by the arm to be washed in an adjoining room.

"How did that happen?" Moses asked.

He went to the door, opening and closing it, looking to discover how the boy got in when his back was turned.

Moses glanced at Sahadeva, noticing that he was trembling and his face was still red.

"Tell me, Sahadeva. What is wrong?"

"I ran into a rickshaw driver or rather, he ran into me. He recognized me. I am sure of it."

Moses' field of vision narrowed and Sahadeva became irrelevant. The inexorable tragedy moving in his direction sapped what was left of Moses' recent resolve.

"We're finished," he managed in a whisper. "This time I know it."

Sahadeva was disgusted by Moses' reaction; nothing had yet happened and it was possible that the threat would never manifest. He called out to Sita, "Are you all right in there?"

Sita emerged, holding the boy by the hand. The boy's hair was slicked and he looked even more like a small man.

A spear went through the boy's neck. The rickshaw driver stood frozen in the doorway, horrified that he had hurt a child. The boy seemed to hang from the wooden stick, now embedded in the wall behind him. Sita screamed and Sahadeva and Moses looked instinctively for weapons, but there was nothing that could be used.

Moses ran out of the room through a second door and the villagers rushed past Sahadeva and Sita, determined to find him. Moses ran through a series of rooms looking for somewhere to hide. Most rooms were empty and he saw nothing to use to defend himself. He looked back for a moment and saw two villagers chasing him. Even in his frenzied state they looked almost comical to him: small men with bow legs who appeared to have no upper body strength. One of them had a forked stick, which he had lit in the fire. Moses bounded up the stairs, raced through the ashram, and jumped into the open, still in his sarong. The crowds were thick at the entrance and he realized that progress would be slow. He turned to face his attackers.

The two villagers emerged from the ashram on his heels and then stopped. They came close with the sticks and prodded him warily, as if he were some dangerous, unknown substance. Moses saw Sahadeva run his way with Sita behind, yelling in Hindi. The villagers stepped back, lowering their weapons. Sahadeva shook his finger at them in admonishment, and they stood together like scolded boys, looking at him as if he were still the teacher in the ocher robe delivering a sermon on the Gita. Yet violence hung in the air around them like static electricity.

Moses watched Sahadeva talk to the villagers in an animated manner, wondering what he said to quiet them. Moses leaned against the ashram wall, aware of the wetness of fear. He closed his eyes, seeing himself before a mirror. He was transparent, he could see his heart, his bones, and most of all a chamber under his heart in which his soul — a grey, wispy smoke with no shape or movement — resided. He saw he had no strength and his only defenses were primitive, atavistic habits.

Sahadeva talked to the villagers about the Mahabharata, about Arjuna, the charioteer, and about Arjuna's holding back, as he had done on the advice of Krishna. He spoke loudly, like a madman, but with knowledge. He spoke of the atman, the soul, and the importance of the guidance of Krishna. One of the pursuing villagers sat to listen, while the other shifted his feet, glad to receive the traditional teaching, but confused in his competing desire for violence.

Sahadeva fixed Moses with a stare to indicate he should stay in place and not antagonize the aggressors. He noticed Moses had his eyes closed and was especially sallow. He saw Moses shrink and weaken, until his presence almost disappeared.

The villagers, who had been joined by other rickshaw drivers, were shifting their weight as a new collective will brewed. Sahadeva stopped talking, and, all of a sudden, the tension reformed and exploded. The villagers shouted and yelled at each other. They looked at Sahadeva, then at Sita, startled and desperate.

Moses awoke from his dissociation at the first shout, perceiving he had to run. His mind pushed him forward but his legs did not follow. He looked around for direction. The sun was directly in front of him, shining intensely through a gap in the monsoon clouds. It flared, as if in direct response to Moses' fear. He looked toward it, momentarily blinded by the glare. At the same time, the driver emerged from the ashram, and seeing Moses, quickly looked about for a weapon. He snatched the forked stick and lunged at Moses. When the driver pulled back the stick, there was blood on the points. Moses howled and raised his hands to his head — a head now without eyes.

4

Completion

1 THE HONK OF A HORN UNDER HIS WINDOW roused Moses from his deep sleep. He could tell by the burnt smell of toast that it was morning. In a moment, the ceiling would squeak and groan as the tables upstairs were unstacked and made ready for the patients. As soon as the noise stopped, he would be given several "shaloms" as the orderlies came and went, checking whether he was still alive. He felt for the raised hands of the clock, determining that it was seven.

"Good morning, Moses," said the nurse, in a sing-song voice, as she burst into the room without knocking. She checked his pulse.

"You can get yourself up, can't you?"

Moses waited for her cold touch to fade, then slid his feet from the bed, groping for his slippers. He walked to the toilet without hesitation, having taken these steps for a decade; he often wondered if the carpet was bare along that stretch from his repetitive journey. He relieved himself and showered, the hot water taking some of the ache from his neck. He reached and grabbed his dentures, shaking off the water and putting them in his mouth, reminding him of the ridicule of aging.

He returned to his bed where his clothes had been laid out while he showered, dutifully put on the regulation tracksuit pants and shirt, and sat on the bed, waiting for the orderly to take him to breakfast.

He heard Clayton as he came down the hallway; his heavy steps contrasted sharply with the shuffling and halting gait of the patients. The steps came closer, and he turned to greet the man who had escorted him to breakfast for what seemed his entire life. He knew Clayton was obese, and as the door opened, he waited for the heavy breath of exertion and the familiar smell of Indian Chandrika soap.

Clayton loved anything Indian and had long since drained Moses of every odor and vision of Banaras. Without a word, Moses moved off the bed, taking his big arm. He could easily have made it to the breakfast room by himself, but this was the regulation for all blind residents and Clayton was the only person for whom Moses had any feeling — that is, if familiarity was feeling.

"It's raining outside," said Clayton. "Big fat drops."

Moses turned to Clayton.

"Unusual for October. It is October, isn't it?"

"It's October and if we have rain now we are in for a long winter."

Clayton positioned Moses in front of his chair in the dining room and took his leave. The clatter of chairs being pushed into the table was particularly offensive today and the strong, greasy smell of eggs was overpowering. Moses was surprised that after all these years he could have a reaction to anything here.

He sat by himself, poking his fork on the plate, then touching the eggs with his finger to pinpoint their location. No one spoke to him, and, when he finished, he promptly stood for another orderly to take him to his room.

Moses shuffled to his bed and lay back, listening to a radio station that played songs with soothing, beneficent messages. He had the window open slightly, enjoying the crisp morning air, which provided a respite from the overheated institution. The Jewish Agency home was set back from a main roadway carrying commuters into Tel Aviv, and even though the rush hour was over, the stream of traffic remained constant. Moses was used to the continuous whoosh of traffic, and over the years the monotonous sounds had been comforting.

He was usually left alone for an hour after breakfast, unless the doctor made his monthly rounds. At this time, and again in the afternoon, he would lie back on his bed, his mind floating over issues of substance. Today, his thoughts wandered lazily back to the recent resident outing and then forward in anticipation of lunch. There were times when he primed his thoughts to resolve some issue, but his introspection always dissolved like an eddy in a stream as he drifted off to soporific sleep.

Moses imagined himself a glowing wick in the last wax droppings of a spent candle. He now understood why his father had stared aimlessly from a window: when there is no hope, there is nothing to observe. If he tried hard, he could evoke past memories, but they took mere seconds to traverse. Occasionally, a distinct image formed, such as the visage of Sahadeva, but this was usually prior to the sedative rolling him off for the night. The only clear memory he retained was the glowing forked stick approaching his eyes.

The period with Sahadeva, after the blinding, was a blur. All he still possessed of it were lingering feelings of impotent hatred toward his attacker. The villagers had walked away from Moses; his blinding had absolved him of his crime. Sahadeva placed Moses in an airless room in a small hospital a few miles from the village, bathing his eyes in the morning and again at night, before lying on the floor next to him to sleep. Sahadeva spoke little during the hospital stay. He remained with Moses for a month, leaving only for a week to visit his brother in Patna to ask for money for Moses' care.

His next distinct memory was Sahadeva telling him that they were on Jew Cemetery Road approaching Jew Town. They had used some of his brother's money to travel by train into Kerala and down to Cochin. Sahadeva led him down the road until they came to the Paradesi synagogue. The Cochin Jews opened their arms to Moses, as they did to thousands of other Eastern European Jews.

Sahadeva and Moses parted with a formal handshake, like strangers.

His hosts, a family of spice traders, gave him the daily job of counting paise, the small coins paid by customers in the markets. The gaiety of the Jews of Cochin never lifted Moses from his despair. The family at first tried to drag him to the markets or the synagogue, but Moses refused to move. Soon he was ignored and left in his misery. He lay there, month after month, year after year, emerging from his room only for food, rarely venturing out in the heat. His blindness and his guilt combined to make him morose and without hope.

He did not seek to go to Israel but was carried along by the wave of immigration of almost all Cochin Jews — precipitated by fears of riots around the country and Gandhi's assassination, which happened to coincide with the creation of the State of Israel.

He had no notion of how he now looked. He felt loose skin on the back of his hands and his hair was almost gone; the remaining patches were wispy, like weak thoughts floating from his scalp. He was very thin and his body felt the itinerant aches of a man of his age. He believed himself to be nothing other than an inmate in a state home for the aged, without family or acquaintances, with no other function than to eat and sleep until death.

This was his second institution. The first, which he had occupied for five years, was smaller and noisier. In this home by the roadway, there were two hundred souls who shared no interests, except abandonment and disability. His neighbors on either side had been there since he arrived; he had barely said a word to them in ten years.

The fact that Moses was a Jew who had escaped to India and come to Israel was no longer relevant. With the exception of Clayton, no one was interested in his past or future, except perhaps as concerned the eventual use of his room. He suspected Clayton's interest in India was really for Moses' benefit. No doubt he gave equal attention to other residents about their only remaining asset: the past.

If Moses had been asked why he was in this suspended state, he would have had to answer that he was stuck. Not stuck physically, for he could perhaps have mobilized himself, finding a place to live on his state pension, but weighed down in the sticky substance of his history. He could no longer dissect the moments of his past experience or recall the grain of each incident, but they combined to hold him in a state of residual fear, unanswered questions, remorse, and, to a great extent, despair.

Jung had told him to find the shadow: his insecurities, unacceptable impulses, and shame. Instead, the contents of his shadow fell into the unconscious, and he was crippled by what lay inside him.

"Lost in your head again?" Clayton said, entering the room, waiting for Moses to take the bait.

"Am I not entitled to a knock?" Moses asked.

"Feeling down?" Clayton responded, ignoring the question.

"What I have done," he said to Clayton, "you would have done. The only difference between us is that you have a stronger ordering principle. If you have done nothing wrong, it is because you don't strive, and if you don't strive, you are an animal."

"What have you done that I don't know?" asked Clayton.

"I have done what every man would have done and every man does. I tried to rise."

Clayton was surprised at the conversation. Moses often spoke philosophically but always in abstractions, never about himself. He started choking, as if food was stuck in his throat. Clayton slapped him on the back but Moses pushed him away.

"I gag on myself," said Moses, "the entrails of my life. I am not about to explain it all to you."

Clayton understood the ugliness of age and was not about to let the conversation develop further.

"Lunch soon. But I have a surprise for you, Moses. Eat all your lunch, get your strength up, and I promise you a treat."

Moses turned in the orderly's direction. He answered clearly, "I'll be ready. Try to collect me before the soup gets cold."

The clock next to his bed ticked loudly, progressing toward dinner. He had been restless since lunch, pacing in his room. He knew

Clayton well enough to appreciate that a treat would not be hinted at unless it existed. Moses hung by a thin thread — the defeat of this small hope could plunge him into further dismay.

The cool breeze stopped blowing and the traffic stilled for a moment. He strained to hear the sounds of the roadway, but instead discerned, closer, two sets of feet walking his way.

Some primal sense of survival was piqued, and Moses listened intently to the movement in the hall. He could feel a vector of energy directed his way and he was alert and tense. As the steps came nearer, he went through possibilities. If it were two people, it must be important. It could be he would have to move or share with another decrepit soul, doomed by circumstance to pass empty days. The news reader on the radio spoke of cuts to the health budget, and homes for the elderly had been mentioned in some context. Perhaps they saw him as clinically depressed; his remarks today had been a bit extreme. They could force some intrusive treatment on him, denying his flimsy dignity. He was amazed by how many options he could concoct in the time it took two people to walk down the hall.

He heard his door open and then the sound of two people clearing their throats simultaneously.

"Moses, I brought you a visitor," said Clayton softly. "I'll let her talk."

"My name is Mrs. Giterman."

She moved closer to his bed.

"I am a health worker," she said to him in Hebrew. When he remained silent, she added, "I can speak to you in English, if you prefer."

Moses found her tone soothing and suspected she was interested in the health of his mind, not his body.

"English is better. My Hebrew is still poor after all these years. So what do you want from me?"

Mrs. Giterman moved closer; he sensed she stood only inches from the bed.

"I would like to work with you. I have been told you are unhappy, just sitting or lying here all day long. Could I come and talk to you?"

Moses was about to speak when she answered the question she knew was forming in his mind.

"Yes, I am a psychologist."

"A psychologist," Moses interrupted. "Why do I need a psychologist? I've been to see Carl Jung in Zürich. Does that count as enough analysis? He interpreted my dream and sent me packing — and I mean packing." Moses laughed for the first time in years. "I am not depressed, I am blind, with nowhere to go at sixty. So maybe you should choose someone else."

Moses realized she was pressing against the bed; he also realized that despite all he still enjoyed human contact.

"Or maybe I am as good as anyone as a subject. Mind you, I don't feel anything is wrong. I feel fine. I don't mind sitting here or lying down and listening to music." He paused thoughtfully. "A bit empty, but what do you expect from being in institutions for fifteen years, eating bad food with nothing to do."

She took his hand and he jumped. She let go, stepping back.

"So, good, we can talk now. Is that a good idea?"

"I have, as you can see, nowhere to go."

Moses waved in the direction of Clayton.

"You can leave us. She won't bite — or so it seems."

"Perhaps you can start by giving me some history. Where you are from; things like that."

Mrs. Giterman sat in a plastic chair and took out a small pad for notes.

"I am taking notes, I hope you don't mind."

Moses sat up in the bed, swinging his feet over the side.

"Tell me first what you look like so I can visualize who I am talking to. You sound young."

He tried to push the wisps of his hair down, but they sprang back instantly.

"Well, I am twenty-eight years old. I left Poland as a young girl when the Nazis came and have been living in Israel ever since. My mother died some years ago and I now live alone. I was married for a year, but we divorced. I practice in Tel Aviv. How does that sound?"

Moses was surprised she volunteered personal information when he had asked for a description of her appearance. He raised a finger, but she went on, "and yes, my appearance. I have brown hair, cut short. I am tall, five foot ten, and I am thin; some say too thin. Let's see, I wear glasses and prefer to wear pants to dresses."

Moses was silent. It had been so long since he had spoken to a woman who in his mind was attractive that certain dormant instincts stirred to life. There had been no tenderness or caring in the institutions and he had gradually lost any desire for contact with others.

"Why so quiet? Do I sound that awful?" she asked after a minute of silence.

"Oh, no, I'm sorry. I was lost in my thoughts. I have not had a conversation with a woman for so long that I didn't believe it was real."

"Have you been asleep for all these years?"

"Do you really need to ask?" he asked. "Can't you see what I am? What I have been reduced to."

"I am not sure what I see," she said, interrupting. "A very thin man with silver hair and a beard. His face is lined and pale, and his clothes sit on him as if they were two sizes too big. That's what I see. But there is a person there, and I am interested in the person behind this appearance. Who is he? What is he thinking? Why is he here?"

She stood up abruptly.

"Actually, this is not really our first session," she said. "I came only to introduce myself and to ask if you and I can work together. I will be back this afternoon and, if you agree, can come and see you then."

Moses was about to apologize for being so obstreperous but instead said, "I would like that."

He did not wait for a reply and turned on the radio, moving the dial to find some classical music. He was not aware that she stood by the door, staring at him. Moses found some music to his taste and lay on his side, facing the radio and the wall. She left the room quietly.

Mrs. Giterman opened a floodgate of memories for Moses. He was already seduced by her companionship and, like a person who goes into surgery, he was resigned to being cut open. The warmth of the nightly sedative could not drown the barrage of visions and feelings. He thought of Jung in his big chair, animated, excited by Moses' dream. Snapshots of Trichy and Banaras swirled wildly, a vendor of oranges, a sadhu with scholar's glasses. He jumped from one image to another, but unlike the past, these were floodlit and full of vitality.

He thought of Nadia at the dinner table, her small hands holding a glass. Her hand reached under the table and her small fingers held his, sharing an intimacy that belonged only to them. He quickly put this image aside to avoid the intense pain each recollection brought. He recalled meeting Sahadeva near Banaras Hindu University and felt elation. He visualized the jail cell and felt humiliation and shame. He loosened his shoulders and chest, stepping back into himself to observe the memories.

He recalled that the Zohar talked of the importance of visions. Would the Zohar still consider him alive? The mysteries buried in that ancient work used to serve as his inspiration. He had taken the parables and sayings as the guideposts for his striving. He shook his head, remembering how the touch of the bindings had once invoked a higher purpose. He lingered over his tactile memory of the book, the smooth fabric of the cover. The remembrance of the Zohar filled him with inspiration, and the ember was reignited; his new direction suddenly became clear.

Moses sat on the bed, shaking his arms and legs, trying to throw off the sedative. He poked his fingers into a glass of water, wetting his forehead to forestall the warmth of the barbiturate. The loss of hope and the disappointments of the body had thrown a heavy blanket over him. He struggled now for air.

He held his mind back, aware how quickly he jumped to solutions. His pattern was to latch onto a hypothesis rather than nurture a thought. Yet, in the corner of his mind, or perhaps in the middle, stood the old attraction of the Zohar. This unfathomable pile of quotes, tales, and illusions had one fundamental purpose: to show the soul the way to progress.

He turned on the radio, trying to raise himself as he ordered his thoughts. He wondered if he could open the Zohar and hear it as an oracle.

A speaker on the radio was talking about Jesus and the meaning of the Church. He listened intently for a moment, fascinated at the mind that could live on faith alone. He turned down the radio until it was barely audible and, after what seemed like a long time, fell into a deep sleep.

Mrs. Giterman and Clayton sat in the cramped document room adjoining Moses' room. She was reading Moses' file, which was remarkably thin, considering he had been institutionalized for fifteen years. Upon arrival in Israel, he had been taken to the first home, carrying nothing of significance. There were no notes as to how he was blinded or came to be in Cochin before making his *Aliyah* — his immigration to Israel. He was characterized, even at that time, as depressive. She could tell, however, that Moses was not clinically depressed. Instead, she saw a man so lost in an administrative system that he had ceased to exist.

"He told me a lot about India. None of this is on his record." Clayton spoke proudly, as if he had some insight into Moses. "He lived in India, and spent months wandering with a monk. He was attacked by some bandits and he lost his eyes in the battle. That's as much as I know."

"Yes, but what has made him give up? Why hasn't he tried to leave? Blindness is not a life sentence. What is it about him that has kept him tucked away in this dusty attic?"

"No one has tried to find out," Clayton admitted. "He keeps to himself. I guess he simply fell between the cracks."

Clayton listened as she read the file out loud, "Moses Banaras is from Poland." She paused. "This last name — Banaras? I don't recognize it."

"It's not his real name," said Clayton. "It was on his immigration papers. He gave it as his last name but he told me that it's a place he went in India. He immigrated with Jews from India, so I guess no one questioned it."

She looked puzzled and continued reading, "He left Poland in 1939, just after the Nazis entered Warsaw. Apparently he escaped without his family." She closed the file on her lap and paused. "It looks as if he went to India after he escaped. There is nothing in here about how he got there."

Her instinct was to jump to the conclusion that he had the psychological profile of a Holocaust survivor, but in this case she was not sure. Moses had not only obscured his identity but, in that brief encounter, appeared to be hiding. Yet he immediately grabbed at the chance to talk to her. What did he want?

"Has he asked for anything since I saw him?" she asked.

"In fact, he has. Just this morning. He asked for a Jewish book called the Zohar. I telephoned the local bookstore and they said they didn't carry it."

Clayton took out a small piece of paper with the word "Zohar" on it and showed it to her, as proof of his quest.

"Let me phone a synagogue," she offered. "If he asked for it, it must be important. From the way you describe it, I assume this is a rare request."

She did not wait for an answer but took the telephone book from under the phone and looked for a listing for a synagogue.

"You might find it by calling the synagogue."

Moses was standing by the door in his hospital robe and dark glasses.

"I heard you talking," he said. "But don't go to any trouble about the Zohar. I just thought it would be interesting to have it read to me. I used to read it. Or try to read it."

She looked up at Moses. His face, though hidden behind large dark glasses, betrayed a new energy. His fingers adjusted his glasses and he smiled, perhaps sensing that she was looking at him. He reached into his pocket, pulled out a folded piece of paper, and unfolded it for her to take.

"This is the full name, 'The Zohar — The Book of Splendor.' I hope it is legible. I owned all five volumes in Warsaw and hid them under the bay window overlooking the street. I took one of them with me but I lost it eventually."

Moses paused for a response. When none came, he added, "I know this sounds strange, but when we were fleeing I had to hide things or, rather, this thing."

"Is that all you hid?" she asked. "Nothing else?"

"No, that's all. Nothing else. It was important to me at the time."

"I will try to get it today, before I come to see you," she said.

Mrs. Giterman left immediately and went to the Great Synagogue on Allenby Street. She entered as the morning service was commencing.

An old woman approached her. "Dzien dobry, shalom," she said first in Polish, then Hebrew.

The woman had fine lines etched on her cheeks and forehead. She reminded Mrs. Giterman of the women who shuffled in the streets of Tel Aviv, crushed in spirit, barely alive. Unexpectedly, the woman took Mrs. Giterman's hand.

"You have come to shul or are you a tourist?" Her hand was soft, but cold.

"I am on a mission," said Mrs. Giterman. "I am looking for a copy of the Zohar."

"I know nothing of the Zohar. What is it?"

"A book of Jewish mysticism, I believe."

The woman pulled Mrs. Giterman gently. "Come with me." They walked through a doorway to the left of the entrance and into a small room, full of old books, parchments, and photos. The woman said, "This is your mysticism." She took down two photos, placing them on a table. There were pictures of smiling children, exchanging Purim gifts, and a yeshiva boy with "Vilna, 1938" written on it.

Mrs. Giterman smiled compassionately and was about to speak, when the old woman hurried on to say, "The mystery is in life, these beautiful lives, and their destruction. This is the mystery for the Jewish people. My husband studied Kabbalah in a basement in Mukacheve and was one of the first to perish. The mystery is not in books; he found that out. It is at the edge between life and death. Some look elsewhere because we Jews never fit in, so we can't lose ourselves in society. Something is always left that gnaws away, like a rat."

For Mrs. Giterman, the Jew was a pioneer, with strong values, powerful intellect, and character. But the Israeli is not the only Jew, and the woes of some are the anguish of all.

"I see you are not interested," the old woman said without animosity. "It is of no consequence. I have some of my husband's books. Come with me and we will see if we can find your Zohar."

They walked from the synagogue and hailed a taxi to the Ramat Gan district. Mrs. Giterman was surprised at the spacious rooms, so tastefully decorated. Somehow she had expected something more modest.

The woman opened a trunk packed with books in disarray.

"I am only looking for one book."

"The Zohar. You are looking for the Zohar. It is five books, not one."

Mrs. Giterman looked surprised.

"Married to a mystic, I know this."

The woman's initial denial and sudden reversal intrigued Mrs. Giterman. What was it about the Zohar that should be hidden and denied?

"They are in Hebrew. That should be no problem for you. I have looked at them, but they don't make much sense. It looks like a prayer book, a midrash, but my husband said they are bombastic. You look in the box. I can't bend over."

She found two books with the same title, "The Zohar — The Book of Splendor."

"They are yours," said the old woman. "They are supposed to be read by men over forty with at least two children, so I'm not sure what you will do with them."

"They're not for me. They are for somebody special. A man over forty."

Mrs. Giterman thanked the old woman and stepped out into a strong wind. She walked several blocks towards the institution before she stopped into a café. She opened one of the books at random and read:

> A man should go into the synagogue to the distance of two gateways and then pray. These gates are two grades and they are found far within; they are the grades Mercy and Fear, at their commencement, and they are the gateways of the inner world.

She closed the book, looking out at the busy traffic. "What would Moses want with such a book?" she wondered. She finished her coffee then quickly made her way back to the institution.

Moses was sitting in a plastic chair, his back erect. He appeared to be meditating or otherwise inwardly absorbed. Mrs. Giterman gently knocked on the open door.

"I've got two of the books," she said. "There was no problem."

"Can I hold one?" asked Moses. "I want to feel one, if I could."

Mrs. Giterman placed a book in his hand. He gently felt its bindings and its pages.

"Can I ask you, Moses? Why are these books so important to you?"

Moses moved his head in her direction.

"I don't really know. They are impenetrable, but I long believed, perhaps because of that, the secrets I longed for were lodged somewhere in here."

She sat facing Moses, increasingly aware that he had been in such a dormant, passive state that he had remained unnoticed for decades. The connection with the Zohar had been sparked by her attention, she was sure of this.

"The Zohar contains the promise of an unseen world that can be understood." As he spoke he fought to push away any feelings of doubt. He had not found the answer in the mysterious East at the side of a sadhu. Was the Zohar just another false hope? He half-wished it was so, as that would allow him to return to his deep sleep, the best method to keep the gnawing anguish at bay. But the presence of Mrs. Giterman had turned on a switch, and there was nowhere else to look but the Zohar.

"Perhaps you can read me some passages," Moses suggested.

She stood to turn on the lights.

"Please leave them off, if you can. I prefer it dark. As long as you can see."

Mrs. Giterman sat down closer to the window and reached for the other book of the Zohar. Moses leaned forward in anticipation. The rain started hitting the windows and the room closed in.

"Open the book to any passage," Moses said, "and just read at random."

She placed the book on Moses' lap. He pushed it back.

"No, you choose," he said.

She read:

> Sitting one day at the gate of Lydda, Rabbi Abba saw a man approach and seat himself on a ledge which jutted out over the hollow ground far beneath. The man was weary with travel and fell asleep. Rabbi Abba beheld a serpent crawling toward the man and it had almost reached him when a branch hurtled from a tree and killed it. Now the man awakened, and, seeing the serpent before him, he jumped up; at this instant the ledge collapsed and crashed into the hollow below.
>
> Rabbi Abba approached the man and said: "Tell me, why has God seen fit to perform two miracles for you, what have you done?" To which the man answered: "Whosoever wronged me, at any time, always I made peace with him and forgave him. And if I failed to effect peace with him, then I refrained from going to take my rest before I forgave him, and along with him, forgave any others who had vexed me; at no time did I brood on the injury the man had done to me; rather, I made special efforts of kindness from then on to such a man."
>
> At this Rabbi Abba wept and said: "This man surpasses even Joseph in his deeds; that Joseph should have been forbearing toward his brethren and shown them compassion was only natural; but this man has done more, and it is meet that the Holy One, be blessed, work successive miracles for him."

They both sat quietly. She watched him, carefully gauging his reaction.

It felt to Moses as if his sightless eyes had been suddenly opened. The message of the Zohar was revealed to him: forgiveness was the key to the door. But who had wronged him? Rather, it was others *he* had wronged. The institutional smell of lunch being prepared — fried meat — wafted into the room. He was starved, lightheaded, about to lose himself in the demands of the body when he brought himself back to the Zohar.

"I need forgiveness," he said to Mrs. Giterman.

"What do you mean?" she asked.

"Just that. I need forgiveness. I need to walk back through my life, stopping at each place, seeking forgiveness, and, in some places, offering forgiveness."

"The passage of the Zohar is just a parable."

"Exactly! A parable for me. I need to start. I need your help. I want to start." Moses' voice was strong, and for a moment he looked determined.

"Where do you want to start?" she asked, excited by the strength with which he had seized the passage.

"With my daughter."

"What about your daughter?"

"She was eight when I left. I abandoned her and the rest of my family. No, that's not quite fair. We were fleeing Warsaw. . . .They were captured. I escaped. I tried to find them but . . ." He paused and though his eye sockets were dry, his lower lip trembled visibly. "I have to find her or find out what happened to her." He shook his head. "An impossible task, I know."

Mrs. Giterman waited to hear more.

"Tell me about her. Her name. And Moses, please tell me your *real* name."

He shook his head, fighting against himself, wanting to remain buried but also ready to slough off decades of remorse.

"Nadia. She is my starting point for forgiveness."

Tears welled in Mrs. Giterman's eyes. She said, in the smallest of voices, "That is my first name, Moses. And I was born in Poland, too."

Nadia was not sure what to expect. Her professional responsibilities initially overcame her feelings. To shock a depressed man with news that could tear him apart was against all her training.

She had not come to this institution to find him although she had been searching for him. Consistently, over the years, she had written to every relief agency, hoping to come across his name or some clue as to his fate. Habitually, when she started visiting institutions, she always checked the files for the name "Aarons."

She had the name but no real memory of her father. He was, in the image repeated over decades by her mother, a scholarly man with a refined intellect, prominent in his field in Poland, respected by his colleagues and students. This had left Nadia with a glimmer of understanding, but she was unable to probe her mother for more. The conversation was always the same. "But what was he like?" she would ask.

"Your father had a refined intellect. . . ."

"But what was he like as a person?"

"He was well regarded."

Even on her deathbed, she would not say more.

As the one-dimensional memory seated itself over the years, she had come to perceive him as a distant, aloof academic, without passion. She visualized him in a dusty academic chamber with disordered piles of papers and books stacked to the ceiling, lost in some intertwined theories of no use to anyone. Now she realized, as she sat in his room, that that image was more accurate than she could possibly have imagined.

She looked at him and then gazed around the room. With the exception of the radio, the clock, and the still unmade bed, there was no evidence that the room was occupied. Moses had not imposed himself here; his presence was virtually undetectable. Somehow, he had managed to disappear.

Slowly, Moses removed his dark glasses; the empty eye sockets were covered with ugly scar tissue. Yet he had a smile on his face, conflicting with his dreadful injury.

"Your voice," he said. "Something about your voice made me think, at one point, you might be my Nadia. But I banished the idea immediately, the idle hope of an old man." He held out his hand to her. "Is it really you, Nadia?"

Nadia took his hand. Her grip soon shrank to that of a little girl holding her father's commanding hand. Moses stood straight, his shoulders back and head high. His smile broadened and she felt genuine warmth flowing from him for the first time. Yet neither of them knew how to bridge the gap.

Without pause, Nadia told him what she herself had been told of their escape. She felt he had to hear it before any relationship could be formed. It was the story of the family, the myth that bound them together.

Within hours of being captured by the Germans, they had been released. At one point it seemed they were to be shot, but the Germans were called away on some other investigation and left them standing in the street. They had made their way back to find Moses, and instead found Moses' father lying on the floor, covered neatly. Moses' mother had surmised that Moses had come up the stairs and gone to look for them, but Sophie believed he had run to save himself. Nadia added, "I only have a memory of you behind a barrel, nothing else."

Moses was about to speak, to try and change the topic, but she continued the narrative. They had followed his path through the sewer and were also given passports to Romania. In fact, they were only days behind him into Bucharest. They had heard he had arrived before them and searched everywhere for him, but eventually they gave up. Sophie, Nadia, and his mother had made their way by freighter to Palestine, escaping Bucharest and obtaining entry permits with the help of their remaining precious stones.

"There was a rumor that you had gone to Ceylon," she said. "That's why I kept looking for you all these years. I always believed that you were alive."

Moses' mother had died within months of their arrival in Palestine, her will to live left in that Warsaw building. Sophie had survived, living a secluded life as a seamstress. Two years ago, she had died from cancer.

Moses had to press on. To dwell on the past would destroy any chance of waking from his deep sleep. To know the ultimate fate of his wife and mother was enough. Too many years had gone by to really mourn them.

"Well, now what?" he asked. "This is a question I have asked myself in so many situations. It's the same question your grandmother always asked, and, you know, I never seem to have an answer." Moses laughed. "I am one of those people who can never wait for life to unfold. That's not really true — I sat on a bed in a home for fifteen years waiting for something to happen. But this is different. 'Now what?' is a good question, under the circumstances."

Moses sat on the edge of his bed. He gestured for Nadia to sit.

"The Zohar is a powerful book. Don't you think? You, of all people, brought it back to me."

She was confused that he had veered away from the story of his family. She surmised that perhaps he could only hear it in small doses. She put it to one side and joined his conversation.

"I don't know anything about the Zohar," she added.

Moses cleared his throat, spitting into a handkerchief. "Sounds of India, I used to call that. Now I do it myself." He paused. "In the Zohar it is said that the Torah is a beautiful handmaiden, secluded in a chamber. Adam Kadmon, the inner man, the primordial soul, the soul of the first man, looks in all directions for her and passes constantly by her gate, not knowing what lies behind. Occasionally she thrusts open the door and for a moment reveals herself before quickly withdrawing. That is what the Zohar is about for me. I thought of it for years, remembering limited parts, but, just like that, in the first reading after all these years, it reveals a small door. What do you think?"

"You mean I am the door?" asked Nadia.

"In part, but no, the door is forgiveness. That's what the Zohar has given me. This is what it has shown me."

Moses still had a faint but discernable smile on his face. He stood, making up the bed mechanically. The traffic noise grew louder and Moses turned on the radio, lying down as if Nadia was not there. She was about to stand when he spoke again. This time, he spoke slowly and clearly, as if he wanted his words to be understood and accepted.

"I have to go back to India, Nadia. Will you take me? I have to go back to Banaras and complete what I started. I want to go back with you."

Nadia held up her hand, then dropped it, realizing Moses could not notice the gesture.

"What would you accomplish in India?" she asked. "The book is speaking about forgiveness for things done to you. It doesn't say that you have to go door to door asking for forgiveness. In fact, it doesn't say you have to go anywhere. The man in the story says he would not take rest until he can forgive the person who did him harm. It means staying in one place and forgiving, not going to his home and knocking on the door."

"True," Moses said. "But the Zohar is not a book of instructions. It is meant to encompass the life of the soul and has hidden meaning. It may mean different things to different people, depending on their understanding. Can't you see that for me it means a way to re-organize, put my life in some order, finish what I started."

Nadia thought she understood — not the parable, but the man. Her father was buried in time and now, no matter what the source of the inspiration, he wanted to start again.

Before finding him, she thought a daughter's love was innate, but as she watched him stare at the book with empty eyes, she now felt only pity. She noticed he had specks of drool on his chin and turned away in disgust as he continued on about the meaning of the Zohar. This was a familiar crossroads: should she let the lesson teach or turn her back and escape?

"So," Nadia said. "When do we go?"

Moses moved from the bed with an energy she had not thought

possible and hugged her. She smelled his musty hair, felt his bony body, the sticklike arms encircling her, then let herself go in his embrace.

The seats on the plane were cramped and Nadia saw that Moses was uncomfortable. She asked for the emergency exit seat, where there was a bit more room, but the airline would not allow a blind man to occupy that space.

Moses sat clutching the first book of the Zohar as if it might fly out of his hands. The other volume was tucked away in his luggage, wrapped in waterproof paper to prevent damage. Since he had taken possession of the books, his conversation was filled with philosophical puzzles. Prior to leaving, he had asked Nadia whether his shadow was showing on the wall, explaining that Rabbi Isaac, in the Zohar, understood his impending death from his lack of shadow. She assured him that his shadow was intact and he looked healthy and strong. Now he appeared to be looking out the window, working out some other enigma. She leaned forward and saw her reflection next to his, noticing the strong facial resemblance between them.

It had taken two weeks to get the tickets, his passport, and visas. The hospital manager had barely looked up when she had announced that Moses was her father and that he was leaving with her. There were few forms to sign; she came to his room in the afternoon and helped him pack a small bag she brought for him. In five minutes he was finished, leaving the radio and clock for Clayton with a note that bore his name but no message.

Moses appeared to have talked himself out; he fell asleep an hour into the flight. The plane was quiet during the night, as if each person was gathering strength for the onslaught that is India. As soon as lights were turned on, she gently shook him awake. He stirred, rose, and moved past her to the toilet. He struggled defiantly down the aisle, accidentally placing his hand on sleeping heads instead of seats.

The plane made a skittish landing at Bombay airport, and they stepped out in the emerging dawn, the air thick with humidity. Nadia wondered at the scores of Indians squatting everywhere, doing nothing but watching the passengers exit, as if this was their main source of entertainment. As they emerged from the terminal, boys in tan shirts and pants fought for their luggage. Moses appeared oblivious to the chaos. She wrestled their bags away, making her way to the airport bus. She helped Moses onto the bus and lugged their bags through the narrow door. The bus was clearly not air conditioned and the windows were mysteriously sealed shut, so that the passengers immediately began sweating profusely. Nadia, her patience thin, went in search of the driver, who was smoking a cigarette and squatting in front of the bus.

"We are sweating on this bus. Can you tell me when it goes?" Nadia asked.

The man shrugged and spoke loudly, as if he was talking to a retarded person. "We are waiting for another plane, Madam. This bus always waits for another plane."

Nadia stepped back from the shouting.

"Another plane? When is that supposed to come?"

"In about an hour, Madam."

Nadia stood still in disbelief, then boarded the bus to tell Moses. He put his hand on her arm when she sat.

"I heard. Welcome to India."

To him, it was as if he had only been away for a week, returning to the same chaos, dirt, and overpowering smells. The bus dropped them at the famous Taj Hotel on Apollo Bunder and they walked around the corner to find inexpensive lodging. The man at the reception, with a badly pockmarked face, sneered at them as if they were illicit lovers. Nadia was too tired to be angry, and eventually, after some argument, they were given a room with two beds.

The next morning they wandered past the stalls on the waterfront, then returned to the Western-style coffee shop in the Taj. Moses had asked the concierge for the train schedule to Banaras, and gave it to Nadia for inspection. She noticed that he was servile to the Indians, and when spoken to, his voice was soft as he bent solicitously toward the speaker. He was not self-deprecating but appeared to be making a genuine effort to be kind.

They had not spoken again of the Zohar or the purpose behind the trip to India. He told her that he needed to travel to Banaras in the state of Uttar Pradesh in eastern India, for what exact purpose she was not sure. She had, initially, rejected the manner in which he vaulted onto the pages of the Zohar and embraced the concept of forgiveness, but a small fiber of the parable had settled on her, as if it was relevant to her as well as conveying a universal fact. The trip was, in part, her journey. The mystery in Banaras also belonged to her.

The Taj Coffee Shop was sparkling clean, full of American families and Arab sheiks. The children ate hamburgers and drank Coca-Cola. Nadia ordered Darjeeling tea for Moses and herself. In this setting, her father appeared as a retired scholar, with a dignity born of experience and wisdom. She felt proud of him, in the gaze of other eyes, and glad to be seen in his company. His sunglasses looked acceptable in the bright light of the restaurant. For a moment, the constant anxiety of looking after an invalid vanished and she was able to relax in the elegant environment with the pleasant odors of cleanliness, tea, and cakes.

"Who is it we are going to see in Banaras?" asked Nadia.

"It is not just Banaras," he said. "I have to go to other places as well. I have not thought out exactly who I will see or what I will do, to be honest. Instead, I have been propelled along by an idea to return. It is as if I had to do what I did, so I can now return and make it right."

"What did you do?"

"Every time I acted or reacted, it seemed as if the lord of chaos — Wotan — stepped in and everything went wrong."

Moses sipped his tea, deliberately savoring the aroma. This was the first time that Nadia had seen him relax; his jaw slackened and a slight hint of color appeared on his paper-white cheeks.

"I can sum it up, I imagine, by saying that I felt though my intentions were often good the results were not, and people were hurt," he said.

"If you felt you did nothing wrong, then what is the problem?" She spoke in a near whisper, fearing the man behind them might be listening. "You can't blame yourself if people were hurt."

"If only it was that simple, Nadia," Moses said, getting to his feet, his tea unfinished. As he started toward the door, he bumped into a man just in front of them, knocking a sandwich from his hand.

"I am sorry," Moses said to his victim. "So very sorry." He bowed, and was quietly reassured to feel Nadia's firm fingers on his arm.

Nadia was amazed this was called "first class." The beds were hard and the dust blew through the train window as they crossed India. She found the dinner inedible; she contented herself with two oranges she had bought at a stall. Moses, on the other hand, ate his meal with gusto and fell asleep instantly on the bed below her.

She went to the end of the car to find the toilet, which proved to be a hole in the floor. She took the mirror from her purse, staring at her image. "You are a sight," she said to no one but herself: the small wrinkles she hid with makeup were pronounced and her eyes badly bloodshot. Through the window, she saw people walking in the night across fields, others huddled by fires. It seemed all of India was awake in the middle of the night, unable to rest. The train stopped periodically at stations whose platforms were swarming. She had hoped to find India fascinating and exciting, but so far it was simply overwhelming.

The train was swaying violently from side to side and she pictured an incompetent driver asleep at the controls, hurtling them wildly across India.

At Banaras, the orange-yellow light suffused the dust and the colors bled into each other. Families cooked breakfast over fires of cow dung, sadhus meditated, and throngs passed in haste. Nadia first, then Moses stepped down and immediately, as if a button had been pressed, scores of boys ran in their direction. Nadia recoiled, but Moses called out something in the few words he knew in Hindi and they dispersed just as quickly as they had appeared. Nadia approached the first rickshaw driver, as Moses had instructed. The driver hoisted the bags precariously onto the floor of the rickshaw and Moses spoke to the driver authoritatively.

India was no longer the hell it had once been for Moses. He was not lost, running, with the burden of guilt and horror. He was a visitor with his daughter, and she had sufficient funds, by Indian standards, for them to have a comfortable stay in a decent hotel. The heat of Banaras struck like a hammer blow. He sat back in the rickshaw, taking in the sounds and smells. He wondered for a moment how they looked together, an elderly man and his daughter, almost like a scene from the Raj: the officer and family going for high tea.

The rickshaw driver yelled, and for a moment Moses was petrified. A loud response resounded into the rickshaw with the same intonation as that of the driver who had blinded him: the identical guttural beginning and final inflection. He attempted to ward it off, but it was too powerful. Nadia pressed against him in the rickshaw, and he struggled to put down the rising fear the remembrance of that terrible day had thrust upon him.

An opening emerged in front of the rickshaw and the driver rose from his seat, pumping. The small breeze from the increased speed was gentle on Moses' face and brought spice odors that added a sweetness to the air. He turned to Nadia, saying softly, "Yes! I am back. I can *feel* it."

Nadia smiled, too absorbed by Banaras to respond. The city swooped in like a low-flying bird, carrying her away in a sudden movement. One moment she was analyzing the experience and the next she was bombarded with bursts of color and smell.

The rickshaw meandered up the long road to Cantonment and the Hotel de Paris. Their bags were taken and Nadia led Moses up the stairs to their room overlooking a dark, luxuriant garden, whose plants and trees seemed mangled and misshapen, except to the Indian mind. Their reservation, as Moses feared, had gone astray and it was fortunate a guest had checked out early. While their room was being serviced, they strolled down the lane of hotels on Cantonment. Moses walked as if he had a place in Indian history, standing straight and stepping quickly, forcing Nadia to hold him back occasionally to keep him from colliding with others.

They returned, took showers, and lay down on their beds for an afternoon nap. Within minutes he heard Nadia cry out, a single whimper, perhaps a moan. Moses wondered about her demons; he had been so focused on his own that he had not given any thought to hers. He listened to her breathing until she awoke.

They dressed quickly, went downstairs, and started walking toward the Lahurabir district.

"Can I ask the psychologist a question?" Moses began.

"I left the psychologist back in Tel Aviv."

"But can a psychologist ever not be a psychologist?" Moses asked playfully.

"Perhaps not," she admitted.

"You must please forgive my rudeness," said Moses. "I have yet to ask about you. You told me you were divorced. I heard that. What else?"

His interest piqued and pleased her.

"I have had bad relationships with men," she said. I always seem to choose men who are cold and unemotional. You would think as a psychologist I could have some insight. My husband, Uri, was distant, sometimes cruel."

Moses smiled and she immediately regretted the admission. But Moses went on and his voice was filled with compassion.

"Men are cruel. Not always but too often."

"Not *all* men are cruel," she said. "Some are kind, generous, caring. I just don't seem to meet them." She was guiding him along the street and felt his arm tense.

"Everyone is cruel. Some don't mean to be. Like me. I tried to help. God knows how I tried."

This was the topic he had come back to again and again; it was obviously a major part of the reason he was in India.

"Where are we going now?" she asked. "Why are we walking to this Lahurabir district?"

"Because they have the best sweets. Then we can come back and have a good dinner to get ready for tomorrow. Tomorrow is the day I have been waiting for."

2 THE CLOCK IN THE TOWER WAS FOREVER AT 2:00 P.M. It had often been repaired, but the repairs lasted only weeks. It was fundamentally flawed and heads no longer lifted for its message. Sahadeva glanced at it, forgetfully, then looked at his watch to see if the lunch break had arrived. Below him, another train rambled into Patna station, its roof as packed with passengers as the seats inside. He reached mechanically, pulling a lever, and somewhere up the track a switch raised a red flag and lowered a green one.

He climbed from the tower and walked along the platform, an invisible old man in a uniform; another functionary with the mindless job of pulling a lever. In the Indian division of labor, one man lifted a lever and another lowered it and neither would, no matter what the emergency, infringe on the skill of his colleague.

He had an hour for lunch and made his way out of Patna Junction Railway Station, up Fraser Road, toward the large oval of Gandhi Maidan. He was as unnoticed as a wandering Indian cow. He crossed the street to the Maidan, toward its center. The wind was so intense that the area was empty except for a few intrepid fathers helping their sons launch homemade kites made of branches and rags. He unwrapped an egg sandwich, which sat well with his ulcer, and crouched on his haunches to eat. The wind blew straight for him and he felt the new snows of Nepal carried aloft on the air. He sat still and his mind drifted; it flashed on the intense movement in and around the train station, then his undone washing.

He strolled to the British Library at the end of the Maidan, walked into the building, and sat down in an old leather chair by the window. He sat quietly at first, enjoying the respite from the wind, but then made his way to the same familiar shelf and took down the poems of A.E. He always left the book on the same angle to see if anyone else ever read it. The pages were smudged from his hands, and he had come to think of it as his personal copy. He opened the pages and read: We must rise or we must fall / Love can know no middle way / If the great life do not call / There is sadness and decay.

He closed the book, placing it on his chest, as if the words could filter through the pages to his heart. The librarian looked on benevolently; she had seen him do this often. She smiled kindly at the old railway clerk but as usual he did not notice. He took the book, inspecting its edges to make sure it would last, and replaced it in the same spot.

Sahadeva walked from the library, turning down Buddha Marg, then on to a side street toward the house of his brother. He wanted to go unnoticed and walked on the opposite side of the street, peering across at where he lived. He saw his brother's children spinning a top on the front step. Even they did not notice him; they barely saw him when he sat in front of them at dinner. He was Uncle Sahadeva, as much an invisible part of their lives as the old ripped sofa on the back veranda. The spinning top careened into the street and the little boy, Dilip, chased after it. He grabbed it, then looked up quizzically at Uncle Sahadeva, who came home only when it was dark.

"Is it time for dinner?" the little boy asked.

Sahadeva patted him on the head.

"No, Uncle Sahadeva is just taking a walk. You go back and play."

The boy ran back and Sahadeva headed back to the station, walking slowly.

He scanned the faces of the passengers, as if expecting some hint of recognition. Instead he saw harried, weary gazes looking for a place to move or sit. Another train, clanging and hissing as it was brought to rest, overwhelmed the noise of shouting. In another instant, the sounds of babies crying, porters hustling, and sighs of exasperation combined and rose to the rafters.

Sahadeva walked up the flight of stairs to his office and shut the glass door, which muffled the sounds only slightly. His desk was piled high with lost tickets and other debris that one day must be examined or at least filed. Usually he would move papers around mechanically, carrying out a meaningless set of tasks which, if put to the test, were unnecessary for the proper functioning of the railway. His brother, through his connections, had sat him at this desk twenty years ago and he had long since lost any desire to better himself or start on a new venture.

At first Sahadeva had been relieved to stop wandering and have a measured order of life. The regular schedule of walking to his office, spending a day stamping forms, pulling a lever, taking a walk for lunch, and then returning to a dinner already prepared by his sister-in-law was nourishing. His brother welcomed him generously when he arrived from Banaras and never asked why he came empty of hand and spirit to his door.

He sat and cleared the desk, stacking the unstamped tickets and papers to one side. Some of the papers had stuck to his desk, adhering from the sticky tea dripped daily. If he tried to pry them loose, they would rip and leave vestiges on the wood. He put his head down on his arms, closing his eyes. For two decades he had blotted memories with routine.

When Sita was taken away, she did not look back at Sahadeva. The villagers led her by the arm, as if she were an escaped convict, and sat her in a rickshaw that meandered up the road. He had left Moses writhing on the ground while he watched the small window in the back of the rickshaw, hoping she would turn around. He needed a memory to take away, to give meaning and shape a future. When it was not forthcoming, he was only left with the horror of the past.

These memories, dim from disuse, came to him now. At first he tried to clear them away, as one unsettles smoke, but they re-formed and hovered. He tried to picture the man he had been, obsessed with an illness that over time had dissipated like scattering clouds on a sunny day. He knew it was his words and his fears that had stirred Moses to act like a madman and end as a blind man. He had panicked and made Sita the source of his deliverance, when he could have continued as a sadhu, however mediocre. He found no lever, and his body threw him out of its secrets in a manner that was utterly humiliating. He lived on because he did not die, that was all.

He stood up and went into the little washroom that adjoined his office. He looked in the mirror, broken years ago by vandals and never replaced. The strands of white hair had no direction and were swaying slightly from a breeze through the open window. His forehead was lined and his eyebrows tangled. What he saw was not to his liking and he stopped the inspection abruptly, turning to urinate with the unsteady stream of his enlarged prostate.

Sahadeva felt the familiar taste of self-pity. It rose in his throat, making him pucker his lips in distaste. He looked at his watch, calculating that he had four hours before he could sneak away to the solace of a warm meal and family noises. He would have to settle for small talk as a distraction.

He washed his hands, replaced the papers on his desk, and then walked down the stairs into the ticket booth, where three of his colleagues sat watching a cockroach scurry up a wall. They jumped when they saw Sahadeva, expecting an emergency. He had never been to talk to them, and although they acknowledged him with a wave or a nod, he had become as transparent as the harijans that cleaned the toilets at night.

"What has happened?" one of them asked, in a worried tone.

"Oh, nothing really. I actually wanted to inquire about getting my mirror fixed. The one in the washroom next to my office."

The three railway clerks looked at one another in astonishment. It was clear that nothing essential got repaired, much less a luxury item. To raise this was as bizarre as asking that they get new uniforms, or someone clean the rubbish from between the tracks.

"Well, here is a form."

One of them pulled out a gray piece of paper with yellowed edges.

Sahadeva dutifully sat and placed a request that his mirror be repaired, looking up occasionally to note that he had quickly gone from a benign figure to a ridiculous one in their eyes. Decades of anonymity were instantly washed away and each clerk reformulated the story in his mind to make it ripe for the retelling. He was about to speak with them, his original intention, but realized he no longer could count on a civil response. He finished the form, listing the "Reason for Repair" as "necessary for grooming according to Railway Regulations." He handed one of them the form and left, hearing ripples of laughter following him like shock waves after a blast.

The water dribbled from the metal cup and down Sahadeva's shirt. His little nephew laughed and the rest of the family tried to hush him. Their eyes darted back and forth at one another and soon the banks broke, a wave of hysterical laughter erupting. Sahadeva sat with water on his shirt, deeply embarrassed. The ridicule of the railway workers was still fresh in his mind; this was just one further agony.

His brother realized he was suffering and calmed everyone down. For the rest of the meal, Sahadeva was ignored as usual. He was about to have another drink when he saw a light in his nephew's eyes and decided against it. Instead, he excused himself and made his way to the corner room that was his home.

Sahadeva lay on the hard bed, lifting his arm over his eyes to shield them from the glare of the bare bulb. He smelled the fumes and railway dirt on his shirt, mixed with the spices of dinner. The street was quiet except for crickets and the occasional rickshaw bell. It was too early for him to try to sleep and he had no interest in sitting with the family and being a sullen nuisance.

He involuntarily moaned, much to his surprise. It was as if a small, wounded animal inside him was making its presence known. He could not always trick himself into sleeping; sometimes his inner life would make itself heard, usually by a small protest such as this. If he had lived a quiet life from the start, he could have accepted his lot as a natural evolution into a dull, colorless passage of time. In his case, the heights he once hoped to climb made the depths even more profound, bringing nothing but disgrace to his cherished aspirations.

His moan became a sigh of grief for lost hopes. Tears rose and pushed aside the dust of ignominy that had crusted his eyes. With the tears rose an ephemeral wisp that could be sensed but not described. Sahadeva recognized this as his forgotten spirit. He relaxed and let it rise, not throwing it off as he usually did. This time it did not offer him hope or a way out but only itself; it existed and was still there.

Nadia looked up in the dark room. Moses was sitting on the side of her bed; she could just make out his outline. He was wearing a long Indian shirt and smelled musty.

He said loudly, as if the sun were shining, "I just had a dream of a river. The Zohar says a dream of a river is a presage of peace."

Nadia sat up in bed, glad to see her father full of hope.

"Tell me about it," she said. "I can't sleep anyway."

It was absolutely quiet outside. Nadia got out of bed and looked out the window. People on the ground were tossing and turning in their sleep. A toddler was walking among them, but they were all too exhausted to care.

"Well, there was not really much to it," Moses said. "I was sitting by the bank of a river, watching it flow by."

He wore his dark glasses, though it was the middle of the night.

"What color was the water?" Nadia asked.

She saw Moses' body slump, as if he had been struck.

"What did I say? What happened?" she asked.

"The Zohar says that all colors seen in a dream are a good omen."

He paused. "That is, except blue. My river was blue. Maybe it means nothing. I had to tell you about the dream. The Zohar says you must unburden yourself of a dream to a friend."

"So am I a friend?" asked Nadia.

"Jung told his dreams to his gardener," Moses said. "Everybody must have someone to tell. I better go back to sleep; my mind is covered with a mist these days. I start something, then a minute later forget what I was talking about. Years ago I could remember everything. My mind was clear then, but now I don't seem to remember things at all."

"How about just calling me a friend?"

For a moment, Moses felt his father peering out of him: the blankness of his stare and the heavy dullness in his heart. It was not a broken heart, but one that stayed blunt to avoid the pain of a struggle. If Moses stayed asleep, he could hide away, but if he awoke, he would surely disturb that sleeping monster another time—and there might not be a retreat. Moses knew he would not have another chance. This time he was not naive, able to be comforted by the solace of his weak rationalizations. He was creating all this, and although no inner voice could be heard, he was being called forward. He had wanted this: the chaos of India, the proximity of his daughter, the stirring. All he needed to do was turn around and tell Nadia she was his friend. He didn't have to crack open the Zohar or write to Jung. He just had to turn around and speak to Nadia and let it be known, by those simple words, that he was back, that he had not given up. He knew that once he did, the gods would awake and he would get what must be given. He remembered the Hindu edict: "Don't start, but once you start you must see it through." He was given a last chance to stop — or was he? All this was a wave that had gathered in Poland and had yet to break. Even his long sleep in the institutions may have been part of the journey, he mused, as if he needed to lie still and let the accumulated horror of his ways sink into every cell, forming a fabric of guilt, of remorse. Whatever it was, he was now called upon to take the step that would launch him to his life or his death.

He turned toward Nadia. "You *are* my friend. Oh, yes, Nadia, you are my dear friend."

Moses half expected to see again or at least hear a thunder clap to recognize his return. Instead, he felt suddenly sleepy, as if he had taken a sedative and the drug was just drifting over him.

For Nadia, they were the words she had been waiting to hear all her life.

Moses kept nagging Nadia to describe each scene. She kept up a continuous commentary on the sights, from Banaras to Sita's village. Moses was waiting for her to announce the large tree at the village entrance, and his spine tingled when she described it to him. Moses grabbed her by the shoulder.

"I have not really thought this through. What exactly am I supposed to do here?" he asked aloud of himself.

Nadia motioned the driver to stop and he pulled off to the side of the road. The driver looked agitated, and they both disembarked, Nadia paying the agreed fare. The dust kicked up as he hurried off, making them both step back and cover their faces.

"I am not really sure where you are going, Father. Tell me why this village is so important to you."

Moses knew it was hopeless. He did not expect to find anyone who remembered him, nor did he have anything in mind to say or do if they did. Yet he had nowhere else to go; this was the single image that had galvanized him at the institution. The Zohar had spoken of the divine quality of forgiveness and this journey of return was necessary for him to be released.

"No, we must carry on," said Moses, moving back onto the road. "This is what I came for and I have to follow it through. If I don't, I'm not sure where else to turn, what else to do."

He took a step on the road, then paused for a moment.

"I *do* want their forgiveness. Years ago, I caused harm here, out of my own stupidity. I knew it at the time, but I couldn't avoid it. I thought I was helping a dear friend — a soulmate — but I acted instead of thinking. I tried to help, to do something to help him. Now, at last, perhaps I can make amends."

Moses said this last half-heartedly. The possibility of confrontation with his past tormentors made walking difficult. What would really be accomplished, he wondered. How would talking to ignorant villagers about a long forgotten incident twenty years ago help relieve him of his mistake?

Moses and Nadia entered the village and were immediately noticed. It was unheard of for foreigners to come to this enclave of rickshaw drivers. Everyone turned away from the intruders, all except for Sita, who recognized the man. She saw him as if he were twenty years younger, filled with trickery and malice.

A wedding was commencing and the village was filled with gaiety, which swept everyone along in laughter and shouting. All were dressed in their best clothes; even the ragged children had their black hair matted down with oil. The smell of food frying had brought flocks of huge black crows, who added their cries to the rising sounds. Occasionally, someone would gaze up to gauge the passage of the sun in order to estimate the time the festivities would commence.

Sita sensed the total confusion that the presence of Moses brought. She heard the sound of mridangan drums moving their way and saw how Moses picked up his head in anticipation. She moved farther from him and back to where the villagers were mingling.

Moses continued to walk along, steadily and purposely, a smile on his face. Nadia walked hesitantly next to him, not sure if they would be the object of warmth or hostility. She noticed gaily dressed villagers standing outside one of the huts. For a moment, she thought that perhaps they'd had word Moses was coming and prepared the festivities for him. She saw a small Indian woman walking directly toward them at a rapid pace and Nadia grabbed her father's arm to slow his progress.

"Someone is coming. We had better stop."

Nadia could tell the attitude of the woman was not inviting. She carried a bitterness with her that could only be rooted in deep disappointment. She felt Moses brace himself. The woman walked up to them, looking over her shoulder from time to time. Her voice was low and menacing. The two she addressed did not need to understand the context of the words; their meaning was clear. The words were finally able to escape. They had been constructed years ago, just waiting for this moment, which she had never expected to see.

Moses stood erect. He moved Nadia's hand off his arm. He recognized Sita's voice and the passion of her words. He made a small step forward toward Sita, who did not budge. He spoke to her softly and gently, hoping that his words might calm her down.

"I have come back to say I am sorry," he said. "It has been a long time, but I want to heal the wounds that I have in my heart and that I caused to others. I won't stay long. I just want a chance to apologize. I may not be able to set things right, but I want to apologize."

Sita yelled out in English: "Go!" She yelled so loudly that the wedding festivities stopped and they all looked in her direction.

"I am not going anywhere," said Moses, still with a soothing voice. "I need to talk with you and with all the people in this village, even if they don't remember me. I have to, Sita, and I will."

He took another step closer to Sita. She examined Moses closely. His skin was pasty with small red blotches, and he spoke with a slight wheeze. She closed her eyes.

Moses spoke to her in Hindustani. It was one of the four greetings he knew. "*Atma ko shanti*. Peace on your soul."

"Go," she said loudly again, as if insulted by his use of her language. "Go!"

Nadia saw that the villagers were quiet, their former merriment now a mixture of fear and hate.

Sita turned and walked away.

Moses sighed. His legs trembled. He fought to steady himself. He broke away from Nadia's grasp, groping for Sita with his hands.

"Just listen to me, Sita. I have to talk to you. Please hear what I have to say."

To save the village from further embarrassment, Sita turned back. A teenage boy, part of the wedding party, walked over and caught up with Sita. They stopped for a moment and spoke. The boy approached Moses and said clearly, "My name is Govinda. I speak some English."

"Govinda," said Sita. "Tell him word for word."

"I will try," the boy said.

Sita began and the boy's words followed closely behind, like a high-pitched echo.

"You are a fool, Moses, and an asura — a devil. You think you can walk in here and cleanse your soul by some admission. What hole do you have in your heart that you don't realize you have sucked the life out of me? You killed my parents. You took something from the village. It has never been the same, as if a light has gone out in all of us. You plunged a knife in my heart and ripped out a part of it. You took away Sahadeva's dignity and you stole my future: a husband, a family."

Sita paused for breath. Her head lowered and tears welled in her eyes. She continued, the boy still only a miraculous beat behind.

"What is worst, Moses, you insulted the gods. My parents loved Siva and he loved them but they died *outside* the sacred circle of Kasi. The unimaginable sin is that they have lost their *moksha* — their liberation."

The drums drew near and Nadia looked over her shoulder to see the groom arriving on a horse. The drumming slowed, and the groom slid off the horse, confused by the pall of despair overhanging his moment of triumph. The villagers milled around, talking to him, glancing in the direction of Nadia and Moses. There was nothing that could ignite their pleasure again, Nadia was sure.

Without speaking, they walked away from the village. Rickshaws pulled alongside them, soliciting, and eventually they chose one. They both sat silently. Nadia was holding back despair and frustration. The journey of her father was her journey as well, and it seemed over now, stifled in minutes.

The rickshaw stopped in front of the hotel. Nadia paid the driver the agreed amount, but the driver looked shocked, holding out his hand for more. She ignored him and helped her father off the rickshaw and into the garden. She took a handkerchief and put it on the iron bench to cover the crow droppings.

"Sit down, Moses. I want to talk to you." Nadia needed to understand.

Moses settled himself onto the bench. He seemed shaken by his experience and distracted. Before Nadia spoke, she examined him. There was a frigidity about him, as if he had been mummified; only his hands were shaking, either out of fear or as a remnant of feeling. He was in a heightened state, almost hysterical. She spoke to him softly, in her professional voice. "Maybe you can tell me about it all later. No need to trouble yourself now," she said.

Moses let out his breath. "Oh thank you. That is very kind of you."

She finally understood why he had become lost in an institution. "Sit here; I will get us a drink."

She sat on a patch of dirt under a tree, closing her eyes, listening to the pipe of the snake charmer at the adjoining hotel. She despaired of helping him back to life. But she had to: within him was what she needed.

3 SAHADEVA'S BACK WAS SORE from moving files to his new office. The move was occasioned by an administrative decision to restructure his department, changing the name from "Railway Administration Department" to "Railway Operations." All employees above a certain rank, including Sahadeva, were given new titles and new offices. Each was left to move his own files and old, rusting typewriters.

"There is a man outside to see you. He is a white man and he has a white woman with him." The orderly at his door was shifting on his feet, as if embarrassed at making such an announcement.

Sahadeva immediately visualized tourists from America in ill-fitting Indian clothes, swallowed by the Indian Railway system.

"Please ask them to wait."

Sahadeva returned to papers on his desk.

"The man is blind and the — "

Before the orderly could finish his sentence, Sahadeva was off his chair and out the door. He headed halfway down the platform when he realized that he had failed to ask the orderly where he had put them. He rushed back to his office and the orderly was standing exactly where he had left him. Sahadeva followed him down the platform to one of the waiting rooms.

Moses and Nadia, in the noisy railway office, did not hear the approaching steps. They sat on a wooden bench, which was the only furniture in the dusty room. Sahadeva came quickly to the waiting room but stopped outside to look in, to see if it was indeed his old friend. He saw a frail, old man with liver spots on his hands and bushy white eyebrows. He wanted to retreat but hesitated, caught between a bond that could never be expunged and his knowledge of this man's potential for disruption. He saw Nadia look up at him with a quizzical smile. In an instant, he saw resemblance in the cheekbones, the fleshy lips, and the heavy eyelids. He stepped forward and she stood up to greet him. Moses moved his hand over to her empty seat.

Sahadeva held Moses responsible for his loss of faith. He had decided to disrobe before they crossed paths, but Moses had corrupted him by sweeping them up in evil. As quickly as he had entered the waiting room, he walked out. He sensed Nadia sitting down and was relieved that she did not follow him. As he walked back up the stairs, the orderly was agog with curiosity. Sahadeva turned to him when he had returned safely to his office and shut the door.

"Tourists. Not my responsibility. You should know that, shouldn't you?"

The orderly was surprised at the force with which Sahadeva expressed himself and backed quietly to the door. With his hand still on the doorknob, he whispered, "But they asked for you by name."

Sahadeva turned and glowered, then returned to his papers, pushing them aimlessly around on his desk. He stacked them in arbitrary piles. He tried to feel his muscles and sensations to ground himself, but all he felt was a numbness as waves of anxiety washed over him.

"Are you so afraid of me?"

Moses and Nadia were standing at his door. It was too late, he could not hide.

"You brought back too many painful memories. I am sorry."

Sahadeva now stood, in deference to Nadia.

"My daughter, Nadia."

Sahadeva did not seem surprised and clasped his hands together. "Namaskar. Welcome to Patna."

He turned to Moses. "How did you find me?"

"You said your brother worked for the railways in Patna."

"You never were shy."

Nadia glanced around the hot office for a place to put their bags.

"Forgive me," said Sahadeva. "Please take a seat."

He cleaned the papers off two chairs, swatted them with his dhoti, and then returned to sit behind the desk.

"Are you from Warsaw?"

Nadia looked at her father.

"We both live in Israel."

Moses abruptly spoke. "Enough pleasantries. We have to talk. We went to see Sita." The name hung in the air. "She was in the same place. She threw me out."

Sahadeva's voice was agitated.

"Why did you go? Didn't you cause enough harm in the first place?"

Nadia looked at her father, waiting for the illumination she longed for.

Moses took a deep breath and spoke everything he had to say in one exhaled sentence, "I can't go on, Sahadeva. I need forgiveness and for it all to end."

"You ruined her life and you want her to forgive you? You are an old man like me. Why don't you just lie down and leave the mess you made alone. You can never get things right. Your life is hopeless and a blight. Now get out. You have left me sitting here in this office with no life."

"I have no life either. Can't you see that? I am a Jew looking for my salvation in India."

Nadia again looked at him, listening to determine who he might be. She said gently yet firmly, "This is shame that you both have. You are both haunted."

The two of them turned away at the same time, unable to face the glare of her words. She knew she had discovered the truth, although not the cause of their shame.

"You are both cowards. Two old men hiding away from the world. I am frankly surprised you are both alive, that God would allow you to exist so long, for so little purpose."

Moses reached for her arm but she pulled away and went on, "I don't care what you did."

"Enough!" Both Moses and Sahadeva shouted at the same time as if the words had touched their cores at the same moment. After what seemed a full minute, Sahadeva spoke. "You may be right, Madam. You *are* right. Two naked old men. Not a pretty sight. Shame has eaten through us like rust. It *is* a mystery we still live. We should both have died the moment that stick blinded your father. In fact, that day we both did die, in a sense, did we not, Moses?"

Moses, slumped in his chair, did not respond or look up.

"Now that you know this, you can be redeemed," she said.

Her words had no impact on Moses: they glanced off him and fell heavily to the ground. Moses suddenly lifted his head and addressed Sahadeva. "Come with us. Come back to Banaras. See Sita and talk to her."

Sahadeva turned from them and stalked from the room, leaving them to wonder if he was gone forever.

"We should leave," Nadia said.

"No, wait," her father said. "He will be back."

Sahadeva exited the station and stood stock still in the passing throng, oblivious to the commotion around him. He deliberately closed his eyes, withdrawing into himself.

Nadia's words had taken him to the truth. Suffering and redemption are links in an endless chain, he realized. The inadvertent harm he caused contained the seed of redemption, which could carry him closer to the divine. He was still on the path; living with awareness was the path: truly acknowledging what one has done and is about to do.

He was still a sadhu in his heart; he had never really given up.

He turned back, entered the station, and returned to the office. He felt calm, alive again, wanting to reenter life. Moses and Nadia were sitting in the same place as if time had stood still.

"I won't go with you, Moses," said Sahadeva. "I have no need of Sita's forgiveness. You must come to your own resolution; it can't come from anyone else."

Nadia noticed that his voice was soft, detached. She repeated his words in her mind. This man, her father's old friend, was more right than he realized. Moses was not the answer to what she was missing. She was searching for the father he had once been and this wound had to be healed by her alone.

"I won't go with you either, Father." Nadia also spoke softly. "This is a fool's errand. Sahadeva is right. Sita can offer you nothing. You must resolve it yourself."

"The harm I caused is larger than me," Moses said softly. "No man or woman can truly gaze upon the horror of what they have done, then put it aside. It can never be resolved by the person who has caused the harm. It takes forgiveness and I intend to get it, even if you abandon me."

Moses groped his way toward the door, feeling in his pocket for money. He took a book of the Zohar, ignoring his other luggage. Recklessly he walked out of the office, staggering along the station wall. Eventually, he came to the ticket booth and grabbed its iron bars.

"Banaras," he said.

Nadia and Sahadeva followed him, amazed at his fearlessness, his determination.

Sahadeva was walking with a surprising spring in his step; he wanted to return to Banaras, but not to accompany Moses. Or to see Sita. It was time for him to sit at the feet of his guru, this time as a man with some wisdom.

"Don't do this," she pleaded. "Come back with me to Israel. There is nothing that can be resolved in Banaras."

He turned to face them, a ticket in his hand.

"My father once told me he had lived a shallow life. At the time I felt sorry for him, thinking my life would bring me insight and wisdom. I now know what he meant. The compromises you make, the harm you cause, dampens — no, kills — your spirit. I would be just as blind if I could still see."

"I am leaving now, Nadia." Sahadeva addressed her warmly. "You may not know it, but you have been the catalyst for me to return to the adventure of my soul. I will return to being a sadhu."

The significance of his admission was lost on Nadia. He gave her a namaskar and left the station.

Nadia recovered Moses' bag from the office before buying a ticket. She sat next to him, waiting for the train.

"I won't abandon you," she said.

He reached over and took her hand, awkwardly but tenderly.

A train whistle jarred Sahadeva from his reverie. He realized that he had been walking in the wrong direction. The man beside him was shouting, his fists waving at the sky. Sahadeva slowed to distance himself and opened his eyes to his surroundings. The man's plaint could have come from any of the wretched people rushing along the street. They all seemed submerged in despair, many bent with heavy loads.

Sahadeva observed a thread of his own despair, the author of the grand scheme to return as a sadhu. He, too, lifted his head to the sky as sadness flooded him, dissolving his inspiration.

It had been years since his feelings had been given free rein. He always withdrew, aware that he would be drowned by them. This time he surrendered, letting them rise and expand. The feelings swirled within him: regret that he had never returned to find Sita, fear that he was hopelessly lost, shame for his part in the tragedy, and self-hatred for his weakness. This time, however, the feelings did not stick or wound; they rushed about aimlessly, then dissipated. He sensed them leaving through the pores of his skin, rising in the dust of the day and then disappearing. A new wave gripped him but just as quickly left, as if no longer welcome. There, in the chaos of the crowd, he became truly still.

Sahadeva walked slowly, uninterested in where he was going. Deep within him something opened. For an instant, he visualized Moses' door, sliding out on smooth hinges. There, in that place, was the lever he had found so long ago. The lever, as he observed it, transformed into a small fire. All that had taken place, he realized, had only occurred so that he could witness this fire at this time. And the fire is the mystery.

Sahadeva saw the truth of who he was: an old man used to the comforts of the room in his brother's house, yet in whom the mystery burned. He could go anywhere, to the marketplace or to the ashram; it made no difference. The train whistle taking Moses and Nadia to Banaras sounded again. He turned back to the station, ready for the next part of his life.

Nadia was pleased that they were again able to find a room at the Hotel de Paris. She unpacked her small bag and arranged Moses' clothes neatly in drawers. They were pretending that nothing was wrong, but Nadia had tears in her eyes. She was now experiencing the real loss of her father: he was obsessed with his quest for forgiveness and there was nothing left for her. Her legs felt like stone; she sat on her bed, unsure of what to do or say.

The window was open and Nadia watched the night quickly descend on Banaras. It was an important day in her life. She had unraveled, if only slightly, the history of her father. She tried to picture him as a younger man, walking barefoot in the dust with Sahadeva, striving for spiritual insight. Instead, she gazed up and saw him lying on his bed in his underwear, rubbing his eye sockets.

"We will go in the morning," he said, as if feeling her gaze. "I will get this right and then we can move on. I will stand naked before her. Then she will have to let me free."

"It won't accomplish anything," she said firmly.

Moses stood up, gaunt and tall, his face flushed with anger.

"Enough of this negativity," he shouted. "You have done nothing but insult me or stand in my way. Don't you see this is something I have to do. With you or without you."

Nadia was outraged but she hesitated. Moses was speaking the very words of her first husband. She had heard them all before, the context different but the anger the same.

"Please don't yell at me," she said. "I am sorry, but I do not deserve such anger."

He lay back on his bed and continued rubbing his eye sockets. Nadia pressed her own eyes, stemming fresh tears.

She lay back on her bed but was unable to sleep. Soon Moses was snoring, now and again shouting in indecipherable Polish. The language brought back a memory of her teasing him about his snoring. They were at the breakfast table and he angrily denied he ever snored. She was surprised that there were any residual memories. The only one she had consciously retained was the anguished, horrified look on his face when he had been hidden behind the barrel.

She thought of her first husband, Uri. He had not stopped talking about politics and philosophy from the second they had met at a party He had mesmerized her, seduced he completely. She could picture his face that first time, with its broad smile and eyes all alight. But as soon as they married, he became moody and detached. She never understood why. Little by little she stopped talking to Uri about her father and put away without even mentioning them the letters from agencies that had tried to find him. For reasons she never understood, he became angrier and angrier in the evening. He paced around their apartment as if he were a caged animal, jumping at her for interfering, accusing her of being a burden around his neck. When she finally suggested he might need some therapy, he shouted that this was the final insult. Still Sophie thought things would work out, but they never did.

All her training did not help to understand Uri. He was interesting and insightful but with a primitive connection to his feelings. She could not fathom what she had done wrong. Even the reasons for their separation, and later their divorce, were completely unknown to her. Perhaps, she often thought, she had tried too hard. Now was she doing the same thing with her father?

They left the rickshaw at the entrance to the village. Moses walked unsteadily, as if held together by wires and elastic. However awkward his gait, he felt inwardly focused, certain that the step he was taking was right. Now and then he sighed a small sigh, barely audible.

They walked into the village but this time were totally ignored. Nadia looked around, attempting to make eye contact with the women walking to the well, but they acted as if Moses and she were invisible.

"Sita may not be here," Nadia offered. "There may be no one from whom you can seek forgiveness."

Moses cocked his head, listening. "I can hear people talking," he said. "Take me to them."

"They are just peasant women." Nadia noticed he had a book of the Zohar in his hand and was pointing it in the direction of the women. She took his arm and led him to the well. The women still did not look in their direction, and it was clear now to Nadia if it had not been before that they were being consciously ignored.

"Sita," Moses yelled. The women went about their chores, stepping around Moses as they walked off. Nadia noticed a few boys unable to hide a look but sufficiently fearful that they lowered their eyes as they walked away.

"Hopeless," Nadia shook her head. "They are ignoring us deliberately. Sita must have told them to ignore you if you came back. What shall we do now?"

"We have no choice," Moses said firmly. "I must stay here until I find her. Or until she returns. It is here I must seek forgiveness. Nowhere else. I will sit here until she returns or comes to talk to me. Take me somewhere in the shade where I can wait."

Nadia sat Moses down under the banyan tree. She saw the shimmering heat floating in layers and the eddies of dust trailing the women carrying water home from the well. The village was desolate, and Moses was under the only natural shelter, the branches sufficiently intertwined to provide a canopy from the relentless sun. He could not survive for long without water and, as the heat of the day increased, he would quickly dehydrate.

"You'll die if you stay here," said Nadia. "Come back with me. We'll try again tomorrow."

Moses lifted his head and removed his dark glasses. "This is the end for me, Nadia. I don't want to leave. I *must stay*."

Nadia was exhausted — hot and exhausted. All of the anxieties of the last month suddenly overwhelmed her. She sat down next to him on the root of the tree.

"I'm exhausted, Moses. I can't sit with you here forever, so I will go back to the hotel and come for you later in the day. Promise me you won't do anything foolish. Just sit here and call out for Sita."

Nadia did not wait for an answer. She kissed Moses on the forehead and headed toward the dusty road where Sahadeva had first entered the village decades ago.

Moses eventually stood up and walked toward the well. When Nadia left, the villagers had crept up around him, examining him and looking at one another in amazement. As he sensed their presence he stood up and moved in their direction; they moved quickly out of his way.

An old rickshaw driver, too frail to ply his trade, walked closer up to him, then circled him several times, examining him carefully. Then he walked over to another driver. They were both old men, toothless, bent, and bowlegged. Together they sneaked up on Moses and one of them grabbed his arm. Moses started to react but instead thanked him in English and asked how to find Sita.

"This way," one of the drivers said in pidgin English. He steered Moses to the end of the village, close to the night soil pit, and stopped.

"Is this it? Am I near Sita?"

The driver edged him even closer. "Yes," he said, "this way." Then the other driver came up quickly behind him and pushed him over. The two slowly walked away as they heard him scream.

He pulled himself up and on all fours crawled out of the pit, covered in dung.

Boys in khaki shorts ran up to him, sensing his complete vulnerability. One rushed up and grabbed his jacket and Moses did not have the strength to resist. They cared little that the clothes were soiled. Another grabbed the sunglasses from his face but, seeing the scars, dropped them as he ran. Moses stood unmoving. Another boy ran back and stripped Moses of his shirt. He rushed off, but returned almost immediately and undid Moses' belt, pulling it expertly through the loops. The boys were like jackals, furtive and quick. They darted off with their booty, then returned for further possible pickings. One of the boys resembled the man-child who had run into the ashram just before Moses was blinded. His features were perfect but mature; his nose had already grown an adult bump and hook. Deftly reaching into Moses' pocket, he removed his wallet and passport. Boldly, he inspected the wallet and thumbed through the banknotes with a look of rapture. The other boys quickly assembled, like flies to a carcass, to count it with him. They ripped off Moses' undershirt, then yanked at his pants, rifling in the pockets as they fell, slowly as in a dream, about Moses' ankles.

Moses stirred as if awaking from a sleep. The boys dashed away, glancing over their shoulders to see if he could follow. Moses tried to pull up his trousers, looking vainly around.

A hot wind blew in his face. His body was standing there but not his spirit. Suddenly, Moses opened his mouth and roared. The sound filled the village, drifting to the sky. Finally, he went hoarse and sat back down on the ground almost naked.

Several widows approached him, still carrying their buckets. Some of them remembered Bhakti and Rohini; others remembered hearing the story that had changed Sita's destiny. One of them walked up closer and brought her bucket down on his head. Moses fell, blood running from the wound in his skull. Now others approached him one by one, as if in a lethal chorus line, beating Moses with their buckets until his breathing became very shallow. They left him there and went back to the well to wash the stain from the buckets.

After a long lunch of south Indian thali, Nadia sat reading a magazine in the air-conditioned lobby. The rickshaw driver who had taken her from the village was still outside, waiting for her to return. When she told him she would be a few hours, he immediately lay down in the shade of the canopy and went to sleep.

German tourists with cameras were talking loudly in the lobby, trying to gird their loins for another sojourn into the heart of this strange city. They had risen before dawn to take the obligatory boat trip up the Ganges and now were yawning as the day wore on. She envied them the frivolity of travel, where India was a curiosity rather than the harsh, bizarre reality it was for her.

She woke up the rickshaw driver, who seemed annoyed by the interruption. He gazed up at the fierce sun, playing his opening gambit for an increased fare. The now familiar sights and sounds rushed at her as they meandered out of Banaras.

The village was quiet, but Moses was nowhere to be seen. She told the driver to circle the huts and then drive around the banyan tree. It was so hot that even the crows stood still in the shade of the tree. She made the driver drive up to the huts then behind them. Dogs barked lethargically at the intrusion but without conviction. Then she saw him.

Moses lay by a ditch, clothed only in his underpants, his pants at his ankles, covered with excrement. He had cuts and contusions all over his body and fresh blood was dripping slowly from a wound above his right eye. The Zohar was still clutched in his hand. His dark glasses, she noted, lay beside him.

Nadia stepped from the rickshaw and stood over her father. The rickshaw driver turned his head and looked for the fastest route away from this disgusting sight. Knowing instinctively she would need him, Nadia reached in her bag and showed him fifty U.S. dollars. "Wait," she said. He took his feet off the pedals.

She pulled a handkerchief from her purse and started wiping away the blood from Moses' forehead. She cleared his face of the excrement and then tried to push away the rest from his arms. She removed his fouled pants and threw them in the ditch. She threw the handkerchief away and tore off the bottom part of her blouse, which she ripped into rags. Bending over him, she silently worked at cleaning him up, trying to restore his humanity. Moses was still unconscious, but he seemed to cooperate as she lifted first his arms, then his legs.

She struggled to lift him into the rickshaw. The driver started to protest but remembered the green dollars. Still, he turned away, unwilling to help. Somehow she got Moses's chest up onto the floorboards of the rickshaw then pushed the rest of his body in, so that he lay in a heap in front of the seat. Gingerly she wiped off her hands, then climbed into the seat.

"Ganges," she said, with such force that the driver sprang into action. She could have said "Hotel de Paris," but she knew her father needed spiritual help more than physical assistance.

The rickshaw stopped at Gola Gali, just above the lanes that lead to the Manikarnika Ghat. She struggled to get him down off the rickshaw, and as soon as his foot touched the ground, the driver hurried away. Everyone stepped out of her way, unwilling to be involved in other than their own *samsara*, the daily drama of life and death.

She put his arms around her neck, hoisted his weight onto her back, and made her way, slowly and painfully, down the narrow lanes toward the Ganges. The heat and smell were unbearable, but her mission was instinctive: she had to save him. The Ganges sparkled with white light, and the water was alive with flowers and small clay oil lamps floating in the strong current. Nadia carried her father down into the waters of the Ganges. She stepped in up to her waist, and cradled him in her arms. He was lighter now, buoyed by the swirling water.

The liquid flowed over Moses, washing away the filth. The force of the current bathed him, she had merely to hold him. She dipped his head momentarily under the water, then gently removed the caked blood from his forehead.

Moses himself was submerged in a black ink. No thought could rise from its depths, just feelings of pain and horror. It was more than guilt; it was a paring back of his self-deception, an abandonment of explanations. In this mass he sank further. It was an absence of light.

He felt the water around him but was uninterested. All he knew was what he had done. It did not come in words or images, he just knew.

He felt a book, which he realized was the Zohar, in one hand and he reached out with the other until he touched Nadia.

She saw that he was finally conscious. "You are at the Ganges, Father. In the water. I have taken you here to wash away what happened in the village. I don't think you are badly hurt, just cut and bruised."

"Take me out to the river bank." Moses said softly. "Please let me stand up."

Under his own power he climbed from the flowing river and turned to face the Ganges. He was holding the Zohar high above his head, looking at it as if he could see the pages.

"Nadia," he said. "I want you to open the Zohar one more time and read it to me. And when you are finished, throw it away."

"Really, Father?"

"Really," he said.

She took the book from his hand, opened it at random — ignoring the pages that fell from the ripped binding — and read: "Man's destiny depends ultimately upon repentance and prayer, and above all upon prayer with tears, for there is no gate that tears are unable to penetrate." As the last word of the Zohar was spoken, Moses stood stock-still and put his hands to his face. A deep moan from the pit of his stomach rose from him, spreading over the water, audible to everyone bathing nearby. The moan was dispatched from his soul. As instructed, Nadia threw the Zohar away. When it hit the ground it split open, pages flying into the river.

Moses began the Kaddish, the Jewish prayer for the dead. "*Yisgadal . . .*" He paused. He shouted, so that his voice boomed over the water. "For Satya!" He began again. "*Yisgadal, Vyiskadash . . .*" Each word was clear; the sounds of his prayer melted into the songs for Siva being sung by a sadhu and the chant of "Hare Krishna" intoned by the widows in the temple above the ghats.

He finished his prayer and turned to Nadia. She noticed that his eye sockets were filled with tears that had forced their way through the scar tissue.

"Tell me where I am standing," he said. "Where have we come to now?"

Nadia closed her eyes and spoke. She knew where they were.

"You are in a holy place. The Ganges is flowing strongly and upon it are garlands of flowers. The water — you can hear it — murmurs as it flows. It swirls in eddies around the bathers, who are holding their hands together in prayer before they dip silently under the surface."

"Yes," Moses said. "I can hear it."

Nadia moved over to Moses and encircled him in her arms. He in turn wrapped her in his. She felt very small in his embrace, yet she could feel his bones almost bereft of flesh. She rocked back and forth, holding him tightly. She imagined she was rocking in a boat on the Ganges and in front of her the small waves gathered together to form Lord Siva, the Hindu god whose image she had seen in every alcove and shop window since she had arrived in Banaras. She sank into this image and felt herself cradled by this deity. It was *that* she was missing, she understood, not Moses. It was the deity she lacked: the presence of an incorruptible value.

Nadia stepped back and held Moses at arm's length. He spoke before she could explain her feelings. "Now, there is another task," he said. "Find me some stones and I will build a shrine to Sita's parents, Bhakti and Rohini."

She looked at him, almost naked but with a renewed energy that matched the coursing waters. She left him there, foraging for stones that she brought him. She did this from love, not from duty.

He walked unassisted until he felt a small wall. He knelt in the dirt and placed the stones in a small pyramid. They stayed in place and he sat down in front of them and spoke to the stones. "Without wailing, without disease, without pain, I dedicate this shrine to your memory. I do so with the greatest respect to you both and your daughter, whom I also have greatly wronged. I pray that your soul be liberated and that it find its way into the arms of Siva." Moses did a namaskar and then stood.

He turned in the direction of Nadia.

"I am finished now, Nadia. You can go home. You don't need to look after me and you don't need to have me at your side. I will stay here in this holy place or near it and tend to this shrine. I will tend to it until I die." He paused for what seemed to Nadia like an eternity. "In that embrace with you, I was made light by your love."

Nadia took some money from her purse.

"Here," she said, "take this. It is all I have."

He reached out and took it, crumpling the notes. He opened his arms and again she embraced him. But this time, though with him, she was separate.

"I will come back to see you," she said.

"There is no need," Moses said.

"Still," Nadia said, "I will be back."

She walked up the ghats and Moses sat down again, making sure the stones were steady and able to endure.